BOSS GIRL

LILY KATE

Interested in receiving *Love Letters from Lily?*
Sign up for her new-release newsletter at:
www.LilyKateAuthor.com

To my other half.

ACKNOWLEDGMENTS

W.A. for being the other half of my brain.

Virginia for your sharp proofreading eyes.

Scarlett Rugers for the fabulous cover design.

All of you, readers—beta readers, ARC readers, bloggers, and the entire book community—each and every one of you are fabulous!

And, of course, to the very best of friends . . . you know who you are!

BOSS GIRL

Good things come in extra-tall, smoking hot stilettos.

Things like Jocelyn Jones.

Jocelyn "Ice Queen" Jones is the hottest agent in town, and I'm determined to make her mine. My agent, that is. She's the best at what she does, which is why I'm intent on keeping our relationship strictly platonic, even if the sexual tension between us is thick enough to slice with a skate. After all, I already have a woman in my life. My daughter, Charli, and we're not sure if there's room for someone else.

Until Jocelyn Jones breaks all the rules. She lets her icy exterior begin to melt, treating me to a view no man has ever seen before. Suddenly, I'm no longer certain if I want to be on her roster, or in her bed—for good.

Tangling business with pleasure has never been on the agenda. Then again, neither has falling in love.

They say it's bad business to sleep with the boss.

But *they* haven't met Jocelyn Jones.

CHAPTER 1

Jocelyn

"I WANT YOU, Boxer."

The silence in the room is palpable, edgy even, as I wait for the man seated across from me to respond. I'm the one who called this meeting, and now—in the wake of my brutal honesty—I'm afraid I've pushed him too far.

Sucking in a breath, I survey Landon "Danny" Boxer's every twitch, every flicker of movement around his lips, every glint in those blue gemstone eyes—but it's impossible to read him.

I've finally met a man whose thoughts are a mystery to me, and I don't like it.

I clear my throat and try again, slower this time, a hint of gentle. "Did you hear me?"

"You want me?" Eyes the color of worn blue jeans rove across my face. Leaning back in his seat, Boxer stretches his huge form across the chair, dwarfing it with his size. "That's forward of you, Miss Jones."

"I want to *work* with you." I fight off the heat inching onto my cheeks. "Sign with me, and we can do great things together."

To my chagrin, he gives an unimpressed shrug. "I'm doing plenty of things already, and they all feel great."

I let out the breath I've been holding, and then attempt a few of the moves they teach us in my overpriced yoga class. I'm not cut out for this deep breathing crap, mostly because it makes me hyperventilate. "We have a great agency here, and I have a number of clients who've—"

"I *know* who you are." Landon Boxer flashes a big, toothy grin. One of his front teeth is significantly chipped—from a distance, it looks like he's missing it completely. His nose is a little crooked. His mouth a little too wide. His eyes a little too shiny. Yet despite all of this, he's attractive in an odd, quirky way. "Thanks for your offer, but I'm not interested, Miss Jones."

"Just Jocelyn. We're friends."

"Friends? I hardly know you."

"Well, we can definitely fix that," I tell him. "What do you want to know?"

"That's not how you become friends."

"Okay, then." I try for patience, but this deep breathing business is driving my blood pressure through the roof. "What should I be doing differently?"

He shakes his head. With the toothy smile gone, the pale blue of his eyes more serious, he's almost handsome in a gruff, Neanderthal sort of way. He's not my type, but I can appreciate the raw maleness about him.

I can also appreciate his career, which is why we're here. Boxer may never know the difference between cufflinks and paperclips, but he has one of the most promising careers with the LA Lightning before him. With any luck, he'll be my next client.

As a bonus, Boxer has the potential to score endorsement deals out of the wazoo if the Lightning does well this year—and I suspect they will blow through regular season at the top of their league.

With the right guiding hand—a bit of a haircut, a trim of the nails, maybe the waxing of a few stray hairs—Boxer will be raking in the advertising dough by letting huge corporations slap his face on the side of cereal boxes.

As for the guiding hand? That's where I come in. I'm the best woman for the job. I just have to convince *him* to let me take control. Together, we can do great things. I'm sure of it.

See, I haven't become the best agent in the business by slacking off. I work my ass into the ground. It's earned me a few nicknames along the way, many of them unpleasant, but I look past all that— keep my eye on the prize.

This is a male dominated industry, and if I show any sign of weakness, it's the end of the game for me. The respect I've worked years to achieve will be gone. So unfortunately, if that means people call me the Ice Queen—or worse—behind my back, I have to deal with it.

The only thing worse than being called the Blonde Bitch would be to have earned the nickname for nothing.

Boxer, however . . . he's different. He talks to me like a normal person and, I must admit, it's refreshing. I can't help but wonder if this is part of the reason I'm attracted to him. As a client. A *potential* client.

"Duke's retiring, Boxer. I know you're loyal to your current agent, but he won't be sticking around another year." I hand him a sheet of paper with a list of endorsements for which he'd be perfect. "Let's work together."

Boxer scans the list, an eyebrow raising. "This is a lot of endorsements."

"I have contacts at all of them. These are warm leads, and I've already pitched you to a few. This one, I think, is perfect." I point to a company that sells men's undergarments. "They love you. Big payday, here."

He frowns, thinking on it for a long moment.

"Look, I'm not trying to steal you away from Duke," I tell him. "I just want you to consider a deal with me. Will you think about it?"

"I still don't know anything about you, Miss Jones, and you don't know me. Duke isn't just an agent, he's been a friend to me. I need to know that the person I sign with is looking out for my best interest, not just the bottom line."

"Okay, well, we can fix that." I take a deep breath and exhale. I've been known to do a *lot* of things to secure a client for my roster . . . but becoming BFFs is a new one. If this were anyone else, I would've sent them packing by now because I don't have *time* for friendships. However, something in his eyes, the way he speaks so earnestly, as if every word comes from his very core, holds me attentive. "Tell me what to do."

"You want to get to know me?" Boxer stands and extends one massive hand. He's got tattoos winding up both arms, adding to his brawny appearance. "Let me buy you an ice cream cone."

"An ice cream cone? How about I buy you a drink? There's a bar just downstairs."

"I don't drink," he says. "But I do love sprinkles."

"Sprinkles," I say, mystified. "Well, then, let's get ourselves an ice cream."

"Great." To my surprise, he covers my hand with his, pulling me toward the door with a grin. "I know just the place."

CHAPTER 2

Boxer

I *DO* LOVE sprinkles. And I'm more than happy to share my favorite ice cream joint with the notorious Jocelyn Jones.

See, I am well aware she's one of the best agents in the business. Hard-working and tough-as-nails, the woman knows how to make things happen for her clients. However, if she thinks I can be wooed over endorsement promises, she's got me pegged all wrong. I don't deal in cold contracts, bleeding my signature onto their pages. I deal in handshakes, loyalty, and trust.

I'm aware of her reputation. Around town, people call her the Ice Queen. I've heard her called worse, but I don't care to repeat that sort of language around a woman, especially when it's not true. Anyone who thinks Jocelyn Jones is made of ice simply isn't looking hard enough. There's more to her than meets the eye, that's for sure, and I want to find out *what*.

But if Miss Jones thinks she can win my business without taking the time to know me, she's not understanding my game. I don't *want* the polished exterior she shows to the world—I want more than that. I need to know she trusts me, and I need to trust her.

If Jocelyn Jones lets the ice around her heart melt, we could make an excellent team.

See, there might be more to Jocelyn Jones than meets the eye, but there's a side of me she hasn't seen yet, either. And if I'm going to trust her with my career, she's going to have to trust me, too.

CHAPTER 3

Jocelyn

"THIS LOOKS . . . GREAT!" I try to give a cheery smile, even though nothing could be further from the truth.

He's taken me to a complete and utter dump. I have to step over a pile of melted green goo on the sidewalk.

Boxer gives an enthusiastic nod, and I try not to wonder whether this place has ever received an A-rating from the FDA. The ice cream shop is hardly more than a hut built into a truck and parked along the road near my office in Century City. I thought it was a mistake when Boxer stopped his car in front of it. We could've walked, but thanks to my high heels, he offered to drive.

I keep that smile on my face, following Boxer to the window, watching as he gives a complicated handshake to the man behind the window.

"Gabe, you know what I'll have," he says. "The lady will have . . ."

I give a stupefied shake of my head as he looks to me. "Boy," I say, scanning a peeling menu that looks thoroughly unappetizing. "Where do I even start?"

"Dip cone, extra crunch on the outside," Boxer says smoothly, half to me, half to Gabe. "Yeah?"

"Crunch is the best," Gabe agrees. "Sweet treat for the sweet lady."

I laugh at this; the thought of anyone calling me sweet is a little bit funny. My cheeks turn red and I look away, however, when Boxer nods in agreement.

I reach for my wallet, but Boxer rests a hand on my arm, halting me in the process.

"Let me pay," I say. "It's business. I can expense it."

"No, this is personal." With an amused shake of his head, he moves my hand away. "We left business back at the office."

"Well, then, thank you."

Boxer hands over a twenty, waving away the change. On the ice, this man looks intimidating. He's big—his sheer size a presence in itself. The features on his face are a little too dramatic, the chip in his tooth a testament to his many battles on skates.

However, when he smiles, his eyes brighten into pools of crystal blue under a slightly-too-long mane of dirty blond hair. My eyes wander toward the bulge of arm muscles as he tucks his wallet back into his pocket.

"Here you are," he says, handing one cone to me and holding onto the other. "I guarantee you've never had anything better."

I take the dessert, calculating just how long it's been since I've had any of it: the waffle cone, the crunch, the full fat ice cream. I don't *diet*, but I do stick to a regimented meal plan of coffee for breakfast, salad for lunch, and a Lean Cuisine for dinner. I just don't have the time to *really* enjoy food. For me, it's a tool to keep energized and nothing more.

Boxer watches me carefully. "What do you think?"

I make a show of my first lick from the top of the cone, raising my eyebrows in pleasant surprise. I'm shocked that I don't have to fake my amazement. The ice cream is *delicious*.

"It's wonderful," I tell both men as they watch me like hawks. "Best I've ever had."

Both break into smiles at my words.

"Great," Gabe says. "I love to hear it. Any friend of Boxer's is a friend of mine. Come back soon and bring Charli."

"Charli?" I look to Boxer.

"Let's walk," he says.

It's a surprisingly warm January day in Los Angeles, and the burst of cool treat sends tingles across my flesh. The sweet crunch of sprinkles against a backdrop of vanilla and chocolate twist brings back the sensations of summer that I haven't felt since childhood.

When Boxer rests his hand on my elbow and turns me down a side street, it's comfortable, as if we've been here before, danced to this tune. We stay quiet for some time, and the peaceful hum of midday sounds is a nice change of pace.

We walk until Boxer finds what he's looking for—a bench tucked into the high-rise buildings of Century City. Despite the corporate feel, he's managed to find a small section that feels like a park. I'd never noticed it existed.

Only once he's gotten me seated does he remove his hand from my arm and sit next to me, perching lazily across the space. He owns the air around him with quiet confidence, how a cat might lounge in a windowsill.

"Tell me about yourself, Miss Jones."

I run a hand over my pencil skirt. "I thought we left business at the office. Call me Jocelyn."

"Jocelyn," he tries the name out. "Okay, then. Where'd you get that name? It's beautiful."

"Thank you. It was my grandmother's."

"Were you close?"

"Oh, I never . . . never met her."

He glances toward me, swift and curious. "I'm sorry to hear that. I'm sure she would've loved you."

His choice of sympathy surprises me. He doesn't even know me, yet he sounds sincere. It's odd. Because I don't have a good answer for him, I take another lick of my cone. I don't talk about my family much because there's no point. They're not here anymore, so there's no sense bringing up an age-old ache in my gut.

"Tell me something else about yourself," he says. "Something happy."

"Something happy?"

Another lick of my ice cream cone. Boxer is an anomaly, all right. I showed him the money already—most clients would've signed on the line and popped the bubbly. Not him.

Lost in my thoughts, I don't realize that Boxer's staring at me. I've completely forgotten the question.

"Miss Jones . . ." Boxer gives me a thoughtful expression over his own ice cream. "It shouldn't be so hard to come up with something that makes you happy."

"Oh, of course not . . ." I smile at him, but he doesn't return it. Instead, I find a sense of contentment there, a quiet calmness. "At the moment, I'm happy you're excited to meet with me. I really believe that together, we can do great things, and—"

Boxer gives a low laugh, and I stop talking.

"I didn't ask for a sales pitch," he says in his deep voice. "Work doesn't count. What else makes you happy?"

I narrow my eyes at him, thinking on it. It's harder than I'd like to admit.

"I enjoy my spin classes in the morning," I begin. "The endorphins make me happy."

"Fair enough."

"Tell me something about you," I say before he can pester me for more. "What's something I should know about you?"

"Oh, Miss Jones—"

"Jocelyn."

"Anyone ever call you Joss?" Boxer asks. You seem more like a Joss."

I blink in surprise. "Only my dad."

"Well, your dad has good taste."

"Yes," I agree, not bothering to correct Boxer with the correct tense. My dad *had* good taste. "I haven't been called that since I graduated high school. It just didn't seem as . . . professional."

"I get it. My name is Landon, but my brother called me Danny growing up. I prefer Boxer."

I size him up, pretending to study his physique. "You look like a Landon to me."

He gives a quiet laugh. "Only my mom calls me that."

I catch a drip of ice cream on my tongue before it falls to the ground, surprising myself with how long I've gone without looking at the clock. Even more surprising, I'm in no rush to leave. "What else should I know about you?"

"I have a daughter," Boxer says, his face lighting at the word. "Her name is Charli. Well, it's Charlotte, but she'll poke your eyes out if you call her that."

"A daughter." Another drop of ice cream snakes down the side of my cone, but I'm not quick enough to stop it from skidding toward the ground. "Are you married?"

"No. Never was, actually." He stands and reaches a hand out to pull me to my feet as I finish the last of my cone. His has long since vanished. "Are you ready?"

"How old is Charli?" I accept his proffered hand, allowing his giant one to engulf mine. His fingers are warm, gentle even, as he guides me onto the sidewalk.

"She's five, almost six. Hard to believe how fast the time goes."

"That it does. Do you have other children?"

"It's just the two of us at home."

"You've been raising her alone?"

"For almost five years, yeah."

I shouldn't pry, but I'm genuinely curious. "You can tell me to bug off if I'm being inappropriate, but I'm just curious how she came to be yours."

He laughs, and I realize the awkwardness of my question a beat too late. I don't deal with kids often, and I've rarely considered having any of my own. Talking about children feels alien, so I cringe and apologize.

"No, it makes sense, but that's a funny way to ask it." We walk side by side, Boxer's face beaming at the mention of his daughter. "I don't suppose Charli came to be mine—she's always been mine."

"Of course."

"You're not prying. This is what friends do," Boxer explains. "As for Chali's mom? We fell in love about seven years ago. I proposed, but she told me *no*."

"*Why?*" The word comes out a gasp, and immediately I'm awkward multiplied by ten. "Er . . . she wasn't ready to get married?"

"I suppose she was young and hopeful, among other things." The blue of Boxer's eyes darkens, masking a flash of hurt. "She liked the *idea* of dating a hockey player more than the reality of it. I tried to keep up with her—the parties, the events, the premiers, but that's not me. Eventually, it wore us down."

"Oh."

"Then, Charli happened," he says. "Nearly six years ago now. We tried to make it work for another year after she was born, but it only lasted a few months. Lauren—that's her mother's name— took off for greener pastures. Last I heard, she's dating a football player in Miami."

"Oh, Boxer."

My hand reaches for his of its own accord, and I give a concise squeeze. I've never been much good at offering sympathy, but this feels right. And when the touch happens, a rush slides through me, a zing of excitement and sympathy and compassion.

"I'm sorry that happened to you." I pull my hand away before I lose my train of thought. "I really am."

"Why?" He looks at me in surprise. "I'm not sorry at all."

"But Lauren—"

"It wasn't the life for her," he says. "But that's okay—this is *my* life. I can't imagine a day without Charli. If anything, I'm a very lucky man."

It's a good thing I let go of his hand when I did. Otherwise, I might've slipped my fingers between his and left them there. I'm not known for my emotional intelligence or my ability to comfort my friends—I don't expect sympathy from others, so I've never learned how to gift it in return.

However, Boxer's not looking for sympathy, and this throws me for a loop. I can't think of the right words, so I settle for a smile and a nod.

"Do you have kids?"

"No," I tell him. "None."

"Any desire?"

"Oh, I don't know." I shrug. It's the truth; I haven't thought about it much. "I haven't figured out how to balance a career and a family yet, I suppose."

We approach his car, and he stops walking. "It's not that hard."

"Of course it is! There are blogs and books and advice on the subject *everywhere*," I say. "I've read half of them, and none of them make it sound easy."

"Well, I'll tell you my theory." Boxer opens the passenger door to his SUV, and I note a doll upside down on the backseat. "Hop in."

I slide in, brushing against his arm as I do so. A jolt shoots through me, just like the last time we touched. It jumbles my thoughts.

"There you are," he says, tucking the strap of my purse into the car. "You liked the ice cream?"

"Loved it."

Boxer shuts the door, then makes his way to the driver's seat. Once he's settled, he looks across the center console, studying my face for a long minute. Eventually, I'm forced to look away—I pride myself on my ability to maintain eye contact in tricky situations, but this one is different. He's not looking to intimidate, but to understand. In a world of business, this is unusual.

"There are only a few things you need to know about me," he begins, finally dropping his gaze from my eyes to my lips—for one moment only—before he looks through the window. "I'm a pretty simple guy."

"I'd beg to differ."

He grins. "Then you're making this too difficult."

"Humor me," I say, unable to hide my own smile. "What am I missing?"

"I love my daughter more than anything," he says. "And I love hockey a close second. That's all there is to it."

"That's . . ." I struggle to comprehend, stumbling for a response. "That doesn't sound so simple at all."

"Well, there's one more thing."

"What's that?"

"Ice cream," he says. "It's a close third."

CHAPTER 4

Jocelyn

LIKE A GENTLEMAN, Boxer drops me back off at the agency's building, waiting until I open the front door before pulling away. As I walk through the lobby and hit the elevator button to bring me to the office, I turn and watch his taillights disappear into the distance.

I'm still thinking about him when I reach the office. I close my door and sit down to work, cramming in one meeting after the next until the agency is technically closed. When a knock on the door alerts me to the darkness outside, the late hour, I'm startled to find he's still on my mind.

"Diana, that reporter, called." Lindsay, my assistant, pokes her head in. "Sorry to startle you. I just hadn't heard from you, and I was wondering what I can do to get you home before midnight."

"Haven't I told Diana a hundred times that I'm not open for an interview?" I blink and look at the clock. "*Lindsay*! It's eight thirty. Didn't you say you had a date tonight?"

"I cancelled. And I already told Diana *no*; I just thought I'd run it by you. It's never too late, you know. Might not hurt to do one interview."

"Go! *Shoo.* If it's not too late, un-cancel your date!"

"I don't mind. I wasn't all that excited about it anyway." She shrugs. "Plus, I finished up some paperwork."

"But—"

"How'd it go today?" Instead of evacuating the premises like I'd suggested, Lindsay slides inside the room and grins. "You had a meeting with Boxer?"

"It went . . ." I pause, sitting back in my chair. "It was interesting."

"I've heard he's a great guy."

"From who?"

She shifts her weight from one foot to the next, her long, flowy skirt rippling around her legs. On anyone else, it'd look a bit hippie in style, but she's paired it with a sharp tank top, a jacket, and a beautiful pair of black heels to make the outfit complete. "Well, Duke used to come by on business sometimes. He always spoke highly of Boxer."

Boxer's current agent is turning seventy-five next month. Someone finally convinced Duke to retire—probably the saint of a wife he's held onto for over fifty years. Whether Boxer wants to or not, he'll need new representation, and soon.

"Did you eat dinner?" I ask. "Let's order something."

"I'll pick something up on the way home."

"Look, Lindsay, I appreciate you working so hard, but you don't have to stick around until the middle of the night every time I do." I wave a hand across my desk. "You shouldn't cancel your dates to stay late."

"Meh, I'm using you as an alibi. My date seemed like a loser. He asked the color of my underwear, and we've never *met!*"

I laugh, which is a refreshing change of pace from my normal workday. When I'd hired Lindsay as an intern, she'd been a cute brunette with bright brown eyes, eager to please. She'd worked round the clock on a measly intern's stipend.

Four years later, she's still with me. We've upgraded her salary, her job title, and her responsibilities. I live in mortal fear that one day, she'll up and decide there are better career paths for her elsewhere.

I'd die before I let that happen. She runs my life, so I make sure to pay enough that it's worth her while. People like Lindsay are hard to come by. Media may call me the Ice Queen, a cold and ruthless bitch, but they've never called me stupid. I know when I have a good thing, and Lindsay is a great thing. So is Boxer.

"At least let me buy you dinner," I insist. "I'm happy to be your alibi anytime."

"I'll put in an order of lasagna from Peretti's Pizza."

She bounces out of the room, and I wonder, not for the first time, how she's managed to keep her pleasant, rose-tinted view of the world firmly in place. She's a few years younger than me—she's pushing twenty-five, and I can't help but think that when I hit twenty-five, I'd been scrambling my way up the corporate ladder. I'm now twenty-eight, and I'm still not sure where that ladder is leading.

Though I'm proud of my career, a tiny part of me wonders what it's like to live life like Lindsay. She leaves the job at the office, has fun with her friends, texts boys about her underwear color . . . It's all so curious to me, but it makes her happy.

I'm in the middle of jotting a note down about needing to call Duke—maybe pick his brain about this whole situation—when my phone rings. It's the direct line to Lindsay, so I hit speaker.

"There's someone here to see you."

I pick up the phone and put it to my ear, confused. "Who is it?"

"Andy Rumpert."

"Andy?" I groan. "What does he want?"

"Business. But if you have dinner plans, I can send him away."

I think on it for a minute. Lindsay's sharp. She's given me an easy loophole if I want to send him away. However, Andy's like an annoying wart that won't go away, and I decide it's better to deal with him now. Otherwise, he'll just pop back up, more annoying the next time.

"Miss Jones?"

"Send him in." I sigh. "I'm in a good mood tonight. Let's see if he can ruin it."

"Aww."

"You can head home, Linds. I have a feeling I know what this is about."

"You're brave," she whispers into the phone. Then louder, she speaks to Andy. "She'll see you now."

Footsteps approach my door. I'm about to hang up the phone when Lindsay comes back on the line.

"Miss Jones?" she says in a hushed voice. "Last week, I heard one of the PR girls blabbing on her phone in the lobby that Andy's going through a divorce and is extra mean. I'm sending in lasagna in twenty minutes, and you can make me kick him out if things go south."

"You're a lifesaver."

"Jocelyn." Andy appears, giving a useless knock on the door, seeing as he's already halfway inside the room. A smile tilts his mouth upward. "Just the beautiful woman I wanted to see."

"Your wife won't be happy to hear that," I say, trying to remain calm. Andy is pond scum, and I don't say that lightly. He's been known to lie, cheat, and steal clients from various agents in a very public way. "What do you need, Andy?"

"Nice to see you, too," he says, a flash of anger shooting across his face.

"What are you here for?"

"Boxer's mine," he says, sitting himself in the chair across from me without an invitation. He's wearing an expensive suit and he's shiny, I'll give him that. Shiny hair, shiny shoes, shiny glint in his eyes, but it's all fake. "I just wanted to give you the chance to back out of the race for his business with grace."

People might not like me or my boldness, but nobody has ever called me a liar, a cheat, or a fake. That's the difference between Andy and me—we both work hard, we can both be ruthless, but I won't cross certain lines. Andy doesn't have the same scruples. He calls it a weakness. I call it morals.

"Back out of what?" I ask, trying for polite. "You're free to try and recruit Boxer. So am I. When did this become a race?"

"Of course it's a fucking race," he snarls, temper flaring up. "Duke's retiring, we both know that. The old ball and chain is making him hang up his skates."

"Mrs. Landingham is a nice woman. I'm glad they'll be able to spend some time together.

"What the hell are they supposed to do at that age anyway?" Andy shakes his head. "Sit around and wrinkle? I want to be working or dead at that age, if you ask me."

"I didn't."

"I'm going to take Boxer on as my client," Andy says. "So why don't you give up now and make things easier—and less embarrassing—for both of us?"

"I could say the same to you."

"Not clever enough to come up with your own retort?"

"Not bothering to waste my breath on it." I stand, fold my hands in front of my body, and give him a smile. "Did you walk into my office tonight to intimidate me, Mr. Rumpert? If so, it's not working."

"You going to run crying to the press? Feed them a story about me?"

"Of course not."

"I'm sure there's some law you could bend to make this about harassment." His eyes challenge me. "Go ahead, give it a try."

I've never once run crying to my boss, screaming to any authorities, or whatever else he's suggesting. The man's got some sort of complex about being challenged by women in the workforce, and I don't intend to fuel his fire. I intend to beat him. Fair and square.

"Good night, Andy. Please see yourself out."

"Is this defeat?" His eyes glint. "Let me buy you dinner as a truce. Come on, my treat."

My stomach roils at the thought. I'd rather stick the Peretti's lasagna into my eyes and starve than have dinner with him.

"No, thank you," I say, resting one hand on the door. "But if you think you can walk into my office and try to intimidate me away from the biggest deal of the year, you've gone about this all wrong."

"Is that right?" He leans extra close on his way out, breath reeking of smoke. "What's the right way?"

"Give up on Boxer now," I tell him. "You don't deserve him."

"And you do?"

"He's mine."

"Feisty," he says. "I like it."

"Not feisty, let's call it focused. I'm the best in the business, Rumpert. He'll sign with me."

Andy takes a long look at my chest, and it's everything I can do not to punch the smirk right off of his face. I practice that stupid meditation breathing again, though I'm pretty sure the only thing I need is a kickboxing class and a pack of Tums.

"You going to make this deal go as smoothly as the one with

Ryan Pierce?" He raises an eyebrow on the way out. "Good luck, sweetheart. We all know how that went. You'll *need* the luck."

With that, he's gone before I can throat punch him for calling me sweetheart. I know, I know, I should be meditating the crap out of this moment, but he brings the violence out in full force. I slam the door shut and return to my desk, dropping my head in my hands.

I'm shaking, trembling from head to foot. There's a knock on the door, and I assume it's Lindsay with the lasagna, so I tell her I need a minute. I take one deep breath, then another, wishing my heart to stop racing and my body to steady.

When I trust my voice not to crack, I call Lindsay in, mumbling some excuse about needing a second to jot down notes. She doesn't believe me for a second, wrinkling her nose in disbelief.

"Don't worry about him, Miss Jones," she says, putting the food on the corner of my desk. "He's slime. Everyone knows it. Even his clients know it—I overhear things working the front desk, remember, and I've never heard a single good word about that man."

"I know. It just pisses me off that I let him get under my skin." I stand and pace back and forth before the floor-to-ceiling window that gives a stunning view of Los Angeles by night. "Can you see if there are more of those yoga-whatever-stupid classes down the street? I can't seem to keep my temper around him."

"Absolutely."

"I'm going to need my temper in check," I tell her, "because he came to say it's a war."

"A war? Over Boxer?"

"Boxer would make for a great client—easy to manage, lots of endorsement potential, a strong player focused on the game. I want him."

"He's also a really nice guy," Lindsay says. "What if you just talked to him? I don't think he'd like Andy much, but if he got to know you . . ." She shrugs. "It'd be an easy choice. He'd love you."

I bark laughter. "Love? No. I'm not sure there's anybody who could say that about me."

Lindsay stills, her shoulders rigid. "Miss Jones—"

"I'm not asking for pity," I say, waving a hand. "I was kidding."

"Of course you are," Lindsay says, sensing it's time to back out of the room. When she reaches the door, she turns back and gives me a look, a bit of sadness in her eyes, though no sign of pity. "You're a strong woman, Miss Jones, but sometimes it's not about fighting with your fists."

"What other way is there? Andy leaves me no choice."

"Maybe Andy doesn't," she says, her voice a soft tinkle of bright cutting through the silent room. "But Boxer does. Get to know him, and I'll bet you there'll be opportunities you never knew existed."

"I'm not sure I'm the world's most likeable person. Maybe *you* should have lunch with him and win him over."

"You're being ridiculous." Lindsay offers me a bright smile. "You don't let many people in, but when you do, they like what they see."

"Now you're just asking for a raise."

"I don't work for you because I love the hours," Lindsay says with a wink. "I happen to have a great boss. Don't be afraid to let Boxer see the real you. He'll like it, I promise."

Lindsay leaves then, and the smell of lasagna draws me back to my desk. Even though my stomach growls, I can't bring myself to eat. I wait, listen as Lindsay lets herself out of the building and does the locking up, and then I rise to my feet once more.

Looking out over the buildings, I wonder what Boxer's doing

right now. Is he with his daughter?

An absolutely crazy notion crosses my mind.

What if I called him?

For no reason at all except . . . to check in with him.

I dismiss the idea just as quickly because that's ridiculous. What would we talk about? I don't have anything in common with the man. He's sweet, calm, patient. I'm uptight, skittish after my meeting, and staring at a now-cooling plate of lasagna.

No, we are no match for one another in any world except business. I package up the takeout, catching a glimpse of my black suit in the windows on the way out, my blonde hair wound tightly in a bun, skirt neatly pressed and standard. Practical. In Boxer's eyes, I'm nothing but business; I'm sure of it. I haven't made it this far by making friends. I've made it this far by making deals.

Two hours later, I'm reheating the lasagna in the microwave and loading up my TiVo'd episode of *The Bachelor*. Ten minutes into it, and I know I'm going crazy because an advertisement for cat food makes me tear up.

There's an old couple holding hands, and I can't help but think of Duke and his wife taking time to be together and retire. When I'm that age, will I be alone with the cat, or will I have a hand to hold?

To combat the tears, I find a Spinning class online and sign up for it at once. Probably, I'm low on endorphins. Endorphins help everything. So does lasagna, and so does deep breathing.

I think.

CHAPTER 5

Boxer

I TIPTOE DOWN the hallway toward my daughter's room, which is more difficult than it sounds. Moving quietly when I weigh as much as a small elephant is a skill I haven't yet mastered.

I push the door open to Charli's room. The muted yellow walls glow under the first dregs of morning sunlight, the brightness washing through me like a gentle breeze. This might be my favorite part of the day.

Inching around the corner, I'm careful not to step on the squeaky stuffed dog guarding Charli's bed from intruders. I rest there, leaning against the doorframe as I watch my daughter's rose-colored cheeks, cherubic in their plumpness. She's an angel like this, a perfect sleeping princess.

Curls as tight as a spring wind naturally across her pillow, spreading in all directions. This is a better representation of her personality than her calm, sweet cheeks. Charli's a wild one, unruly on her best days, but I wouldn't have it any other way. She's got spunk, the kid, that's for sure.

There's a heart of gold underneath it all, however, and I know that too. My heart constricts as she takes a deep breath and lets out the faintest of sighs as I watch the rise and fall of her chest.

She looks more and more grown every day.

When did she lose the baby fat? I wonder, wishing she could've stayed small just a bit longer. Already, she's playing soccer, hockey, and tee-ball, and she's as fierce as they come. Her room might be yellow, her pillows might be purple, and her favorite color might be glitter, but she's a tomboy through and through.

The harsh jolt of the radio clock gurgling to life gives me a start, and I stumble backwards out of the room. Charli's taken on a violently independent streak lately, and prefers to get up to her own alarm.

She also prefers to wake *me* up, which is why I jog back to bed and climb under the covers. I've already been up a full hour—ran a couple miles on the treadmill, watched the news, showered and dressed in fresh pajamas. Just so Charli can wake me up again.

Footsteps pad down the hallway, tiny in size, and a giggle filters through the open door. I pull the covers over my head, just the way she likes, and squint my eyes shut.

"Dad?" she whispers softly. "Daddy . . . it's time to wake up."

I roll over and grunt. Another giggle.

"Daddy!" Her voice grows louder, and she takes a few more steps into the room. "Wake up! It's time for school."

"I'm sleeping."

"But, *daddy!*"

"Go away," I mumble, taking a peek at her through the comforter as I roll back around. "I'm hibernating."

The giggles turn into a full-on waterfall of laughter. Light and innocent, almost piercing in her joy. "You're not a *bear!*"

"Are you sure . . . ?" I poke a bit of my head outside of the blanket and watch her through one eye. "Maybe I *am*."

"You're not! You're a human. A *boy!*"

Her curls bounce as she inches closer, just a shadow of doubt across her face. That's when I pounce—both hands extended like claws. I give a growl so loud she gets the hiccups, and I immediately feel horrible.

"Dad!" She's laughing, hiccupping, and rushing at me all at once.

I catch the screaming bundle with one hand and raise her above me like a football. She kicks, flails, and yelps some more as I find the tickle-zone near her ribcage. When she gives a hiccup so big it turns into a burp, I lose it, too, and I pull her in for a serious round of cuddles.

She tries to tickle my armpits, but she mostly scratches my shoulder. I go with it anyway because I can't possibly bear to disappoint those huge blue eyes.

"Let me in, it's cold out here!" She wiggles her body underneath the covers and gives me a squeeze with the tiniest arms this world has ever seen. She's strong for her age, but put her next to me, and it's like a fly trying to hug a hippo.

I hold her close, press a kiss to her forehead, and tell her how much I love her.

"How much, daddy?"

"More than you can ever guess. What's the biggest number you know?"

"Ten."

"No," I tell her. "You know bigger numbers than that. How old am I?"

"A hundred."

"Closer," I say, grinning into her curls. "I love you all the way to the moon and back again."

"I guess that's pretty good," she says. "I love you even more."

We stay that way for a long minute, until she gets another case of the wiggles and accidentally sends a foot straight into my gut. It's times like these when I wonder how a five-year-old princess can bring a full-grown man to his knees. A few inches lower, and she would've connected with an area I would prefer to keep intact. Just in case.

In case of what? I find myself wondering as I send Charli to pull on some clothes. In case I invite a woman over? At the rate my dating life has been going, I'll be a born-again virgin by the time Charli can drive.

It's not that I'm opposed to finding love again—it's just that I can't risk Charli's heart. She's a special girl, and it'd take a damn special woman for me to bring someone else into our family.

A brief image of Jocelyn Jones flickers through my mind as I strip out of my pajama pants and pull on a pair of jeans. Why her? I have no clue. She's out to get me—or, my face, rather—when Duke retires. She looks at me and sees dollar signs.

Even so, I have to admit the woman is beautiful. I'm a man, and I have a pulse—it's natural that my pulse speeds up when a gorgeous woman walks into a room, and even more so when she's eating ice cream and looking like it's giving her an orgasm.

Dammit, I think, looking down at my pants which, unfortunately, are too thin for the thoughts I have running through my head.

"Dad, it's pajama day," Charli calls from down the hall. "Can I wear my Jasmine pajamas?"

"Sure," I call back, making sure the door is shut.

"You have to wear yours, too."

I almost argue, but it's a pretty simple request. *Wear pajamas*. There's only one problem, and it's this stupid boner. Maybe I do need to get laid, I think, if Jocelyn Jones—the Ice Queen of Hollywood—has this sort of effect on me after *one* business meeting.

I shift around, glancing down at the pj pants Charli had picked out for me. They're red and have crossed hockey sticks all over them. I look like a buffoon, but I know it'll make her happy, so it's the least I can do.

I am not, and can never be, both a mother and a father, but I do my best. We have fun together, and I hope that makes up for everything I can't provide. A woman's touch, a mother's advice, a date to the mother-daughter events at her school. It kills me that I can't do it all, but that's life.

When I'm finally presentable again, I vow to keep Jocelyn as far out of my brain as possible. I'm not signing with her. I've already decided. I'm not interested in making the most money I possibly can; I'm interested in having a career and a family life with Charli. That might mean turning down some endorsement deals to stay home with my daughter, and I already know Jocelyn would have none of that.

I know Andy Rumpert is out for me, too, and I might be able to strike some sort of deal with him. He seems reasonable, at least from a distance. And he's far less sexy than Jocelyn Jones, which would do great things for my mental health.

"Dad, I'm ready!" Charli's getting the cereal out of the cupboard. "Where's the milk?"

I grab it from the fridge as per our routine. She's not quite strong enough to pour the milk, so her job is the cereal. She dumps the cereal into the bowl, flakes of the stuff scattering everywhere. I pour in the milk, and then Charli sets the timer on her Aladdin themed watch.

"Can I go, yet?" I ask, sinking a spoon into the cereal. "Pretty please?"

"No, dad!" she cries. "Forty more seconds."

Apparently, Charli has determined that fifty-two seconds is the perfect amount of time that cereal needs to sit in order to get soggy. She hops onto her chair, I sweep the spilled cereal into the trash and then pop over to my chair, and Charli starts the ten second countdown.

Once her alarm goes off, she punches a tiny fist to the ceiling and calls for us to dive in. We eat in silence, side by side, and I feel the familiar peace that comes with spending a morning with my daughter.

As much as I need to get stuff done today, I can't look forward to dropping her off at school. If I had it my way, we'd play some street hockey in the back alley, pop in a movie for the afternoon, and make dinner together. She really is the only girl I need in my life.

Except, of course, for the romantic aspect. But that takes second fiddle now, for at least the next few years of my life. I just have to figure out a way to keep myself distant from Jocelyn Jones because that woman is a temptation the likes of which I haven't seen in years. Not since I fell in love the first time.

"Time for school, kiddo," I say, once our spoons clank against the bare edges of the bowls. "I think Marie just arrived, but I'm going to take you today."

"Are you coming for pancake lunch day?"

"There's a pancake lunch day?"

Charli's face goes slack. She runs into the other room, grabs her backpack—the sparkly soccer ball on the outside glittering against the sunlight—and scurries back. "Ooops."

"Charlie . . ." I shake my head as she pulls out the paperwork informing me that, yes indeed, there is a pancake lunch today. "When did your teacher give you this?"

She hops back on her chair and gives me a shrug, feet dangling high above the ground. "Dunno."

"You've got to give me these things earlier," I tell her, resting the paper against the table and tilting her chin upwards. "So I can clear my schedule to come."

"Does that mean you can't come today? Because I was too late?"

I shake my head. "I'll be there. Go get your shoes on."

The front door opens, perfectly timed, as Marie calls out a hello. She's been the nanny slash housekeeper slash burst of sanity ever since Charli was born and, even though I try to do it all, I'm grateful to have Marie to pick up the slack.

"Am I taking you to school today, Miss Charli?" she asks. "I'm hoping it's pajama day, otherwise I have no clue why you're wearing those clothes."

"Of course it's pajama day!" Charli giggles and hugs Marie. "Dad's taking me."

"Great," she says. "Then I'll get some shopping done. Have a great day at school."

"I will," Charli says. "Because dad's clearing his schedule for lunch."

"Excellent," she says. Then she raises her eyes, and catches a glimpse of me standing in the doorway. "Pajama day for you too, Mr. Boxer?"

I've tried to correct her and get her to call me just plain old Boxer, but she refuses. And I've given up arguing. "According to Charli it is," I say with a shrug. "We'll see you later. I'll get Charli from school today, but I'll need you to watch her this afternoon while I'm at practice."

"Absolutely. I'm free all night, Mr. Boxer, no rush."

"No need," I tell her. "I'll be home by eight."

"Because eight o'clock is book time," Charli says. "And we can't have book time if dad's not home."

"Exactly." I ruffle her hair, hoping that book time will never come to an end. Already, five years have gone by too fast. I can't stand to think there will be a day she won't notice if I'm not home to read her a bedtime story.

What'll I do when the only girl in my life is all grown up? I push through the door holding Charli's hand, wondering if, when Charli goes off to college, I'll be alone in this big old house.

It's not ideal, but love is going to have to work hard to find me because I'm not quite ready to share my time with anyone else.

CHAPTER 6

Jocelyn

"YOU ARE MISS Popular today," Lindsay says, knocking briefly before entering my office first thing this morning. "I've gotten five meeting requests, and I haven't even had my latte yet. Also, one date request."

I look up to find her waggling her eyebrows at the name she's scribbled on the notepad. With a sigh, I hold out my hand. "Let me see that."

"You haven't gone out with this one before, have you?" Lindsay rests the notepad on my desk. "Charles Strom? He's the head of . . . what's it called?"

"Intellect. That new company doing something with computers—they were in the newspaper. The article was so dry I skimmed most of it."

"More than I read," Lindsay agrees. "So, can I confirm the date?"

"I don't know. I'm in the middle of a bunch of stuff—I have to follow up with Boxer because I can't rest until Andy's off my case. Then I have the other meetings you scheduled, and I should prepare the papers Brian will need for that upcoming endorsement . . . let's say no."

"You have to eat, Miss Jones," Lindsay says, pulling the note back from my desk. "Why don't you go out for a change of scenery, at least?"

"I prefer to be alone rather than bored by my date."

"Give him a chance. If he's boring you out of your mind, you can find a way to leave. I'll even pick you up if you need. It'll be refreshing. We can always order lasagna and watch dumb reality television shows every other night of the week."

"I don't know—"

"Great. I'll get your date scheduled."

Lindsay's out of the room before I can comprehend whether or not I've actually agreed to anything. A few minutes later, an appointment with Charles Strom pops up on my calendar, as well as a quick note from him—or more likely his secretary—via email. The note promises a pleasant evening and delicious dining. We'll meet at seven.

"Well, that solves that," I say, turning to the next order of business. "Lindsay, you sly fox."

The hours pass quickly as I set into the monotony that is everyday work. Meetings, phone calls, reviewing documents, administrative crap—it all flows, one thing to the next, until I realize it's almost lunch.

There's one more phone call I need to make before I head out to grab a salad from down the road. Sitting back in my chair, I choose my cell phone as opposed to the landline. It's more personal to have my private number appearing than a corporate one.

If I've learned anything about Boxer, it's that he's not signing himself away to the highest bidder—he's looking for personality. I can give him personality.

"Hello?" He sounds a bit confused as he answers. "Who is this?"

"Hey, Boxer," I say, a smile spreading across my face. The image brought to my mind by his voice—the wide grin, sturdy jaw, handsome blue eyes—is entirely pleasant. "It's Jocelyn. I hope you don't mind I called from my personal line—I just wanted you to have my cell phone number in case of emergency. You can reach me all hours of the day."

"Fine," he says. "I'd offer you the same, but it seems you already have my number and aren't afraid to use it."

"I'm sorry, is this a bad time?"

"Actually, it is. I'm at my daughter's school for her pajama day pancake lunch. Can we talk later?"

"Sure, um . . . of course." I'm rarely ever speechless, but this one has me at a loss for words. "Sorry to bother you. When should I call?"

"Later," he says, sounding vague and distracted. "Talk to you later."

When I hang up the phone, I'm mystified. I need a breath of fresh air, a latte, and a nice, crisp salad with some chicken. I grab my purse and stop by the lobby.

"Am I rude?" I ask Lindsay. "Be honest."

"Um . . ." She looks up and winces. "Not usually?"

"I can't figure out Boxer."

Lindsay shrugs. "He seems pretty straightforward. That little girl of his is cute. There was a picture of them in the paper."

"Curious. Very curious."

"Remember what I said," Lindsay calls as I head toward the doors. "Just be yourself!"

"Nope, *myself* isn't good enough." I stop in the doorway. "Andy Rumpert is going to steal Boxer right out from underneath me, just like he did with Donovan."

"This isn't a repeat of Donovan."

"Sure as hell feels like it," I tell Lindsay. "Do me a favor and try to think of something that'll impress Boxer. I'm going to need a leg up on this one."

CHAPTER 7

Boxer

I'M GETTING QUITE a few stares, and I think it's because of my pants.

Not a single parent heard the news it was pajama day. Either that, or my daughter made it up.

I look around, and not one other person—parent, child, or teacher—is wearing anything other than their normal clothes. Jeans, t-shirts, dresses, that sort of thing. In fact, all of the students are in their normal, private school uniforms of plaid skirts or navy pants and white collared shirts.

"So, honey," I say, squatting next to Charli just as we're about to step into the auditorium. "Why aren't any of your classmates dressed in pajamas?"

She shrugs. "They forgot."

"Really?" I struggle to hold back a smile. "Every last one of them?"

Her baby blues watch me, mischief in them, and I see the exact moment she realizes I know the truth. Even so, she sticks to her story. "I forgot."

"You didn't forget, did you?" I say softly. "Why'd you tell me it was pajama day if it's not? You could get in trouble for not wearing your uniform."

"I don't like my uniform."

"Why not?"

She gives a two shoulder shrug, as if it's not worth the explanation to a grownup like me. "You wouldn't understand," she says on a sigh that's ten years older than her. "You get to wear whatever you want every day."

"You'll get to do that, too, when you're as old as me."

She squints. "I don't want to be old like you."

"Thanks, hon."

She giggles. "Those are the rules. I'm little; you're big."

"That's right. So if you promise to stay little, I promise to stay old."

Holding out a pinky, a solemn expression on her face, she makes me swear on it. "Deal."

"You have to tell the truth though, okay? I trust you." I ruffle her hair. "If you tell me it's pajama day, I'm going to believe you. But you can't lie about it or we'll both get in trouble. Why'd you tell me it's pajama day?"

"Because I like my pajamas. And I like your pajamas." She reaches out, her fingers toying gently with the fabric around my knees. "And we're a team like you always say. Teams wear matching clothes."

She's wearing an old Minnesota Stars sweatshirt that goes down to her knees over her pajamas. She wears that thing like other kids hold onto a blanket—with unrivaled ferociousness, especially considering its current state of disrepair. The thing is so thin I can see sunlight pouring through it.

"We are a team," I tell her. "Me and you. We'll always be a team."

"So how come we can't wear matching clothes? I don't want

them to be on our team." She nods toward the rest of her classmates. "I want it to be just me and you, daddy."

"I know, sweetheart, but it's important to make friends, too." I grasp my daughter's hand in mine, swallowing it with the size of my fingers. "I'll tell you what. Let's make friends together."

"You'll sit with me?" Her lips are leaning toward a pout, as if she's unsure of this whole sharing thing.

"Of course I will. Let's grab some pancakes." If I could keep her home with me all day, I'd do it, but that's not what the parent book says to do. "You can do the syrup pouring, just like at home."

"Okay," she says. "Because you're not strong enough to lift it up like me."

"That's right. Let's see those guns."

With a grimace worthy of a tiger, she bares her teeth and raises her hands above her head, eeking out every last centimeter of muscle that she calls a bicep.

I reach out and give the pea-sized bump a squeeze. "Mashed potatoes."

"They're not mashed potatoes!"

"Then go show me how strong you are and load up the pancakes."

As she scurries off, I follow her progress with a smile creeping onto my face. I can't help it. If someone had told me how much joy fifty pounds of pure energy would give me, I wouldn't have believed them six years ago. Now, I don't know how I could live without her.

"Hey there, Mr. Boxer," Charli's teacher greets me as I step into the cafeteria. "Thanks for joining us today."

"Of course, Mrs. Orman," I say, greeting the thirty-something-year-old brunette. "Sorry about the, uh . . . dress code violations. I was under false pretenses that it was pajama day."

Her eyes flick ever so quickly over my pants, her cheeks flushing red before she pulls her eyes up to meet mine. "No problem at all. I chatted with Charli about it, and . . . well, you look great."

"Um, thanks," I say, shifting awkwardly as I glance around the room.

She's not the only one giving me funny glances. Some of the other dads hanging out here look downright stupefied at my getup. A handful of teachers give me a disapproving frown, and then there are the other mothers—the younger ones, some of them single—who are staring with unabashed amusement. I'm not a self-conscious person, but I can feel my heart pumping a little faster than normal.

"I discussed this with Charli," I tell her teacher. "It won't happen again. I don't know what she was thinking making up stories."

"It's clear she enjoys spending time with you, doing things together. I think she just wanted a little attention."

"I give her plenty of attention."

"You do a wonderful job, and Charli's an amazing kid. But, she's also very smart and attentive, and . . ."

"And what?" I press, suddenly less interested in pancakes. "Did something happen in class?"

"No, not so much, but—"

"Why don't I believe you?"

"Look, Mr. Boxer, I don't have to tell you that you are a very talented hockey player and have made a great career for yourself. There's a lot of speculation that you're going to help lead the Lightning to a big victory this year."

"What does this have to do with Charli?" I growl. "Did someone say something?"

I vowed a long time ago that my career wouldn't interfere with Charli's life—at least, not as much as I could help it. I have zero tolerance for paparazzi, media, reporters, or anyone else who'll try to rope my daughter into the spotlight. I'd rather give up hockey than put her in the public eye. She's a child, and she deserves to have her childhood.

"It's more the general population of the school," Mrs. Orman says, wringing her fingers together in front of her body. "And nothing bad, I promise you. We are very sensitive to that sort of thing here at Westwood Prep."

"That's why I'm paying a shitload of money for her to come here," I tell Mrs. Orman. "Sorry about the language, but I thought this was a private school that'd help guard her from some of that."

"It's impossible to ignore. You—your team, at least—make an appearance on the news three times a week. Kids, the boys in particular, enjoy watching you. You're a hero, Mr. Boxer, and a great role model. Please don't take this the wrong way—they look up to you, wear your jersey, beg their parents to stay up late to watch the end of your games."

I don't have anything to say to this. I'm partly flattered, partly embarrassed, and mostly flustered.

"I think Charli feels a little possessive over you," Mrs. Orman explains, her thick eyelashes fluttering against her cheeks. "All the kids here love you. Some of the teachers do, too. You're a popular man, Mr. Boxer. The way I see it, Charli wants to know you're hers, and hers alone. I don't blame her for not wanting to share."

I can't help the frown creeping onto my lips. Surely many men would find Mrs. Orman attractive. To me, she's just Charli's teacher, and I prefer to keep things that way.

I haven't looked romantically at a woman since Charli was born—at least, not with the intent to let anything happen. Until another image flashes through my memory—Jocelyn Jones sitting in the front seat of my car, her lips pouted with curiosity, just begging for a kiss.

I clear my throat and shake my head to get rid of the image, but Mrs. Orman takes it the wrong way.

"Oh, I'm so sorry!" She clasps a hand over her mouth. "I just meant that you and Charli share a special bond, and she's protective of it. Her mother isn't in the picture, from what you've told me, so your daughter's likely going to grab onto the bond you two share and hold it for dear life. She cherishes it."

"I understand," I say, my voice still sounding gruff. "Thanks again for looking out for Charli. You do a great job with her."

"Good luck with your season." She gives me a smile. "Everything will be just fine, I promise."

"I'm going to grab some pancakes," I say, since the conversation is wandering into uncomfortable territory. "Thank you."

"Here, dad." Charli dumps syrup onto my plate once I've joined her at the table. "Let me dress your pancakes."

I don't tell her that she hasn't *dressed* my pancakes, she's drowned them. There's enough syrup on my plate for an entire tribe of pancakes. Still, her teacher's words are fresh in my mind, and instead of giving her a lecture about not wasting syrup, I pull her in close and wrap my arm around her.

"That's perfect," I say, pressing a kiss into her unruly curls. One of the 'Mom' things I haven't figured out is hair. On a good day, Charli's curls are a wild mess. On a bad day, she looks like Michael Jackson with an afro. "I love you."

"Love you too, daddy."

She happily chomps on her pancakes, and I follow suit, mostly drinking mine since the 'cakes' have disintegrated into mush. We're almost through with the meal when I feel a shadow arrive behind me, a large figure that I recognize the second I turn around.

"Boxer." Andy Rumpert has a huge grin on his face. He sticks out a hand as if we're old buddies. "Fancy seeing you here, man."

"Andy." I turn halfway in my seat. Charli's head swivels too, and she gives the stranger a look that's none too excited. "What brings you here?"

"Couldn't miss a chance to talk with my favorite defender in the league."

"I'm in the middle of something."

"Oh, right, sorry." Andy offers a smile that anybody can see isn't nearly sincere enough. "My niece goes here, and I just stopped by to eat lunch with her."

"Who's your niece?" Charli asks.

She's young, but she's smart. Smarter than me. I turn to watch Andy's reaction, but he slides smoothly into the real reason he's here. "I know Duke's retiring. I want you, Boxer. I want to work together."

"Sorry, I don't discuss business at my daughter's school."

"Let me buy you a drink later."

I turn back to my pancakes. "No, thank you."

"I've got tickets to the premier of the Fast & the Fury. A pair of them. Come with me, and we can talk. Tomorrow night."

"I said—"

"I don't mean to interrupt." Andy slides onto the stool next to me at the cafeteria table, and the entire thing sags under our combined weight. We are two big men on child sized seats. "I know this is some special father daughter time, but I need to get some reservations made. I'd love to buy you drinks; we can talk some business and then have a little fun."

"I don't drink."

I fork my pancake, swirl it around in a bath of syrup, and keep my arm snug around Charli's back. Her pout lines are growing deeper, and if I don't get rid of Andy soon, I have a feeling she'll do it herself. God, I love this kid. She's got the taste of a princess and the temper of a grown man with road rage.

"What sort of fun are you into?" Andy asks. "I'm up for anything."

"Ice cream," Charli finishes for me. "He loves sprinkles."

"I'll bet he does," Andy says. "Ice cream, huh?"

Andy winks at me, but he's in for a surprise if he thinks that's code word for something. I gave up drinking and life at the bars when Charli made her appearance, and I haven't regretted it for a day.

"How about we grab some ice cream and then hit the premier? Get you out of the house for a night?"

"I like my house just fine," I tell him. "And I don't discuss business at my kid's school. Bye, Rumpert."

"Tell me you'll come to the event, and I'll get out of your hair."

I hesitate and glance at Charli. The reason I don't go out isn't for lack of invites—it's because I've got all I need at home.

"Look, buddy. You're going to need a new agent. I don't want to be hanging around your daughter's school trying to win you over. Give me a fair shot and, if you don't like what you hear, I'll call it quits and leave you alone."

"One night out?"

"Movie premier. Drink—er, ice cream. A little business talk and then a little fun. We'll have everything sorted by the end of the night, and I won't pull you out on a weekday again."

"Fine."

"Fine?" He sounds surprised. "Great. I'll send a car for you at seven. Look sharp, my friend."

I'm surprised, too, as he stands to leave. I've heard about Andy Rumpert, even talked to him on occasion. He's a cross between a shark and a weasel—he does well by his clients, but it comes at a cost.

The sad truth is that Duke's retiring, and I can't blame the old asshole. He's got a beautiful wife, and he wants to spend time with her. I'd be a jerk if I asked him to stay for me. So, I need to find a new agent, and until now, I'd been considering Jocelyn Jones.

But if images of her keep popping into my head and making my pants incredibly tight, that's just not going to work out. At least I'm in no danger from getting a boner after spending time with Andy.

Charli watches him walk out of the room. "He's weird."

"Yep," I agree.

"You work with him?"

"Unfortunately."

Charli reaches over, her big blue eyes somber as she offers an encouraging pat on my shoulder with her chubby little fingers. "Sorry, dad."

"Me too, honey. Me too."

CHAPTER 8

Jocelyn

"MORE WINE, MA'AM?"

I glance up at the waiter and smile, then shake my head *no*. The last three times he's asked, I've gestured for him to top off my glass. But I know my limits, and if I have one more glass, I'm going to tell Mr. Hot Shot CEO across from me exactly where he can shove his cell phone.

He's been yammering into that thing for the last forty minutes. Our date was supposed to start an hour ago. I showed up seventy minutes ago. He arrived forty-two minutes later, and in our remaining time together, he's pulled the phone away from his ear *just* long enough to call me Jamie.

Why am I still here? I swirl the wine in my glass and stare into the deep-red tornado spiraling in circles. It's probably not worth the effort of splashing it on his shirt. I can't waste good wine on his tie.

I glance at him, picturing the stain creeping over his white shirt, but he's oblivious, staring at the ceiling and yelling about some deal that needed to be done five minutes ago. Definitely not worth the wine spillage. Also not worth the cleanup headache for the staff. Instead, I take another sip, flex my fingers, and try to remain calm. *Deep breathing.*

It's not as if I had other plans, anyway. Heating up a Lean Cuisine and watching re-runs of Boxer's games doesn't count as work, no matter how much I pretend. The man can skate though, and I'd been enjoying my marathon of Boxer highlights pretending it's research.

Once I start thinking about Boxer, however, it snowballs. Suddenly, I can't get him out of my mind. Mr. Hot Shot's grating voice drones on and on in the background while I sink back into the memory of our ice cream date.

Now *that's* a man who knows how to listen. Though I didn't realize it at the time, Boxer hadn't pulled out his phone once. For that matter, neither had I, and I can't *remember* the last time I'd gone so long without checking for an email, a text, or a phone call.

Our dinner arrives finally, drawing me out of my daydreams. I try very hard to wait until Mr. Hot Shot's off the phone, but his lips show no signs of stopping, so I give up on politeness and dig into my food.

Normally, I'd wait patiently. Usually, this sort of behavior doesn't bother me. I get it—I'm a busy woman, and I often field work calls on dates. But tonight, it's extra obnoxious, and I can't figure out why.

So, I tuck into the tiny piece of lasagna that costs forty-two dollars and polish it off in just a few minutes. It's amazing how much eating I can accomplish when I don't have to make polite conversation or worry about what's stuck between my teeth.

I'm already finished when Mr. Hot Shot puts his hand over his mouthpiece, pushes his salmon toward me, and hisses at me. "Can you tell them I asked for no butter on this? Disgusting. Idiots."

Before I can respond, he's back on the phone, this time standing up and pacing to the back of his chair. I survey the salmon which, frankly, smells so appetizing I debate eating it for him. I haven't eaten since lunch today, and that was hours ago.

Instead, I offer him a tight smile and excuse myself to the restroom. This is my third time to the bathroom since we've arrived; I've been using it as an excuse to stretch my legs. My date doesn't notice. This time, however, it's not an escape. I need to make a phone call.

Leaning against a wall in the quiet, mood-lit hallway, I dial Boxer's number. My heart speeds up as the phone rings through once, twice . . . *finally*, he picks up before I pass out from hyperventilation.

"Hello?" He answers with a low, throaty tone.

My heart is stuttering. I'm at a loss for words. *What am I doing calling so late?*

"Jocelyn, are you there?"

"Yeah—yes, it's me," I stammer, closing my eyes and wishing I could pound my head against the wall. "I'm sorry to call at this hour. Are you busy?"

"Uh, a little."

"I'm so sorry to interrupt your evening, but I just wanted to check in with you," I tell him. Sadly enough, though, this is the best conversation I've had all night, and a part of me wants to hold onto it for a second longer. "How are you?"

"I'm fine," he says. "Like I mentioned, I'm a little occupied—"

"I am *so sorry!*" I exclaim, the impact of his words hitting me. *He's on a date.* He must be on a date. *How did I not see this coming?* "Please tell your date I apologize for the interruption. I'll call tomorrow."

To my surprise, he lets out a bark of laughter. "My date?"

"Daddy, who is it?" The small voice registers from a distance. "Can you finish Rapunzel?"

"My *date* is anxious to continue our bedtime story," Boxer says, his voice kind this time. "But I'm sure she accepts your apology. Let me ask."

I can't help but grin like an idiot into the phone as I listen to Boxer's exchange with his daughter. *He's not on a date.* This fact makes me ridiculously happy, almost giddy.

"Jocelyn says hello," he tells Charli. "And she says sorry for interrupting our date."

"Huh," Charli says. "Is she nice?"

"Very."

"Is she pretty?"

Boxer coughs, and then puts a hand over the mouthpiece. His answer is muffled, but it's something about us being business friends and that in business, looks don't matter.

"But is she pretty?" Charli's relentless.

"Yes," he says finally. "Very beautiful."

In the background, my heart's pounding again, thumping like a bass drum, vibrations rumbling through my body. At the same time, my thumb is inching toward the hang up button, thinking it might be best to end the awkwardness for both of us now. It's mortifying! What else can he say with me on the line—*No, darling, she's quite an ugly toad*?

"Hey, I'm sorry," I say. "I shouldn't have called at this hour, it's just—"

"Why did you call?"

I swallow, realizing that none of the answers I'm considering are anywhere in the ballpark of appropriate. *Because I wanted to hear your voice?* I can't stop thinking about you? Because I'm on a date with an asshole, and I wish it was you instead?

"I just wanted to check on you. Personally," I say. "I know it's a busy time what with Duke retiring, and I know you'll be bombarded by requests. Just wanted to stay top of mind."

"Oh. Of course."

It's embarrassing, the way I can't seem to speak like a normal person around him. Normally, I have no problem doing deals worth millions—with male or female clients. Yet here I am mumbling because the man does funny things to my hormones.

"Anyway, Cinderella shouldn't be kept waiting," I say. "Goodnight."

"Rapunzel."

"What?"

"We're reading Rapunzel."

"Right."

"What if I call you tomorrow?" he says. "If you have specific questions we can talk then."

"Perfect."

"Hello?" The thin, high-pitched voice of a young girl interrupts. "Jocelyn? It's me. Charli."

"Hello, Charli."

"Goodnight," she says. "We're busy."

I laugh as Boxer apologizes into the phone. "I'll talk to you tomorrow, okay?" he says. "Goodnight."

I bid the pair goodnight, my stomach fluttering at the image of the two of them tucked into bed together, a storybook on their lap. Never in a million years would I have believed *that* image would be more appealing than my current situation.

However, as I drag myself back out to the dining room, I find my date more heated than ever, his conversation taking a turn for the violent as he slams his coffee cup down on the table.

I sigh, and continue my march toward the front door. I'm still hungry, and the dessert menu looked decadent, but it's going to have to wait. Even seven layer chocolate cake isn't enough to convince me to stay.

Our waiter catches me on my way to the door. "Are you looking for something, ma'am?"

"Actually . . ." I turn, an idea popping into my head. "Can I get an order of the chocolate cake to go? Put it on our bill."

"Of course," he says. "Right away."

When my order arrives a few minutes later, my date is sitting in his chair, ordering another glass of whiskey and not even realizing he's alone.

I hug my dessert and my purse to my chest and climb into a waiting cab. Maybe tonight wasn't so bad after all, I think. I spoke with Boxer and scored award-winning chocolate cake.

Things could be worse.

CHAPTER 9

Jocelyn

"SO?" LINDSAY DRAPES herself over my desk in the most dramatic fashion. "Was he dreamy?"

"Who?" I look up from the papers on my desk. "Oh, Mr. Hot Shot?"

"Uh oh." Her starry-eyed grin turns into a look of mild annoyance. "Another loser, really?"

"I don't even remember his first name. Know why?"

She gives a sympathetic cluck.

"The phone was glued to his ear. Super Glued."

"I'm sorry, boss."

"The waiter didn't even flinch when I asked for the chocolate cake to go. He gave me an extra slice."

"Yikes."

"Yep."

"Why aren't you more annoyed?" Lindsay's eyebrows cinch together, suspicious. "You were humming this morning. I haven't heard that since—well, since the day Billy Reider signed with you."

"Oh . . ."

"Boxer?"

"What?"

"Did he sign with you?" she asks excitedly. "I know how badly you want that deal."

"Oh, not at all." I let out a sigh of relief, thinking she'd read my thoughts. "He's . . . undecided."

"Aw, man."

I straighten my papers. "But we had a nice little chat last night, and I think we have an understanding. He's going to call today."

"That's great!" Lindsay perks right back up. "I'll be on the lookout for his call and send it straight through."

"Yes, please do that." Even as she stands to leave, I find myself hoping the call comes through to my cell phone. He has the number, and I want him to be comfortable using it. "Patch it through even if I'm in a meeting."

"You got it." Lindsay pauses at the door and turns to face me. "Are you still working on that endorsement deal? The one for the undies? He'd be perfect for it."

"Yes, which reminds me. Can you call around to some dentists? They'll probably want to see if they can get that chipped tooth fixed first."

"I'm on it," she says, jotting down a reminder in the notebook at hand. "Oh, one more question. You're not interested in a second date with Mr. Hot Shot, are you? He called this morning to ask."

"He did?"

"Well, technically his secretary."

"Oh, well . . ." I hate that I hesitate. Even as I remember Mr. Hot Shot's horrible manners, I can't help but think ahead to when I'm eighty. I'm not particularly thrilled about feeding a cat by myself. As much as I hate dating, I never wanted to end up alone. Wouldn't having Mr. Hot Shot be better than nothing? I sigh and look to Lindsay. "What do you think?"

"Hell no!" she says. "You deserve better. But it sounds like you're open to a date?"

"No, it's best if I stay focused on work."

"Let me set you up with someone I approve of."

"No, Lindsay, really. I'm busy, and—"

"I have access to your calendar, boss. You're not busy Friday night."

"I *am*. It's Lean Cuisine night."

"That is *every* night," she says. "Don't make plans. You're going out on Friday."

Lindsay shuts the door behind her, and I'm tempted to dial her desk and order her not to do any such thing. But when I look to my cell phone, the second number—just under Lindsay's—is Boxer's. That's *sad*. I need to meet more people.

Maybe a decent date, a connection with a genuine man, is just what I need. It doesn't have to be complicated, and it doesn't have to end in marriage. Who knows? Maybe I'll have my first real fling. It's been far too long since I've been touched by a man, brought to bed and made to feel like a woman. Maybe, if I can find someone who'll fit the bill, it'll help get my mind off Boxer.

Instead of dialing Lindsay, I check my texts and find a message there from Andy Rumpert.

May the best man win.

Instantly, I forget all about *feeling like a woman*. Andy Rumpert is *not* stealing the year's biggest score from my roster. My blood burns hot, and I keep thumbing through my phone until I find the number for Boxer's current agent.

I dial Duke, make small talk with him for a few minutes, and then beg him for an hour of his time. "You name the place," I say, once he's agreed. "I'm buying lunch."

CHAPTER 10

Boxer

FOR THE FIRST time in a long while, I've got another female on my brain as I watch Charli bounce toward school, turning every three feet to wave back at me. And I'm not sure if I like it.

I can't help but remember Jocelyn's voice from last night—a bit strangled, almost shy. Normally, I don't answer business calls when I'm reading Rapunzel, but something had pulled me to answer the phone. Even worse? I'm glad I did.

Even better? I'm supposed to call her today.

Best of all? She told me to call her, so I'm not left looking like the pathetic idiot who can't keep his mind off the one woman he's not supposed to touch.

Charli's curls swish around her pink cheeks as she blows one final kiss before pushing through the front doors. Teachers are there, guiding her inside, but it's this same routine every day. It takes us twelve minutes to say goodbye. Even her teachers have stopped trying to rush the process.

Once she's tucked inside, I pull away from the curb and head onto the freeway. I have no place to be right now, which is a good thing because I've been looking forward to this moment all day. I only wish I knew *why*.

The phone rings over my Bluetooth, and it rings again. And again. And again.

My car slows to a stop in Los Angeles morning traffic, and I curse under my breath as Jocelyn's voicemail kicks on. I didn't plan for this, dammit. Do I leave a message? Is that too much? Why the hell am I overthinking this like a teenager?

"Hey, Jocelyn, just returning your call from last night," I say on impulse. "Um . . . I should have some time today if you want to chat. Business. Uh—call me back."

I hang up and let loose a stream of curses that'd burn Charli's ears right from her head. I've had to tone down my language with a daughter at home, but in this moment, my old creative expletives come back in full force.

"Good talk," I tell the empty car. "Real nice, Boxer."

CHAPTER 11

Jocelyn

MY CHEST CONSTRICTS as my phone buzzes. It's my cell phone. *Boxer is calling my cell.*

Try as I might, it's hard not to read too much into it. Boxer has my office number, he's called it before. Yet he chose to call my cell.

"Miss Jones?" A voice says my name before I can answer Boxer's call.

My heart is beating a million miles an hour with every fiber of my being wanting to answer the phone. Instead, I look up at Duke, wipe my palms against my standard black dress, and reach out to shake his hand. "Duke. Thank you so much for meeting me here. On short notice, too."

"You said you're buying, didn't you?" His voice is gruff. "I told you I'm only here for the food."

"Great. Me too."

He raises an eyebrow and gives me a once-over. "You don't look like you eat all that much."

I catch a glimpse of myself in the window, but it's the same thing I see every day. Blonde hair tied back, button down black dress, high heels—tights if it's chilly outside, bare legs if not. It's a bare leg day today because, frankly, nylons make me itch.

The dress is always knee-length, no longer and no shorter, with just enough of a neckline to let me breathe. Small diamond studs are the only jewelry I wear besides the occasional watch or bracelet, and more often than not I keep my hair tied in a sleek bun. It's just easier this way.

"Table for two," I say, once Duke and I have made our way inside. "I tried to make a reservation, but they don't take them."

Duke grunts. "That's because it's Dougie's."

"How'd you ever hear about this place?" Duke has the same taste in restaurant decor as Boxer. Much like Gabe's ice cream shack, this place is a dump. Crooked sign dangling across the door, sticky floors beneath our feet. "It's . . . unique."

"I've been coming here for years. Boxer and I meet here."

The host, a guy in a stained shirt smelling of meat and grease, leads us to a corner table overlooking a back alley and a dumpster. The air, heavy with cooking odors, smells surprisingly delicious.

I *had* offered to take Duke to Moonshadow—a celeb-heavy bar overlooking the ocean in Malibu—a place meant to impress. Or Sugarfish, the best sushi in town. Or Nobu, a combination of sushi *and* Malibu. But no, Duke choose a hole in the wall that even rats had abandoned for greener pastures.

"Nice place, huh?" Duke gestures toward peeling walls, a grimy floor that, upon closer inspection, has actually been washed clean. It's not as dirty as it first seemed, it's just *ancient*. "Not much on the eyes, but wait until you try the food."

"I can't wait," I lie, wondering if I've stashed Pepto-Bismol in my purse. I suspect one bite of meat from this place will have me hugging the toilet in ways I haven't hugged it since college.

Then, my stomach growls.

"Glad you brought your appetite," Duke says with a smile. "I respect a woman with an appetite."

"That's me," I grimace. I debate having Lindsay cancel the rest of my afternoon meetings so I can be at home to digest this meal in peace. "Bottomless pit."

"Let's get the business crap out of the way. When the food arrives, sorry, lady, but I'm going to eat in silence."

"I'm going to cut to the chase," I say. "I want Boxer."

"Well, I can't say I'm surprised," he says, eyeing me over two sweating glasses of water. "He's a great client."

"I imagine so, and I asked you here to go over a few questions."

"Well, I figured. I'm not an idiot." Duke's got hair coming from his nose, his ears, the top of his t-shirt—everywhere except his head, which is bald. "You want my advice about how to rope Boxer onto your team?"

"Yes."

There's something about this man that almost reminds me of Boxer. An older, less attractive Boxer—maybe his great-grandfather once removed. There's a playfulness in Duke's eyes, an understated taste in accessories and food.

Duke's got money, that much is clear. He's got status and a bit of fame, at least in our industry, but he flies under the radar. Just like Landon Boxer.

"Well, I have a big nugget of advice for you," Duke says, pausing mid-thought to put an order in with the same server who acted as the host. He orders for me, too, without asking. "Listen, Miss Jones."

I nod and inch my chair forward.

"Give up now, doll." Duke crosses his arms and offers a polite smile. "You and Boxer aren't a good match."

"Excuse me?" His words surprise me, and I struggle for patience as I process them. "With all due respect, I'm not quitting. I didn't ask you here so that you could tell me to give up."

"What'd you ask me here for, then?"

"Your advice."

"I'm *advising* you to let it go. Let *him* go."

"Let's say I bite. Why are we not a good match?"

Duke shrugs as the server arrives to top off our water glasses. "For starters, you don't even know the man."

"No, but I am willing to learn." I fold my hands across my lap and lean back. "That's why I asked you here. To learn how I can become his friend."

"I don't know how *I* can help. I've been friends with the guy for years."

"Exactly."

"How do you know my shirt is red?"

I look at his shirt which, as he's stated, is a vibrant shade of cherry. "It just is."

"*Exactly*," he echoes. "I'm friends with Boxer because we get along. I didn't have to fake anything; we just clicked."

"Where'd you meet?"

"Gabe's."

"The ice cream place?" I try not to let my jaw fall open. "You're kidding me."

"We have the same interests."

"What other interests does he have?"

"Give it up, Miss Jones. He's not your type."

"That's not your decision to make," I fire back, no longer trying for polite. "Why are you so intent on keeping me away from him? I can *help* him. I want to help him. If he signs with me, we'll have Charli's college fund set up in three damn months. You know it, too. I'm good at what I do, Duke, and you're retiring. He has to go *somewhere*."

"Listen to me." Duke's voice is calm, softer, and he leans

forward, eyes landing on mine. "Boxer's different than most of the players, and I'm not going to let him sign with an agent who doesn't respect that. He's not out to earn the most money. He doesn't want to be famous, or earn millions from endorsements—sure, he wants success and to earn a living, but that's *all*."

"But—"

"Don't tell me what he wants," Duke says. "Boxer's a simple guy. He loves his daughter, hockey, and Gabe's ice cream, and I'm pretty sure that's the right order."

"But—"

"He's not looking for a boss, he's looking for a friend. A partner. With a guy like Boxer, he's not making every decision with his head."

"What else is he making it with?"

"If there's an endorsement deal across the world, and it promises to take him away from his daughter for longer than a few nights, he's going to turn it down. If you aren't okay with that decision, then let him go."

I swallow, feeling like Duke's walked me into a corner.

He knocks back the last of his water as if it's whiskey. "This is why I took this meeting instead of sitting at home in my undies."

"Care to elaborate?"

"I respect you, Miss Jones, and if it were any other client, I'd happily sign them over to you. But this one . . . he's different."

"He took me to Gabe's."

Duke's silent as he raises an eyebrow. "Is that right?"

"I'm trying to get to know him." I lean forward, steepling my hands over the table. "Andy Rumpert is in the game, too. If I give up now, Andy's going to get Boxer. At least you know I won't lie."

"You're honest, I'll give you that."

The host-turned-server-turned-chef walks across the floor,

balancing trays of food. My time to beg Duke for help is running low.

"Give me a shot," I plead, both hands pressing against the table as I lean in. "A little help. If I fail, I promise to lose gracefully."

"I'm not playing games here," Duke says, so serious he ignores the plates of steaming meat being placed on the table before us. "There is no secret sauce to making a friend, Miss Jones, but I'll give you one piece of advice."

"Oh, thank God."

"The man loves his daughter, hockey, and Gabe's."

"What?" I blink in disbelief. "You already told me that!"

"Well, think about it some more."

Plates clank on the table, the smell of barbecued meat heavy in the air. It's thick enough to taste on a breath, and I can feel Duke's fingers antsy to dig in. Even my stomach is throwing a welcome parade at the sight of the meat.

"Let down your guard, Miss Jones," Duke says. "Spend some time with him, and the rest will fall into place. Now, let's eat."

CHAPTER 12

Jocelyn

"LITTLE GIRLS LIKE Barbies, don't they?"

"What is this about?" Lindsay asks over the phone. "Miss Jones, do you want me to buy a present for someone? I didn't see anyone's birthday on the calendar, and I sent your client's wife—what's her name, Dana?—birthday flowers last month."

"I can handle this," I say, eyeing the aisle at Target. "You didn't miss anything. This is a spur of the moment, no-reason gift. Five-year-old girl."

"I think Barbies are pretty safe," Lindsay says. "But you're going to want to get some fun extension packs—clothes, or a car or whatever. What's she into?"

I stare at a wall of Barbies. I've never been more lost, more terrified, more unsure of myself. "Um, I don't know?"

"Car. Go with the car." Lindsay's voice is soothing, as if she can sense I'm on the verge of panic. "Grab the gifts, bring them back to the office. I'll wrap it and take care of the rest."

"Have I told you I love you?"

"Next time, don't wander into the Barbie aisle alone. Let me be your moral support."

"Noted."

Once I've paid and escaped the dangerous maze of Target, I load my finds into the car and direct me and the Barbie toward the office. I'm not cut out for these things—sentimental, fun gifts for children. I'm in the business of negotiating contracts, representing clients, babysitting athletes or celebrities. I haven't stepped foot in a Barbie aisle in . . . years? Maybe in my lifetime.

While I'm driving, I hit dial on Boxer's number, returning the long overdue message. He picks up on the third ring, just when I'm about to have heart palpitations that we'll spend the rest of our lives playing phone tag.

"How are you, Miss Jones?"

"Jocelyn," I say. "I'm great, how are you?"

"Just dropped Charli off with Marie—the nanny. I'm headed to practice."

"Sorry I missed your call earlier, I was . . . out," I say, not quite ready to explain my meeting with Duke. "Anyway, I wanted to invite you and Charli to lunch tomorrow."

"Lunch?"

"Yes, just a low key, get to know you deal. I figure if Charli's a part of your life, and if we might be working together—you and I—it's best if we all meet. Informal, of course."

"Well, okay, but . . . I don't think tomorrow will work."

"Oh, right. Too soon. Sorry." I cringe. "Any day will work."

"It's not too soon, we just have other commitments. Let's say Monday at noon. There's a nice little diner near your office. I'll pick you up at noon?"

I'm still wondering how this has turned from me buying him lunch into him collecting me from my office as if this is a date. "Sure," I agree. "That sounds lovely."

I can sense him preparing to hang up. But at the last second, he pauses. "Jocelyn?"

"Yep?"

"Thank you, that's thoughtful of you. Charli will be excited. She's been talking about you ever since you called last night. She'll love to meet you."

I laugh, surprised. "Well, I can't wait."

When we hang up, I'm smiling. Next Monday at noon, I have a date. Sort of.

I guess *technically* I am the third wheel of a father-daughter date, but I'll take what I can get.

CHAPTER 13

Jocelyn

"ONE DATE PER month," Lindsay tells me. "Come on, we made a deal. I found a nice guy for you, Miss Jones."

"I have a date. I'm headed there right now." I sit on the edge of Lindsay's desk, reapplying my lipstick in a hand mirror. "So, I don't need to meet anyone else this month."

"But you cancelled the one on Friday. For *no* reason. I know you sat at home on your butt."

"I had plans."

"Your microwave doesn't count as *plans*. Plus, you'll get another free dinner!"

"You have to understand something, Lindsay."

"I'm listening."

"I've worked for all these years—*really* freaking hard—so I can afford to buy my own dinners. If I want to spend my evenings eating chocolate cake in a pair of men's boxers on my own damn couch, I'm going to do that."

"You don't buy yourself quality food; *that's* the problem."

"Lean Cuisine is good for the soul." I hop to my feet, wondering why on earth I've spent extra time applying makeup before heading to meet a five-year-old and her father. "I've agreed to one date per month, and I have a date today."

"Hold on." Lindsay peers at me through critical eyes. "You have business lunches all the time, and yet you've *never* called one a date before. What gives?"

"It's a double date—sort of, since Charli is coming. Boxer's daughter. Hence the Barbie."

"Well, I hope you have fun today."

"Me too," I say. "If I'm not back in an hour, cancel my two p.m."

"You got it," she says. "But I am *not* letting you off the hook for blowing off my friend last Friday."

"We'll reschedule next month," I say. "When my quota is up."

"You're getting old," she calls as I leave the office. "Shall I order you a cat?"

"Goodbye, *Lindsay*."

As I pad down the staircase, even the thought of becoming a cat woman doesn't dampen my excitement. Today's Monday, and I have the chance to *woo* Boxer. I am going to *woo* if it kills me.

I have my Barbie in hand, my makeup on point, and my most casual business dress—which, of course, is still black and knee length and looks exactly like every other dress I own. As I've mentioned, uniforms are just easier.

Now, to impress a five-year-old. Surely it can't be that hard, right?

CHAPTER 14

Boxer

"IS THAT HER?"

My head jerks up to look out the window of our car. We pulled up outside Jocelyn's building not two seconds ago; I haven't even finished the message that says: *We're here.*

"That's her," I say, trying to keep my voice even. "Remember what we talked about?"

I zone out as Charli ticks off the list of things we'd discussed on the car ride over. Being polite, steering away from too-private questions, and anything I could think of that might make Jocelyn uncomfortable.

I only hear two of the items on the list because I'm too busy watching the blonde-haired beauty striding toward me. She's a picture of fair skin, fair hair, and fair blue eyes, outlined by a backdrop of sleek onyx buildings. Her legs, long and slender, carry her gracefully over the sidewalk in a pair of heels that boost her height.

Even though she's taller than average for a woman, when I step out of the car, I dwarf her with my size. She's slight in figure, but not fragile, and I can see the fire burning behind her eyes as she looks up, sees me standing there, and smiles. With her smile, the fire turns to liquid, simmering blue gems twinkling as she reaches the vehicle.

"You look great," I say, feeling as awkward as the words sound. "I like your dress."

I've only ever dealt with Duke when it came to business, and if I ever complimented the man's looks he would've dumped my sorry ass on the spot. This whole 'opposite-sex' thing is throwing a kink in my normal M.O. I'm trying to be polite, but I sound like a nutcase. Somewhere in between flirting and infatuation and loser-ness.

She blinks in surprise, glancing down at the black, knee-length thing. Her fingers fly over the buttons as she brushes a hand down her front, and I bite my lip in response, unable to stop the rush of images as I picture what it'd be like to snap those buttons right off.

"Hi," she says, glancing shyly behind me. "Would this be Charli?"

"Charli." I turn halfway, startled to find a shining face next to my elbow. "Jesus, Charli, you scared me."

Charli giggles. "Hi."

Jocelyn extends a hand to Charli with a grin. "Pleasure to meet you."

"We got a half day at school today," Charli explains, extending her chubby fingers to meet Jocelyn's daintier ones.

"A half day, that's lucky," Jocelyn says as the two share a long handshake. So long that it's not until twenty seconds in that I realize Charli's squeezing too tight and not letting Jocelyn go.

"It's not *lucky*," Charli argues. "It's conferences."

"That's enough, Charli." I wind her fingers back and apologize to Jocelyn. "Hungry?"

"Absolutely."

I open the passenger side door for her and, in a sudden lapse of judgement, rest a hand on her back as she steps into the car. I feel her body tense, freeze for a moment, until I pull my hand away.

She settles in, her face a bit red, and I'm on the verge of strangling myself. Except that outcome would be inconvenient and unproductive for both of us, so instead I keep myself alive and climb into the driver's seat, silent.

"I brought you something," Jocelyn says, spinning her head to face Charli as we begin to drive. "It's not much, but I hope you'll like it."

She hands a box into the back seat to Charli's gleefully clapping hands. I raise my eyes in the rearview mirror and stare down my daughter until she remembers her manners and says *thank you*.

"You didn't have to do that," I mumble, flicking my eyes across the seat to where Jocelyn's staring forward, a lingering smile on her face. "It's sweet of you, but not necessary. She's spoiled enough, aren't you, Charli?"

"Nope," Charli squeals joyfully.

Jocelyn laughs. "It's really nothing. I'm not very good at choosing gifts though, so I hope it's okay. Otherwise, I can return it, or—"

"Don't be silly," I tell her. "You're going to love it, aren't you, Charli? Miss Jones didn't have to bring you anything."

"*Maybe* I'll love it," Charli hedges. "We'll see."

I sigh, but Jocelyn winks in my direction. "At least she's honest. I can respect that in a woman."

"Watch what you wish for," I say. "That girl can be so honest it hurts."

"Have you had au jus?" Charli calls from the backseat. "We're going to the deli where Monica makes it."

"I haven't," Jocelyn says. "At least, not in a long time."

"You'll like it. It's my favorite," Charli says. "Monica is the best. She taught me how to say au jus."

"Monica runs the deli," Boxer says.

"You guys must visit this place a lot."

"Oh yeah," Charli agrees. "Once a week. We like Monica."

"We like the deli," I say. "It's quick and easy."

"And what should I order?" Jocelyn asks. "Charli, you're going to have to help me out."

Ten minutes and a million Charli-words later, we've parked and made our way into Lucker's deli. Monica's there, behind the counter as usual, her dark hair piled high on her head.

"Well, hello, Boxers," she calls. Then stops herself at the sight of Jocelyn. "Boxer family plus one! I'll get you a new table today."

"But I like our old table," Charli whines. Then she points it out to Jocelyn. "We always sit here."

"There's only two seats," I tell her. "We are lucky enough to need one with three today."

Charli gives a grumpy fold of her arms, but when Monica points out a bigger, cooler table, her frown fades. Charli climbs up, patting the chair next to her and glancing toward her dad.

"Can I get your order put in right away? Will it be crème soda and au jus all around?" Monica asks after we've settled into our seats.

"Yes," Charli says, wiggling upright in her chair.

"Hold on, Jocelyn can have whatever she wants." I rest a hand on Charli's and squeeze lightly. "Why don't you ask her what she likes?"

Charli looks over to Jocelyn, her eyes wide. "You don't want the crème soda and au jus?"

Jocelyn grins. "I'll take whatever you recommend."

"Jocelyn will have the same," Charli says. Then she folds the menu and hands it back. "Thank you, Monica," she adds at my prompting.

"Do you want to open your present now?" Jocelyn asks. "If

it's okay with your dad."

Charli hasn't let the beautifully wrapped box out of her sight, setting it down only to handle the menu. I give her the go ahead nod, and she begins tearing into the wrapping paper. The thing looks like it's wrapped in pure gold, and I cringe at how much that tissue must've cost.

My attention, however, is soon distracted by the woman sitting at the table with us. For someone who has claimed to have no experience with kids, Jocelyn's somewhat of a natural. Granted, Charli is pretty easy to get along with, and she likes most people. But Jocelyn doesn't have to try so hard—it's me she wants, not my daughter, and I appreciate the effort and her thoroughness in taking an interest in my life.

However, as the golden paper comes off, there's a sinking sensation in my stomach. That looks like a Barbie box. I really, really hope, for everyone's sake, that it's *not*.

I really should've warned Jocelyn somehow—if only I'd known she was thinking of bringing a present. Charli's never liked Barbies—thinks they're too girly for her, which is something I've never understood. Her bedroom is pink. But who am I to argue if she'd rather toss a baseball with me than play with a few stick figures with big boobs?

The wrapping paper hits the floor as Charli unsheathes the goods inside.

Her face falls, a little frown creasing her forehead.

Shit.

Hello, Barbie.

"What do you say?" I jump in before she can react. "Can you tell Jocelyn thank you?"

"Oh," Charli says, her voice a thin icicle. "Thank you, Jocelyn."

Unfortunately, it's not enough. Jocelyn's fingers clasp together, and she shoots me an apologetic look across the table.

"If you don't like it, that's fine," she says hurriedly. "We can return it and get something else."

"No, this is great." I nudge my daughter. "Isn't it?"

"It's not tickets to Six Flags," Charli says, looking at the doll. "I sort of wished for tickets to Six Flags."

Jocelyn's face is strained, and I can tell she feels horrible. Which makes me feel like the worst parent ever.

"Charli, come here a minute." I grab her hand, excuse ourselves from the table, and bring her out front into the sunlight.

She's dragging her feet, her head hanging when we stop walking.

"What was that about?" I kneel down before her. "Where did all of your manners go? We talked about this, Charli. She brought you a present. You shouldn't complain when someone gives you a gift."

"But I don't like Barbies!"

"How is she supposed to know that? She's never met you before."

"I wanted tickets to Six Flags."

"Well, we're not going to Six Flags to ride rollercoasters this summer if you keep acting like this." My heart aches to threaten this since it's what she's been looking forward to all year. "If you don't like a present, you just say thank you and move on. You know that, honey."

"How come Jocelyn is bringing me presents anyway?" Charli asks. "People only bring me presents when they take you away from me."

"What?"

"That one time the girl brought me a teddy bear. Then you went away for the whole night and missed reading to me."

I blink, surprised to know she remembers the one night I went out with Tricia. We'd met at some event a year or so back, and I'd liked her enough to ask her out for a drink. Turns out, we hadn't been compatible, and it'd been a horrible date. Even so, I hadn't gotten home until after Charli's bedtime.

"The other time that girl brought me a book. You disappeared all night again."

Angela.

I'd gone on two dates in the last year, and neither of them had worked out. But I was starting to see a pattern, and suddenly, it was hard to stay upset with Charli.

"Listen, that was different," I tell Charli. "When those ladies brought you presents, it was because we were going out on a date. This is business—it's for work. I'm not going to go away for the night."

"Promise?"

"I promise." I rest a hand against her cheek and tilt her gaze up to meet mine. "Jocelyn is just trying to be nice for work. She's going to help me with hockey, that's all."

"It's not a date?"

I grit my teeth. "It's not a date."

"Oh, okay." She leans in and kisses me on the cheek. "Sorry, daddy."

"It's okay, but I'm going to need you to apologize to Jocelyn."

Charli grabs my hand and pulls me inside. I can't help the churning sensation in my stomach, a mix of emotions stealing my appetite. This never happens. I'm hungry all the time. But somehow, the mix of feeling as if I'd let Charli down while simultaneously banishing any hopes for a relationship with Jocelyn is enough to do the trick.

Not that I should be thinking about relationships; I shouldn't.

This is business, I remind myself, and it's a good thing Charli's jolted me back to reality.

When we make it back to the table, Charli's back to her usual charming self. "I'm sorry," Charli tells Jocelyn, resting a hand on her knee. "I like my Barbie, even though I don't play with them much."

"Do you want to know a secret?" Jocelyn leans forward. "I never played with Barbies, either. A friend helped me pick this out."

"Really?" Charli moves around to her seat and climbs up to the table as Monica brings the soda bottles and French Dip sandwiches over.

"Really." She shakes her head. "So if you want to exchange it for something else, go ahead."

"Like a soccer ball?"

"Or a baseball."

"Basketball?"

"Whatever you want." Jocelyn smiles. "I'm glad we've got this sorted out."

Monica rests the plates on the table and grins. "Can I get y'all anything else?"

"My dad's not on a date," Charli says, picking up her sandwich to dunk in the au jus. "Don't worry, this is just business, Monica."

Jocelyn straightens, the smile on her face one of forced confusion. "Of course. We're hoping to be business partners."

"That's great!" Monica turns to Jocelyn. "Because Duke's retiring?"

Jocelyn again looks confused, and I'm stuck realizing that it must look like I tell Monica an awful lot. For some reason, I don't want Jocelyn to get the wrong idea that Monica and I are anything more than food-provider and food-eater, but there's no time now to set the record straight.

"That's right," Jocelyn says, sending a meaningful glance my way. "Boxer's on the market for a new agent, and I'm hoping he'll choose me."

CHAPTER 15

Jocelyn

AFTER LUNCH, CHARLI begs for a trip to the park. Boxer gives me an apologetic look, but I quickly agree to accompany them, begging a moment alone to update Lindsay with my schedule. Boxer and Charli race ahead, and I pull out my phone to dial Lindsay's number.

"How did it go?" Lindsay asks when she picks up. "Even your hello sounds . . . defeated."

"I struck out. Big time. I need help."

"Where are you?"

"We're headed to a park."

"Okay, that sounds like things are going well," Lindsay says. "If Boxer and Baby Boxer wanted to leave right after lunch, they would have."

"She hated the Barbie."

"Who hates Barbie?"

"Charli."

Lindsay swears under her breath. "Tomboy, huh?"

"Yep."

"I should've guessed. Sorry, boss. For whatever it's worth, though, it's the thought that counts."

"It's not the thought that counts, this is business," I tell her. "I have to win over Boxer. I'm not doing a wonderful job of it."

"Look, forget about the Barbie. I guarantee Charli has already let it go. Have some fun at the park, and all will be forgotten!"

I sigh. "I don't do well with kids."

"You'll do fine. You were a kid once, you know. It's not like you don't have some experience with it."

"Fine."

"If you need rescuing, just . . . send an SOS message, and I'll call you with an urgent request."

"You're the best."

"Good luck! And, boss?"

"Yeah?"

"I've never seen you so on edge. Just relax. You're the best there is, and if Boxer can't see that, it's his loss."

I'm grinning as I say goodbye to Lindsay, even if I know she's just blowing sunshine up my ass. I remind myself to see if I can finagle some extra budget for her bonus this year. She's paid well, but she should be paid more. She's a staple in my life.

"All good, boss?" Boxer's grinning as he sidles over toward me. "Sorry to keep you from work. We could've dropped you off if you wanted."

"Oh, you're not keeping me. I was just updating my assistant on the change in plans." I tuck my phone into my pocket. "I'm all yours, now. Where's Charli?"

He gestures toward the swing set in the middle of the playground. Charli's already made a friend, a boy of about her age, and they're currently in a battle to see who can fly the furthest off the swing.

"Doesn't that make you nervous?" I cringe. "I can't watch. She's going to break something."

"You get used to it." Boxer laughs, stopping before a bench. "She's tough. If I tell her not to do something, that just makes it worse."

He waves an arm toward the bench, and together we sit. The air is filled with shrieks from the swing set competition and there's a certain peacefulness to the moment despite the chaotic background chatter.

"I'm really sorry about Charli," he says, turning to face me. "She—"

"I should've asked about the Barbie before bringing some silly gift. It's my fault."

"Your fault? That was the most thoughtful thing you could've done. She's just . . . it makes her nervous."

"Barbies?" I watch Boxer, but he doesn't answer immediately.

"No," he says finally. "The last few times a woman brought her a gift, it was because I'd asked them out on a date. I've gone on two dates this year, and both times I missed reading to Charli before bed. She was worried I wouldn't be there tonight for her."

"Oh, poor thing," I say, meaning it. "I'm sorry, if I'd known—"

"Don't worry," he adds quickly. "I explained to her that this is business, and business is different than personal."

"Of course."

He closes his eyes, rubbing a hand over his forehead. "I mean, it's personal, getting to know you, but—"

"I get it. For the record, Charli has nothing to worry about. I wouldn't dream of stealing you away from Rapunzel."

He smiles, relief evident on his face. "As for the Barbie thing . . . she's an odd duck. There's no way you could've guessed that one."

"I don't think she's odd at all! I like her, a lot. Even if I'm not great with kids."

"You do just fine."

I shrug, watching as the kids leave the swings waving in the breeze to dig a trench in the sand. Once again, I'm hit by the peacefulness of the moment, the warmth of the sun on my face, which is why his next question comes out of the blue, catching me off guard.

"Why'd you meet with Duke?"

A chill spirals through me as I look up to find Boxer waiting for my answer. "Duke?"

"We talk," he says in explanation. "He mentioned he had lunch with you at Dougie's."

"Yes, we did." I clear my throat. "I wanted to pick his brain about the agent business."

Boxer leans back, his arm coming up and over my shoulders. We're sitting far enough apart where it doesn't feel romantic, but still . . . I can't help the race of my heart as his fingers brush inadvertently against my shoulder.

"I'm impressed," he says finally. "He doesn't like most people."

"Oh?"

He grins, giving a bewildered shake of his head. "Seems he liked you just fine."

CHAPTER 16

Jocelyn

"I TAKE IT by your message that things went superb?" Lindsay asks.

After Charli had worn herself out at the park, Boxer dropped me back at my office building. Instead of heading inside, I made my way to my car.

"Things were going well. I didn't want to leave." I respond as I buckle my seatbelt.

"Dare I say you sound . . . *excited*?"

"I think the playground went *great*! We got to talk. Boxer is really sweet, and—"

"Hold on." Silence covers the line as Lindsay works through something in her brain. "You counted this lunch as a date. You enjoyed yourself. You sound happy, yet no business deal has been signed."

"But—"

"You *love* Boxer!"

"What?!"

"You have a crush on him!"

"No, absolutely not."

"All the signs are there," she says. "He's calling your cell phone—you *never* give out that number unless you're really serious about someone as a client. You give them *my* number but never yours. You wore extra makeup today—yes, I noticed. You wore your nice black dress with an extra button undone at the top."

My fingers fly near my throat and button it back up. "That's not true."

"It is too. Don't you pretend it's not true because you're buttoning it up right now."

I drop my hand, exasperated. She's too psychic for my taste. "I'm taking a break," I tell her. "I'll be back in an hour."

"Flowers?"

"Yes," I say. "Please hold my calls."

~~

The gravesite is deserted, as it always is. Hidden out of the way from the glamour and glitter of Los Angeles, I pull onto an abandoned road on the outskirts of town.

The cemetery itself is clean, well-maintained, and I wave to the man at the front gates as I pull through. He nods back, just as he always does. We never speak, and I don't know his name, but we've been through this same routine for years.

I park, thinking not for the first time that this might be the only place I don't have to feed a meter in the entire LA metro area. Climbing from the car, I gather the bouquet of roses I bought at the nearby farmer's market and hug it close to my chest.

"Hey, there, mom," I murmur, strolling over to the two headstones placed next to one another. "Hi, dad."

I kneel, clearing away some of the dirt and grime from the top of the headstone. Joseph and Prudence Jones have the same date of death, though my father was born five years before my mother. Five extra years of life.

Both of their lives ended when their car spiraled off the road during a storm and crashed. My mother died on impact, my dad one day later. At the time, despite the shock, I'd prayed for him to recover. Bargained with God, pleaded with the angels, but none of it had worked.

In retrospect, maybe it had all happened for a reason. I'd been only seven at the time, but what I could remember of their relationship shimmered in golden memories, dusted by years of happiness. Mornings filled with laughter and cups of hot chocolate, evenings drenched in moonlight as the three of us huddled under blankets in our backyard and watched for shooting stars.

We'd never seen a shooting star, I think, removing the now-dried flowers from the vase. The city was too bright for shooting stars, too polluted with light. We were going to go camping for my next birthday, but it hadn't happened. That birthday had been spent in a foster home, and I don't even remember how we celebrated. Or *if* we celebrated.

I blink, standing as I look down at the graves. I'd wished for years things hadn't worked out like this, but wishing hadn't gotten me anywhere. Neither had crying, and neither had hoping. Which is why I didn't do any of that anymore.

The only thing that ever made a difference was hard work. If I filled enough hours in my day, I wasn't plagued by the what-if's and what could've beens. Falling asleep on the couch, exhausted, spares me the torturous hours spent remembering all that isn't meant to be.

I miss them still, but I don't cry any more. Not often, at least, and I don't waste my breath on wishes. If I've learned anything in this world, it's that life deals you a hand of cards, and sometimes that hand is pretty crappy. The only thing worse than a crappy hand of cards is giving up on the game, and I'd decided long ago that I wasn't giving up on the game.

"There's a guy," I tell them, my closest confidants. I don't stop to think whether it's pathetic the only people I tell everything to are long dead. "His name is Boxer, and I'm not sure what to do about him."

Of course they don't respond, but speaking aloud makes something feel real. Them? Maybe. Or maybe it's my way of working through problems, and this is the only place peaceful enough to speak from my heart. I don't know.

"He's a really nice guy," I tell them. "I want him on my roster, but . . . *ugh*. I don't know. I just can't stop thinking about him."

There. I've admitted it. Though I've only voiced it to my parents, gone nearly two decades, it's something. Lindsay's right. I like Boxer. I like him a lot—which is a huge problem.

"I don't know what to do," I say, still talking to air, to the whispers of a past life. "I'm a business woman. If I start mixing business and pleasure, I have the potential to lose everything. My clients, my reputation, my sole source of income."

A breeze ruffles the grass, but I'm too distracted to shiver. It's a cool January day, the sun that had shone so merrily at the park is now hidden behind the clouds.

"It's not an option for me to look for something personal with Boxer. He made it plenty clear over lunch today that we have a strict business-only relationship." I cross my arms, unable to ignore the larger gust of wind, and hug my body for warmth. "He's got a daughter, and from the way he speaks about Charli, he's not looking to introduce a new woman into his life—to their life, and their family. I'd be chiseling my way into a place I don't belong."

I pace back and forth, lost in the imagination of what that might look like. A life with Boxer, with Charli. A life as a mother, with one child at least, and the potential for more. It's a future I haven't much considered for myself. And frankly, I don't know why I'm wasting time envisioning it now—I learned long ago that *wishing* doesn't do much good.

I rest a hand against my mother's name. "I think I'm going insane, mom. All of these nights eating Lean Cuisine by myself— maybe Lindsay's right. I'm imagining a life with a man who doesn't even like me. At least, not in any sort of real way. How sad is that?"

She doesn't answer, but there's a melancholy note to the air. It's depressing, difficult to breathe. "I'm trying to sign him on as a client, but it doesn't feel right. He's not . . . he's not out for money. I want him because he'll get scooped up for big endorsements, and we'll both make loads of cash. I'm using him, and it's not fair."

I can almost hear her asking *why.* Why I need him as a client at all. Lindsay's voice pops into my head, too, echoing the sentiment. *You don't need the money, why not ask him on a date?*

"Because!" I stand up and unfold my arms from across my chest. "If he says no, then I'll lose him as a client and as a friend. If I have him as a client, at the very least I can make sure he's taken care of, and Charli, too. That's more than Andy will do."

I'm breathing heavily, my chest heaving as I sort through my options. Business or pleasure, neither or both. The latter two options are just not going to work for me. The second option is too risky. Which leaves me with only one option—the same route I've been on since the beginning.

Secure Boxer as a client. Stop daydreaming that it could be something more, and take care of him and his daughter as best I can financially. It's the only way that everyone ends up happy.

I think.

Before I can wonder where it leaves me on the happiness spectrum, my phone rings, and I'm grateful for the distraction. I click answer, straighten the flowers, and make my way back to the car.

"Jocelyn," I say into the mouthpiece. "Who's this?"

"Matthew Lucas," a clipped, New York accent says. "I'm calling about the endorsement deal for ComfortBox."

"Yes! What can I do for you?"

"Landon Boxer. Are you working with him yet? I'm not holding the spot open any longer. We want him, but if he's not ready to move forward, we're going with someone else."

"Give me a week."

"Two days."

"Done," I say with a smile.

That's why I've succeeded in my career. I didn't need a week to get the job done, I needed twenty-four hours. Now I've got two days, and that'll be plenty of time.

I take one last look at my parents' names, catching myself on the verge of a wish. I *almost* wished they could hear me, offer me advice, lead me to the right answer. To what question? I'm not even sure. All I can say for certain is that I like Boxer too much to corral him like I would any other client. If I can't act on my feelings for him, the least I can do is make sure he's happy.

A sense of peace rests on my shoulders as I turn away, a lightness in my chest. I've never quite figured out if it's the act of speaking aloud, or remembering my parents, or what it is about these cemetery visits that eases my mind, but I keep coming back, and I keep solving my problems. It's a little bit like magic.

And I plan to keep coming back again and again, and maybe a solution to my latest problem will present itself in time.

CHAPTER 17

Boxer

"PLATES, NAPKINS, CUPCAKES . . ." I glance at the list Marie jotted down last minute, but it's nearly impossible to read. Plates? What *color* plates? What size? Should the napkins be white? Red? Which candles go with *unicorn* theme?

Speaking of unicorns, I'm fairly certain one of these mystical creatures galloped into Target and vomited all over my cart. That's the only explanation for the amount of junk I have in here. Glitter and streamers poke out from every nook and cranny.

I'm six foot three, over two hundred pounds, and I can barely push this load of junk through the aisles. I'd thought that getting *everything* would be easiest, but now I'm having second thoughts, and I can't bear the idea of putting *everything* back.

Now, there aren't very many things that make me nervous. I've faced off with the biggest, meanest players in the NHL and not batted an eye. I've stopped a mugging mid-mug, and didn't blink. I've driven over a hundred miles an hour on the 405, and still, I hardly broke a sweat.

Ask me to plan a birthday party for a six-year-old princess, and I feel like I've been told to walk the plank. Except this is worse, because the plank is purple and pink and slick with sparkles.

I hate to do this, but it's the only thing I can think of in my panic. Pulling out my phone, I hit dial on the last number I called.

"Oh, hey, you!" Jocelyn sounds pleasantly surprised. "Long time no talk. We've made it what . . . two hours?"

"I need help."

"Of course. Anything." Her voice turns serious in an instant. "What's wrong? Is it Charli?"

"No, not exactly. Well, yes."

"Is she okay? What happened? Was it that stupid swing set?"

I can't help but laugh. "No, she's fine, it's actually me. I'm in trouble."

"Where are you? I'm in the car."

"Target."

"*Target*?"

"Listen." I pause, flinching as I ask this next question. I know if I loop her into this, I'm stepping beyond the bounds of business that I'd *just* requested we keep, but I can't help it. I have nobody else to ask. "You turned six once, right?"

"Like, six years old?" She gives a tinkling laugh. "As a matter of fact, I did."

"And you had a birthday party?"

She hesitates. "Yes." Her voice is a bit distant, almost sad. "The theme was horses."

"Oh, thank God." I rest a hand on my forehead and pinch away the stress. "I know I'll owe you big time, but I have a favor to ask. Marie's mother just got sick—the nanny—and I sent her home for the week to help out."

"And Charli's birthday is . . . ?"

"Saturday."

"Ah."

"Marie normally takes care of everything. She buys stuff, does stuff, prepares stuff . . . she'll be gone until Sunday."

"I'll be right there."

"Are you sure?" I look over the cart with a skeptical eye. "I have half of Target in my cart, and it's not pretty."

"As long as we're not going down the Barbie aisle, we should be good."

"No Barbies."

"I'm on my way."

"I can't tell you how much this means to me, Jocelyn. If I had someone else to call, I would, but my parents are upstate, and I only have a brother, and—"

"Stop it," she says briskly. "We'll get through this no problem. I'm ordering you to grab a burger or something—you'll need energy—and then sit still. I'll be right there. Which Target?"

"Culver City."

"On my way. Oh, Boxer?"

"Yes?"

"I was actually about to call you. Unrelated to this, of course, I have a favor to ask of you."

"Anything."

"You'll . . . *ahh*," she pauses. "Want to know what it is first."

"It can't be worse than a six-year-old birthday party at the last minute."

"I'm hoping you'll sign an endorsement deal with ComfortBox. They'll fly you out to New York for a two-day shoot, so you'd be spending one night away from Charli. Seven figures."

"One night away."

"Of all that, and you heard one night away?"

"I don't like being gone."

"What if Charli could come with us?"

"Us?"

"Er, *you*. I suppose I could go with you if you needed help to organize and schedule things."

"This is the undies company?"

"They sell men's undergarments, and they want you to be the face of their new boxer campaign. It'll be a quick photoshoot; it'll be fun. You'll look great—I promise."

"I don't mean this the wrong way, but you're not my agent. What do you get out of this?"

"Nothing!"

To my surprise, she sounds downright cheerful. I echo her in confusion. *"Nothing."*

"I just got the call from Matthew not ten minutes ago. I was going to call Duke and hand him the lead. Think of it as an olive branch. Duke will get the agent's commission—it'll be a nice chunk of change to start his retirement off right. You'll have enough to set up a solid college fund for Charli."

"And you?"

"Look, I just think you're the best man for the job. I don't need the money."

She sounds sincere, her voice quiet, and in all honesty, I'm speechless. I clear my throat, pretending to stall, but I already have my answer. Jocelyn's stuck her neck out for me, and I'm not going to let her down. She's thought of everything—including, especially, Charli.

"You've got yourself a deal," I say, huskily. "Thank you."

"Really?!"

"You're helping me with this thing, aren't you?" I gesture to the cart, realizing she can't see me, and clarify. "The party. This is the least I can do to thank you."

"Great! I'm going to call Duke. When he contacts you, pretend we haven't talked. It's best if he sets things up. That's how I wanted everything to go."

"Okay."

"Thanks, Boxer."

"Jocelyn?"

"Hmm?"

"See you soon."

When we click off the phone, my palms are sweaty. In the last ten minutes, my emotions have been taken on a rollercoaster. Panic to relief to surprise to . . . *touched*? God, I'm turning into a pansy. I'm nervous just thinking about Jocelyn walking through those doors; my insides are a pile of goo.

In some odd way, it feels as if we've broken through a barrier. When I needed help, I called Jocelyn. She's coming to my rescue. Isn't that what friends do?

Look, I know I told Jocelyn that I wanted to sign with a friend, not a stranger, but I hadn't meant this level of friendship. I'd just wanted her to tone down the formality and call me Boxer instead of Mr. Boxer. Now she's helping me plan my kid's birthday party. I hadn't meant for things to get so far out of hand.

When did things get so complicated? I just needed a new agent. And now, I'm afraid, I've found something else entirely. I'm starting to fall for Jocelyn Jones, and I'm not sure I can go back to the way things were before.

CHAPTER 18

Jocelyn

I DON'T THINK I've been this giddy since I turned six years old.

We'd had horses and cakes and decorate-your-own-cookies, and even a magician at my party. I'd worn a pretty pink dress and invited friends from school. I still have a photo of me wearing a crown, holding the hand of my mother, who'd worn a matching pink dress at my insistence.

Now, the memories are bittersweet at best. I haven't thought about that time in so long, despite a picture I keep in my wallet of my special day. Though the event itself was bursting with excitement, the years thereafter were not. That was one of the last parties my parents had been alive to see.

I blink, exiting the freeway a little quicker than needed, turning into the parking lot minutes later. It's already mid-afternoon, and I haven't been back to the office since lunch. It's been years since I've felt so irresponsible. Maybe I'll call in sick for the rest of the day and head home right after this. I don't think I've ever played hooky from the office—my job *is* my life. I would have nowhere else to go.

I especially hadn't thought I'd spend my one day free from work at Target. I hadn't thought I'd be back to this monstrosity again this year, let alone in the same week. Getting to Target from my condo is like trying to swim through shark infested waters with little more than a wetsuit for protection—it's just not worth it. Especially not when Amazon delivers the very same things directly to my door.

But if that's what it takes to befriend Landon Boxer, I'll swim through those waters any damn day of the week.

"Hey, Duke," I say into my Bluetooth speaker. I waited to call until I'd parked the car first, so I could give him my full attention. "It's me."

"Jocelyn, what can I do for you?"

"I have an offer," I say. "Listen first, ask questions later."

Quickly, I explain everything to him—the finances, the travel, the endorsement deal. I throw in the rest of the information I've already covered with Boxer.

"I want you to have the deal," I say. "Boxer's the best man for the job. Give Matthew Lucas a call today to set things up."

"Boxer's not going to say yes."

"I think you might be surprised."

"Miss Jones—"

"Do me a favor and ask." I'm in a hurry to get out of the car, mostly because I have ice cream melting in a container next to me. "I think it's up to Boxer to say no, don't you? You get the money if he signs on the dotted line. If he says no, it's five minutes out of your day. Two if you skip the small talk."

"I'll do it because you bought me lunch, Miss Jones, but don't hold your breath."

"Thanks, Duke. I have a feeling we'll be chatting soon."

I get out of the car, but not before I grab the small container of now-melting ice cream I picked up from Gabe's on the way over. It had been directly on my route between the cemetery and

Target, and I hadn't even made the decision to stop. My body did it on its own—paying, ordering, and returning to the car—before I'd realized what had happened.

I march through the front doors, purse on one shoulder, ice cream in hand. It doesn't take long to find the distressed single dad perched on the bench in front of Taco Bell with a crumpled bag on the seat next to him.

In front of him is a cart, and by God he must have a degree in architectural design in order to fill the thing that high. It's like a Lego project on steroids. Paper plates, crowns, and streamers are popping out of every line on the cart, rolls of wrapping paper poking out like tent poles in every direction. On top of it all is a piñata that looks like a cross between a monkey and a giraffe. I don't understand it either.

"There you are." He raises to his feet, blue eyes awash with relief at the first sighting of me. "Thank you so much for coming. I dropped Charli off at her friend's house for the afternoon, thinking I'd get all of this done while she was occupied. No such luck."

A wrinkle of worry eases across his forehead as I smile and extend Gabe's as an offering.

"Sit down," I instruct. "Eat this, and take a deep breath. *Then*, we'll get started."

"You brought . . ." He cracks open the lid of the container. "Crunch cone?"

"I figured you might need to stress eat."

He reaches into the Taco Bell bag and removes two spoons. "Don't ask why I grabbed two," he mutters, offering one to me. "I'm not thinking straight."

I don't complain, instead sinking onto the bench next to him. He offers me the first bite and, even though I'm still full from our French Dip sandwiches earlier, I accept. The moment is too sweet to say no.

It's still the best ice cream I've ever had, and Boxer seems to agree. He takes a bite, his eyes closing in a peaceful sort of rest, the worry sliding from his face like sand through an hourglass.

He's fascinating to watch, the change in expression almost lyrical as he opens his eyes a new man. Where pale-blue worry had hovered before, a glimmer of excitement has taken over, and it has my heart skipping a beat to think I might've helped put it there.

"You're something else," Boxer says with a shake of his head. "I wish I could repay you somehow."

Almost like magic, Boxer's phone rings. He blinks, glances down, and shakes his head again.

"Go ahead," I tell him. "I can wait."

"Hello, Duke," he says, shooting me a skeptical glance as he answers. "How's it going?"

Silence descends on us as the low murmur of Duke's voice rasps in the background. I wish I could hear what he's saying, but it's probably not necessary. I know the gist of it.

"Actually, I might be interested." Boxer finally speaks, giving me a wry grin. "If it's really just one night away, I'll sign it."

Internally, champagne bottles are popping. I'm not even sure why. I'm just happy to help, and I think this is a great move for Boxer. I might not get a cut of the money, but in a way I have a reward. Seeing him happy.

Money will come, or it won't. But I have a feeling that Boxer's friendship isn't something that can be bought, and the fact that he thought to call me to rescue him from Target imprisonment means something.

"Get the papers, Duke," Boxer says. He waits a second longer, then laughs at Duke's next question. He glances at me, and responds. "Why don't you just ask her?"

I'm startled as Boxer hands the phone to me, but I try to play it cool.

"Hello?" I clear my throat. "This is Jocelyn."

"Oh, Miss Jones . . ." Duke *tsks* in the background, and I can't tell if he's chiding me or if he's amused. "Well played, my friend. Well played."

"Why don't you give Matthew a call? I'll text you his number."

"I shouldn't have underestimated you," Duke says. "Well done, Miss Jones. I'm impressed."

CHAPTER 19

Boxer

"LANDON BOXER."

I stop in the middle of the aisle, turning slowly to face a horrified-looking Jocelyn Jones.

"What?" My heart pounds. "What's wrong?"

"Who do you think you are?" she asks.

"Sorry?"

"Mixing *Pocahontas* with *The Little Mermaid*?! Honestly, Boxer."

She holds up one set of paper plates and one package of napkins. Finally, her face blooms into a smile, her light laugh sending tremors across my skin that have me wanting to pull her into my arms. Instead, I rest a hand against my heart and shake my head. "You scared me. I thought you were going to be sick or something."

"*Then* you throw an *Aladdin* piñata into the mix? On top of the weird giraffe thing? You only need one piñata." She removes a fat, bright blue genie from the cart and places him back on the shelf. "It's a good thing you called me, or else this party would've been a mess."

"Horrible."

"Like Disney vomited all over your house." She pauses. "You are throwing it at home, right? I guess I didn't ask."

"Fourteen girls. All at once." I close my eyes, already fighting off a migraine just imagining the high-pitched chaos. "I am about to offer Marie all my signing money from this endorsement deal if she comes back."

"You don't have any help?"

"We're flying to visit my parents the week after, so they're not coming down for this party. My brother will send a present like he always does. I've never had to think about help before. Marie always just . . . took care of us. She sent out the invitations a couple of weeks ago, so it's too late to cancel."

"You'll be fine."

I grimace. "I tried to combine three princesses, and I didn't even realize that was a faux paus."

"It's not a faux pas," she corrects, narrowing her eyes at me. "It's a sin."

I make the sign of the cross, which brings a laugh from her. "What if . . ." I shake my head. "Forget it. We'll be fine. Or, maybe you can draw out a plan for where things go? Never mind. It doesn't matter."

"I'll do you one better. I'll have to bring over some papers for you to sign for that endorsement deal. The party's Saturday? How about I swing by early and set everything up for you."

"You'll come to the party?"

"N-no," she says. "I'll just do the event planning part. I'm good with organization—I'm not as good with kids."

"I beg to differ." I smile, remembering the way she'd talked with Charli in the car. At first there'd been a few awkward pauses, but then they'd gotten along like pals. Charli hadn't stopped talking about her all afternoon. "But I wouldn't force you to be part of the party. If I had a way to escape it, I would."

"But my offer stands. What if I put in for an order of an ice cream cake and drop it off with the papers? I know a great place. I'll get all the streamers and party favors set up, and then I'll leave before the main event. In exchange, you'll sign those papers."

"Okay," I agree slowly. I'd already been planning on signing the papers, even if she didn't set up the party. But I can admit when I'm out of my element, which I am now. I need the help on Saturday, so I will selfishly take it. "Can I ask for one more favor?"

"Name it." She pulls something off the shelf, reading the box before turning to me and waggling some party poppers. "Charli will love these."

I nod, and she tosses them in the cart. "Do you know how to do hair?"

She stills. "Hair?"

"Charli's been asking to wear a braid, and I'm hopeless. I can never manage to do anything more than knot it together, and then we spend an hour crying and trying to untangle it."

"Hard to imagine you crying."

"Well, I do the cursing, she does the crying."

"That seems more like it." Her eyes crinkle as she grins. "You're lucky I grew up braiding my own hair, and a few of my friends', too. Have no fear, a French Braid is on the way."

A weight is lifted off my chest, floating away, as if I'd cut free the unicorn balloon that Jocelyn had tied to the cart. All morning, I'd been dreading this—the party, the cakes, the favors, the poppers—terrified that I'd throw Charli the worst birthday celebration in the world.

Now, with Jocelyn's help, there's nothing left to worry about. She's taking care of everything, including the hair. As I watch her push the cart down the aisle, humming a little ditty to herself that sounds like *A Whole New World*, my heart fills with a warmth that has nothing to do with her looks. Nothing to do with the stunning beauty that's had me captivated since our first meeting, or the gorgeous way her eyes shine when they land on me.

This, this feeling, is more than that. Deeper, having everything to do with the fact that she's single-handedly subtracted the stress from one of the most nerve-wracking moments in any single dad's life. If I can't make my daughter feel like a princess, then I'm not doing things right.

"I have to find a way to repay you," I blurt out. "For doing all of this."

"Oh, you don't have to repay me at all." She looks almost surprised that I suggested it. "I volunteered to help, and I'm having a good time. Plus, you're doing the endorsement deal for me. It all evens out."

"You don't get anything from the deal, either, though. You're doing all of this . . . why *are* you doing it?" I move toward her, and she steps back. I take another step forward, and this time, she stops. We're inches apart. "Does my signing with your agency mean that much to you?"

A flash of something, discomfort maybe, crosses her face. "No, I—"

"Why are you doing all of this?"

"Because I want to," she says. "I'd do it for anyone."

"You would?"

"Any friend." She shifts, her eyes downcast. "Or any client. When I bring on a business partner, I'm willing to help in whatever ways you need."

"So this is business?" I ask the question carefully, watching her reaction. I'm trying to gauge whether she's feeling the same way as me—confused, like things are progressing in a direction entirely different than what we'd planned. "You'd do this for any of your clients?"

"Yes." She tilts her chin upward, defiant. "I have clients loyal to me, and I'm loyal to my clients."

"Like a friend."

The defiant gleam in her eyes flickers. "I suppose."

"Well, it's no wonder you're the best in the business." I take a step back, finally able to breathe. Standing close to her is too consuming, too distracting, and I can't seem to stop talking. The words flow, keeping conversation alive just so I can stand near her. "Well, I appreciate it."

"You shouldn't feel pressure to sign with me," she says, marching forward, her heels clicking on the tiles. "It's no secret that I want you on my roster, sure. But I would do this anyway."

"Even if I told you no right now?"

"No?"

"If I said I didn't want to sign with you, would you still be here, helping me?"

I move toward her again. Her back is to a wall of toys, and she can't possibly do anything except meet my gaze. She does, her eyes glinting as she looks up.

"Yes," she whispers. "I would."

"Why?"

"Because." Ducking around a display of trucks, she disappears down another aisle. "Every girl deserves a great sixth birthday party, and I'm not going to let some clueless man ruin it."

I laugh, following her as she throws a few more packages into the cart. "One little girl is very lucky."

"It's fun," she says. "I haven't had an excuse to do these things in ages."

"Are you sure I can't convince you to stay for the party?" A part of me is longing for her to say yes, if for no other reason than an excuse to spend time together. I can't possibly call what's between us love, or lust, or anything except for curiosity. All I know is that she makes my head spin in ways that have me wanting to find out more. "Charli would love it."

"No," she says. "I can't."

"Can't?"

"It's not my place."

"But—"

"I'll drop off the papers on Saturday morning, and get you all setup, though, so don't worry."

She click-clacks in her heels down the aisle, the conversation closed. I'm frozen to the spot for a moment, watching her calves as they lead the rest of her slim figure through the store. I could watch that woman move all day long, and it'd never get old.

"Hey, big guy, I need some help with this." Jocelyn's a good ten steps ahead of me, and I have to hustle to catch up. "You think she'll like it?"

I eye the piñata. It's a unicorn the size of a small canoe. "She gets to whack something with a stick? She'll love it."

"These were always my favorite." Almost reverently, Jocelyn pulls a package from the cart to her chest. "The poppers."

"Poppers?" I haven't seen these before, but the look on her face has me convinced they're the best thing in the world. "What do they do?"

"You've never seen them before? You have got to try one."

"Fine, then, hand them over."

"But—"

"I'm still going to buy them, I just want to try one."

"But—"

Rebel that I am, I gently remove the pack from her chest, tear it open, and pull one free. It's not hard to figure out that I need to yank on the little dangly string in order to make it work. So I give it a good tug, and let's just say I *shouldn't* have been surprised.

The thing is called a popper.

But somehow, that doesn't register, and I'm fucking terrified after pulling the trigger.

It blasts off, loud and echoing through the store. No *wonder* Jocelyn didn't want me setting it off inside. That, plus the streamers. They're everywhere, flying through the air as I blink in shock.

"Oh," I say. "*That's* a popper."

She's just staring at me now, a look of disbelief on her face. Where I'd normally call her stunning, now, I can't help but think she's adorable. Bits of confetti and streamers decorate her, bright bursts of color against the pale strands of her hair.

"I can't believe you!" she hisses. "You stole a popper, and then set it off in Target!"

"I said I'm going to pay for it."

She's completely oblivious to the fact there's paper all over her, so I reach out and brush a long strand off of her shoulder. It trails lazily to the floor, both of our eyes watching as it swirls through the air.

Then, reality sets in, and she pulls a little circle thing out of her purse and pops it open. A mirror. Fascinating. I had no idea they made them that small.

One look at her face, and she gives the tiniest gasp, her lips parting into the letter 'o' before she turns her gaze on me. "I'm a mess."

"You're beautiful." I don't mean to say it, but it comes out, and then it's just there. I can't take it back, and frankly, I don't want to. She *is* beautiful. "Let me help."

She clears her throat, her eyes fixed on my chest as I step toward her and carefully run a hand through her hair, teasing out the ponytail holder.

"Sorry," I tell her. "I can't get all the confetti with this thing in."

She gives the slightest nod to continue, and I do, picking out the colorful clumps from her silky mane. I could run my fingers through her hair all day. If only we weren't in the middle of the party section at Target.

Maybe I should've waited to test the popper on Saturday where I could've done this in the comfort of my own home with nobody to interrupt us. Until, of course, fourteen girls arrived in hopes of finding a birthday party and functioning poppers—not some old hockey player infatuated with his almost-agent's hair.

"There," I say, teasing my fingers through one last time. "You're all cleaned up. Sorry about the mess."

To my surprise, she leans in toward my fingers, her eyes closed. It's as if she's never been touched like this, and it makes me rock hard and tingly all over. The look on her face—I can only imagine what it'd be like if I let things go further.

"Unless you want me to keep going?" I laugh, continuing to caress her head. "I give excellent head massages."

"What?" Her gaze flicks up as she steps backward, a look of alarm on her face. "No, just . . . a broom. I'm going to find a broom."

"No, Jocelyn, I'll ask at the front desk—"

She's already gone before I can continue.

Awesome.

Great job, Boxer, I tell myself. I scared off the one agent who is generous enough to help plan my kid's birthday party. If I don't watch out, I'm going to lose the one woman who can help me pull of Charli's sixth birthday party, and the one woman who could do great things for my career.

The one woman who I'm finding I can't stand to be without, even if the only thing we have in common is business.

When Jocelyn returns moments later, she's holding a broom with all the tags still on it. "We'll buy the broom too," she mutters. "Need it for the party."

I take it from her hands and sweep up the mess, but it doesn't do much to set her at ease. She checks through the cart methodically, muttering under her breath about numbers and items and invitations and God knows what else.

"Hey," I say, finally. "Are you okay? I don't want to make things weird between us."

"No, of course not." She's distracted, counting out various plastic utensils. "Just figuring this out."

"It doesn't have to be perfect."

"Oh." She gives a throaty chuckle. "It won't be, but we can make it work."

"Jocelyn." I walk over to her, resting the broom in the cart. "I shouldn't have said you were beautiful. I know we're just business partners, okay? I crossed a line, and I'm sorry."

She freezes with the pack of forks in her hand, her gaze slowly coming to meet mine. "Yes, of course."

"I'm sorry. I won't cross the line again, okay?"

"Great."

"But I won't take it back either." The words spill out, and I know that even as I'm promising not to cross lines, I can't help it. There's an emptiness inside those pools of blue; a place that seems lonely to me, as if it's been too long since she's had fun. Too long since she's been touched, told she's beautiful, made to feel like the incredible woman she is. "You *are* beautiful, Jocelyn."

She opens her mouth, but no sound comes out.

"I also respect your work, so I will try my best not to say something stupid like that again." I offer her a smile. "Can we forget about it?"

She nods, her lips curling upward at the side. "Sure thing, Boxer."

"Thank you for your help, again," I say, gesturing to the cart. "I'd be lost without you."

"No, thank you," she says, finding a clear, firm voice. "I had fun. Really."

We haul our treasures up to the front. I check out and pay, and together we walk out through the front doors. She's carrying a bag, so we walk to my car first and unload everything.

I turn to offer her a handshake, determined to stick to my word about keeping things professional.

To my surprise, she gives me a shy smile. Then she opens her arms and eases onto the tips of her toes to give me a hug. I try not to sniff her hair, but it's difficult. She smells like ice cream and sugar, and I want nothing more than a taste of her skin, a kiss on her neck.

Maybe it's me, and maybe it's her, but the hug lingers for a second longer than necessary.

"I'll see you Saturday," she says, pulling away and clearing her throat. "I'll bring the cake."

CHAPTER 20

Jocelyn

"DID YOU GO to the spa?" Lindsay shrugs out of her jacket, resting it on her lap as she slides onto a bar stool. "You look refreshed."

I accept a cocktail list from the bartender and shake my head. "No time for the spa."

"Yoga?"

"Nope."

"It's not your birthday for another few weeks . . ." She frowns, sizing me up. "Are you on some diet you didn't tell me about?"

"If I were on a diet, would I be ordering a margarita?" I set down the drink menu and put in my order with the bartender. Extra salt, blended. Two shots of tequila. "I'm telling you, there's nothing out of the ordinary."

"Oh, there's something." Lindsay picks up the menu, scans it over, and then duplicates my order. "I just can't put my finger on *what* it is."

"You ladies celebrating anything special?" The bartender is an older woman, her voice rocky and worn from a lifetime of over-the-counter conversations. "Birthdays?"

"We're celebrating something," Lindsay says. "But I haven't figured out what yet."

The woman nods. "Well, I'll leave ya to it. Call me Elene."

"We're not celebrating *anything*," I say, once we're somewhat alone. "We're drinking to forget."

"Forget what?"

I sigh, scanning the dimly lit bar that used to be a local hangout. Over the years, newer, trendier bars have popped up in the area, stealing the clientele from this establishment and diverting them to the shinier ones. I've tried the *other* bars in an effort to impress clients, but the music is always too loud, the drinks too expensive, the food too bland. This place is a classic.

"Nothing," I say. "Let's just forget it."

"What happened today?" Lindsay's not giving up so easily. "I thought your outing with Boxer was going well. I could've saved you if something went wrong."

"Oh, no, the park was phase one. *Phase One* went great. After the whole Barbie incident."

"Don't be hard on yourself. You couldn't have guessed she wasn't a Barbie lover. But wait one second, missy." She swivels to face me. "Phase *One*?"

"Yep."

"Why am I not aware of Phase Two?"

"Because I wasn't aware. I'm still not sure what happened."

"Start talking."

"I'm waiting for my margarita."

Lindsay squints at me. "Jocelyn Jones, you're not afraid of anything. The last time I saw you order hard alcohol was when Donovan . . . *oh*, shit. You're falling for Boxer."

Thankfully, Elene, the bartender, plunks down our drinks at that very moment. "This is about a man?"

"No," I say, at the same time Lindsay says, "*Apparently*."

"What's he like?" Elene leans against the counter. "Why are

you still in denial?"

"I'm not in denial. I'm just not interested in him," I argue weakly. "Except as a business prospect."

"Right," Elene snorts, rolling her eyes in Lindsay's general direction. "Name?"

"Boxer," I say, all too quickly.

Elene laughs. "He's on your mind, sugar, whether you like it or not."

I rest my head against the counter, eyes closed, the first sips of margarita swirling through my brain. Lindsay's right—I'm a business drinks sort of woman. One or two glasses of wine, and that's my maximum. I don't *get* out of control.

Now and again, I'll have three glasses of wine for a special occasion, like my horrendous date with Mr. Hot Shot the other night. But I feel as if that one deserves a pass—it was either the third glass of wine or suicide, and I choose to live.

To my surprise, Lindsay's hand snakes out and rubs my back. "I should've seen this coming the second you ordered a margarita. Or before, when I saw your cheeks glowing without a facial peel."

"I'm not glowing," I say, sneaking a glance at her with one eyeball. "I'm terrified."

Elene pours herself a margarita. "Bar's empty, and I might as well be a counselor with all the tears I've wiped off the counter over the years. Spill your beans, ladies."

"I'm Lindsay, this is Jocelyn," Lindsay says. "Jocelyn's the best sports agent around, and she's out to rope in Boxer as her client. But, apparently, we've got a *twist* to this whole thing. Miss Jones wants more than Boxer's signature."

Elene wiggles her eyebrows. "I know who he is, and I don't blame you, Miss Jones. That man's packing a lot of . . ." she gives a raspy clear of her throat. "Charm."

Lindsay laughs, pulling me into an upright position. "See? None of us blame you. It's understandable. Boxer's a catch."

"I don't *like* him, I just . . ." I pause, taking a lick of salt from the edge of my glass, washing it down with a crisp swig of cocktail. Instant brain freeze. "Ow. *Ow*."

"Slow down, boss," Lindsay says, "or you're going to be spending the night on my couch while I hold your hair."

"I'm not good at this."

"The drinking, or the falling in love?" Elene asks. "Because if you want my honest to goodness opinion, you're not good at either. You, my friend, are wound tighter than a spring."

Lindsay nods enthusiastically. "Whenever she tries to deep breathe, she has a heart attack. Basically."

"So? Why not jump in bed for a night with this guy, get the sexual tension out of the way, and then do business with a clear mind?"

"It's not a horrible idea," Lindsay agrees with Elene, which is surprising. Lindsay is a professional in all senses of the word, having never dated anyone in the realm of the sports world. "He really does seem like a great guy."

"It's not that simple." I run my fingers along the bar, the alcohol melting away my previous arguments. "Even if I *were* interested in a one night stand, *he's* not interested."

"Good Lord, woman. Take a look at yourself," Elene says. Then she turns to Lindsay and shakes her head. "Is she always this dense?"

Lindsay nods. "She's the smartest woman I know, but sometimes I want to whack her over the head with her own stiletto."

"Excuse me," I say. "I'm right here."

"What man doesn't want a piece of you?" Elene asks, gesturing to me. "You're clearly successful and smart, and you're stunning.

I *highly* doubt he's not interested."

"Oh, you'd be surprised," I tell her. "I happen to carry a reputation."

"Let me guess. Maneater." Elene folds her arms across her chest. "You're successful in the Boy's Club, so all those men with the winky little wieners have some name they like to pin on you out of jealousy."

"The Blonde Bitch. Ice Queen," Lindsay starts listing them off. When I glare at her, she looks up. "What? It's true. We both know it, and we both know they're completely unfounded."

"Of course they're unfounded," Elene scoffs. "But if this Boxer is a true man, he'll embrace your success, not run away from it."

"He's a true man." Lindsay fans herself. "He's gorgeous, and he's *so* sweet with his daughter.

"This is strictly business, ladies," I say, though I have a feeling my argument is falling on deaf ears.

"Honey, you've gotta loosen up," Elene interrupts. "I don't know you that well, but I know your type. How long has it been?"

"Since?"

Lindsay and Elene laugh. When I still don't answer, Lindsay gapes at me. "Since you've had *sex*, Jocelyn."

"Oh, come on, ladies. I don't know."

"Sure you do," Elene says. "Two months and four days for me."

"Last week for me," Lindsay says. "But only because it was my fifth date with a guy, and I think it's going somewhere."

"You didn't tell me that," I accuse her. "Is this Mark?"

"Yes! He might not last forever, but for now, he's perfect."

"Your turn," Elene rounds on me. "How long?"

It's no use arguing, so I sigh. "Fourteen months."

Lindsay blinks and looks like she's about to pass out. "Seriously?"

"Good God, woman," Elene says. "Call Boxer right now. Screw business—literally. Your health and sanity are more important. Drinks are on me."

"She'll say she's too busy." Lindsay sighs. "She's in a relationship with her job."

"Right, but is your job going to cook you dinner on your birthday?" Elene asks. "Or hell, forget cooking. I just need the man to dial in for a pizza and make me feel nice. I'm simple."

"No," I say quietly. "I can't."

My tone must ring through to them, because both women quiet down, watching my face as I push my empty glass away from me. The margarita is buzzing in my head, and I take a second to gather my thoughts.

"You have to trust me when I tell you it's not that simple," I say. "I don't have time for love from someone like Boxer."

"What's that supposed to mean?" Elene asks. "You deserve love as much as the rest of us. I don't want to hear you saying that ever again, Miss Jones."

"Jocelyn," I correct automatically. "And I just mean . . . ."

The thought is lost, somewhere between the back of my brain and my heart, struggling to surface, struggling to tease out the words I'm trying to say.

"I just have the feeling that when Boxer falls in love, it's *everything*," I say finally. "There's no stepping slowly into the water, dipping a toe and testing the boundaries. He's either all the way in, or he's not."

"Honey, that's the sort of love everyone else is looking for," Elene says. "Every woman wants—no, *deserves*—a man who loves with his whole heart. Otherwise, why not skip the love and go for the sex? It's easier."

"Not for someone like him," I say. "I don't know why, but I

have the feeling Boxer isn't the sort of guy who has sex without there being strings attached. He's protective of his daughter, his family, and when he invites someone into his home, he's going to make sure it's worth it."

"You *are* worth it, boss," Lindsay says. "I still don't understand the problem. You don't *need* him as a client, do you? If you feel this strongly, let Rumpert take him."

"No, I can't do that," I say, blinking back tears. "I just . . . I don't have the sort of capacity for love that Boxer does."

"What are you talking about?" Lindsay asks. "Sure you do."

"He'll do anything for his family, his daughter, his parents. I don't have family, okay? I don't know what that's like. I haven't for a long time." I shake my head as my throat burns with tears. "I almost tore apart a couple in love recently. Because I didn't *recognize* it was love. What sort of psycho does that?"

"Andi and Ryan?" Lindsay asks softly. "You didn't know—"

"I should've known. I should've listened to Ryan when he told me he was falling in love. He called me . . ." I stop, swallow, a wave of shame washing over my body as I remember the night at my co-worker's wedding. Lawrence Pierce, brother to Ryan Pierce. "I'd wanted to sign Ryan, and I pushed him too far."

"You made a mistake," Lindsay says. "When you realized it, you backed off. Did you apologize?"

"I tried to," I say, my voice raspy with hate for what I'd done. "Ryan won't return my calls, and I don't blame him. I don't dare talk to Andi after what I did."

"Why did you try to break them up?" Elene asks. "I don't understand."

"Because I wanted to sign Ryan from the Minnesota Stars and bring him over to the LA Lightning. He deserves it—he's a great player. But I wasn't risking a young kid on my roster who's can't control his . . ." I clear my throat as Lindsay fills in *ding-dong* for me. "I've been burned before. I love the game. I'm loyal to my clients. But I'm not an idiot, and I'm not a sucker—I refuse to sign another player who runs off to South America at the drop of a hat because of a girl."

"Things went south?"

"They were in love," I say, looking away. "Ryan was willing to give up everything for Andi. I'd *thought* they were nothing more than a fling. I tried to get him to break things off so he could focus on his career, but I was wrong. Completely wrong."

"Well, it ain't too late to fix it."

"Of course it is. I botched the deal."

"Ryan got the girl, didn't he?" Elene asks. "That sounds like it's far more important to him than any money he might've gotten."

"True," I agree. "But I was horrible to them. I don't know what came over me; it was like I morphed into someone else. All these old feelings came up, and I turned ugly."

"Can you get her a meeting with this guy?" Elene asks Lindsay. "I'm guessing you run her life?"

"I do," Lindsay says. "And I can."

"No, I should leave them be," I say. "Honestly, no good can come of it."

"Think about it," Elene says. "You can apologize to the couple, ask for their forgiveness or whatever makes you feel better, and then get their advice. Find out what sort of love they have because honestly, it sounds like something worth having."

"I guess," I say. "But I still can't—"

"What's the worst that can happen?" Lindsay says. "You don't get Boxer as a client?"

"No," I say, near silent. Both women lean in, their eyes locked on mine. "That's not the worst."

Lindsay shakes her head. "What—"

Elene shushes her. "Let the woman speak."

I swallow, breathe deeply. "The worst would be to screw things up so bad, pushing him so hard in one direction—my direction, that I lose him entirely."

"Honey," Elene says, "you have to push a little, or at least open yourself up. Otherwise, the opportunities will sail right past you whether you want them to or not."

"And if he doesn't like me?" I've blinked a hundred times, but a tear manages to slide onto my cheek. "What if he sees what's inside, and it's not enough?"

Elene looks down at the bar. "Love is a risk, honey. I can't promise you anything. That'd be cruel of me, so I'm not going to do anything of the sort. But—" she raises a finger. "What I'm going to do is promise that you'll regret it if you don't try."

"But—"

"Donovan," Lindsay says, interrupting. "That's what this is about. It's not about Andi and Ryan."

"It is."

"No, it's not. Sure, maybe you feel bad," Lindsay agrees. "But this is about Donovan."

I fall silent. It's crossed my mind once or twice, but I've never let myself dwell on the past. I made one mistake, and it nearly ruined me. I try not to think about it.

"Sorry, but I need to get going." I stand and toss enough money on the counter to cover the round of drinks, then turn to leave. "Thank you both for the advice."

"Wait, boss—"

"I'll see you tomorrow," I say. "I'm going to call a cab home tonight. Lindsay, use the Uber account with my corporate card."

They call goodbye after me, clearly sensing the end of the

conversation. I'm thankful they give me my space because the second the taxi arrives, I crumple into the backseat. Another tear falls, and then a third. It's been months since I've cried, but there's too much at stake for me to hold it all inside.

The cabbie lets me off in front of my condo. I pay him, dry my eyes, and make it inside while keeping myself somewhat put together. Once inside, I change into my pajamas and grab a pint of ice cream from the fridge.

I ignore the texts from Lindsay asking if I made it home okay and plop down onto the couch. I'm sick of crying, so instead I'm going to blow my diet and dip into my emergency stash of sweets.

Emotions—I hate them. Yet, they still happen, so I've tried to keep myself prepared with Ben and Jerry.

I'm only two bites in when the knock sounds on the door. I stand up, carry myself through the kitchen and look through the peephole. My heart does a full-on line dance at the sight of a familiar face.

Landon Boxer.

CHAPTER 21

Boxer

LET ME BE honest. I'm not completely sure why I'm here.

There's movement behind the door, and the click of the lock has me ready to turn around and pretend I was never here. Except for that peephole. Damn peephole means it's too late for me to chicken out.

Taking a deep breath, I prepare to find the woman I've come to think about obsessively. As if her perfume is lingering around me to tease, drawing up images of her at inopportune moments. Which is problematic when I should be doing other things, like playing hockey or reading bedtime stories or otherwise functioning in life.

My brother showed up in town earlier this evening. He does that sometimes, wandering in and out as he pleases. He remembered Charli's birthday and brought her a present. She's infatuated with him being here and showering her with attention, so much so that she hardly noticed when I asked Steven to watch her for a few hours. Outstanding business, I told him.

Maybe I've come to apologize. Maybe I've come to be honest, to ask for more than she can give. Maybe I've come to push her away completely. I don't know, and I don't have a plan. I just know that my heart, my head, and my feet all led me here tonight.

I thought I was prepared to see her, the stunning blonde from the office, but that's not what I find when she pulls open the door. There, instead of the polished exterior I'm used to finding, is something different.

While the shimmery blonde hair and slim figure are the same, Jocelyn's face is nearly devoid of makeup. Her eyes are pale blue, like the sky viewed through a cloud, just a bit hazy and soft.

She's been called the ice queen, among other names, but I don't see it—not how they mean, anyway. When I look at her, I don't see the sharp icicles, the cold front that others claim to find in her. Instead, I see a crystalline gem, a raw and beautiful work of nature.

Ice, while at times dangerous and sharp, can also be beautiful. There are few things more miraculous than snowflakes, or the sheer white innocence of a frozen tundra. Within her is a certain contentment—like the quiet of a morning's fresh snow.

Maybe I don't mind the ice because I spend so much time on it. It's my love, my career, my passion. Maybe there's a reason I've been drawn to her.

My hands shake as I fold them in front of my body. No matter how strongly I feel for her, if she doesn't feel the same toward me, it means nothing.

"Landon?" Her voice is a windchime in greeting as she waits for me to say something. "What are you doing here?"

It's now that I notice there's a tinge of sadness in her beauty tonight. A hint of redness lines her eyes, and a remnant of makeup is smeared high on her cheek, as if she's been crying.

I spy her shorts, just barely long enough to be decent, and a flimsy tank top that leaves little to the imagination. This puts my mind at odds with my body; while I'm nearly rigid with desire for her, I'm more concerned with the source of the tears, the reason for her pain. I want to hold her until the tears stop.

"What's wrong?" I step into the apartment, not waiting for an invitation. I raise a hand to her cheek, brush my thumb across it. "Why are you crying?"

She doesn't argue or pull away. "It doesn't matter."

"Of course it does. Jocelyn—"

"I'm fine, okay?" Her voice is razor thin, a hint of danger at the edge of it. "Did you want something tonight?"

The way she phrases her question sends a lightning bolt of clarity straight through my body. "Yes," I say, kicking the door shut behind me as I step further into the room. "I do want something. I came here for something. For you."

Her eyes flicker in confusion.

"Tell me no right now if you're not interested," I say, backing her against the kitchen counter. "Otherwise, I'm going to kiss you."

Confusion melts from her expression and is replaced by something else entirely—a warmth that tells me I'm not the only one feeling this way. But I don't move, not yet—I can be patient. I've been patient for years, waiting for the right woman to come along, and now she's here. I'm sure of it. It wasn't love at first sight, I don't believe in that anymore, but there's a chemistry between us, and I'd hate myself forever if I didn't risk exploring it.

She still doesn't say *no*. As I wait, giving her time to push me away, I feel her body arch against mine, her nails digging into my shoulder as one hand comes up to balance herself against me.

I lift her up and deposit her gently on the counter so that I'm standing even closer. Stalling. Making my intentions known. Once this moment passes, things will never—can never—be the same between us.

Then her legs wrap around my waist.

"Are you sure?" I ask, leaning in, our breath mixing together as I pause there, an inch above her lips. "Because this is your last chance to say no."

She blinks once, then nods. The sight of her full lips tilting toward me is enough to spark movement. A rush of desire courses through my body, liquid ice as our lips touch.

The moment's frozen, suspended, like the utter stillness across that frozen tundra. Muted and tender in its fragility. She tastes sweet, like vanilla ice cream. I know then that I'll never be able to get enough.

My hand comes up and rests behind her head, fingers weaving through the silky strands as I pull her lips off mine. Her neck is exposed, vulnerable, and I move in for a taste. When I press my lips to the skin there, she murmurs a sound that sends heat clamoring through my veins.

She hasn't been touched like this in ages, I can sense it. I'm just glad I'm the lucky man who gets the chance to show her what she's been missing.

"Joss." I pull away, leaving only my fingers to dance across her collarbone. She shivers as I find the tiny strap of her tank top and ease it down over one shoulder. "Please tell me if I should stop."

Her eyes are still closed. Instead of telling me no, her legs squeeze tighter around me. My hands reach down behind her, spread over her lower back, and I pull her to the edge of the counter.

The only thing between us is the frustrating friction of my jeans and her shorts—and whatever she might have underneath. Whatever it is, I intend to find out—but first, I need to explore, to cherish, to worship the treasure she is.

Jocelyn beats me to it. She pulls me toward her, eyes fixed shut as if this moment might shatter when she opens them. She's perched for a kiss.

I resist, holding back and brushing a kiss to her forehead. I watch her reaction, the softening of her features, and finally give in. My lips lock on hers and all the tenderness melts away, leaving in its place a ferocious burn for more.

I hold her to me as her fingers grasp at my shirt. My tongue teases past her lips, savoring the sugary sweetness, wondering what she'll taste like elsewhere. Sounds slip from her lips that drive me wild with need until I'm ready to shatter from the pain of waiting.

"Let me take you to the bedroom," I murmur. "Please."

"No," she argues. "Here. Now."

I bring a hand up, ease the hair back from her face. It's messy now, uncontrolled and adorable. "Later, if you want. Not the first time."

"But—"

"Joss, open your eyes, sweetheart."

She shakes her head, eyes still closed. "I don't want this moment to go away."

"I'm not going anywhere." I rest a hand underneath her chin, tilt her face up toward mine, and examine her lashes, still flecked with the last drops of tears. A well of frustration boils up inside of me. "Why were you crying?"

She merely shakes her head.

I kiss one eyelid, willing the tears away, then the other. It's wishful thinking, maybe, but the dampness seems to lessen by the time I pull back.

"We shouldn't," she says, a hand coming to rest on my chest. "This isn't right. We're business partners."

"Does this feel like business to you?"

I raise her up so that I'm holding her weight completely. Her legs are situated behind my back, and I'm absolutely positive she can feel my desire pressed against her. Judging by the soft inhalation of breath at the contact, she's not disappointed.

I don't give her time to speak, enveloping her mouth in a kiss that leaves my intentions completely exposed. It's funny; when I arrived here tonight, I wasn't sure what I'd find. I figured I owed her an apology, maybe, or an excuse.

What I *didn't* expect to find was that I had no control over my feelings for her; I hadn't expected her to sweep away my will-power entirely. But I suppose that, like hockey, relationships are an unpredictable game. Love, lust, infatuation—whatever it is, I haven't played this game in far too long, but the one thing that never changes is that I don't give up easily.

"Which way is the bedroom?" I ask.

She jerks her head backward toward a doorway. I stumble to-ward it like an oaf, moving far faster than I probably should, seeing as I have a woman wrapped around my body. So I pause, resting a hand against the doorframe, and savor the moment with a kiss as sweet as a chocolate strawberry. Dainty, delicious, and just right.

"Boxer," Jocelyn says, breathless as I come up for air. "That doesn't feel like business."

"Look at me." The weight of her in my arms is nothing. My hockey bag is heavier than her. "Joss, please."

Her eyes finally open, and I watch as she studies me, my face, my lips, the flimsy excuse for distance between us.

"I'm here," I say firmly. "And I'm not going anywhere."

"Second door on the right."

I plunge onward, through a small living room where a televi-sion is flickering in the background. I can't count in this state, so the second door is harder to find than it should be. I blame it on the scent of her pheromones clouding my judgment.

I weave briefly into the first door. "Bathroom," I mutter, back-ing out and continuing onward. I've got no more thought power than an animal at this point, my desire laser-focused on one thing, and one thing alone—making Jocelyn Jones mine.

The bed appears like some glorious light at the end of the tunnel. It's large, luxurious, outfitted in a way that looks and smells like Jocelyn. Sleek black comforter and sheets, with the subtle hint of sugar in the air.

I kick off my shoes, then lie her down on the comforter, pushing her hair back, savoring a moment of nothing but closeness to one another. As one, we inch further onto the bed until her head is rested on the pillow, and I'm perched next to her, one hand dangerously low on her hip.

"What are we doing here, Boxer?" she whispers in the near silence. "Why did you come here tonight?"

"I don't know." I move so that I'm positioned over her, straddling her, but not yet touching. We're still completely clothed, but I need to be near her, as close as she'll let me.

"You showed up here for a reason. What about Charli?"

"My brother stopped by to watch her for the night. They're having a birthday celebration, and I wasn't invited. Seemed like a sign."

"To come here?"

"Can't think of a better place to spend my free time." I lean down, brushing a kiss against her forehead. "I can't stop thinking about you. I don't know why, don't ask me to put words to it, but I haven't felt this way about a woman in a long time."

"Me neither," she murmurs. Then her face colors, her cheeks pink as she gives a flustered shake of her head. "I mean, about a man. A man. I'm interested in men, and do you know what? Never mind. If you could just stop me from talking—"

It's no problem at all to stop her from talking.

That's accomplished with a touch to her forehead, brushing a wisp of blonde out of her eyes. Once I've cleared the way, I let the threat of a kiss torture both of us for a long moment, the desire between us thick enough to slice with an ice skate.

"What will happen after?" she asks.

"Mmm." I don't process the question, my hand now trailing past the edge of her tank top. "After what?"

She begins to say something, but my thumb accidentally slides across her breast as I'm exploring, and she sucks in air like it's her last breath on Earth. It's erotic, the way she reacts to my every move.

As a hockey player, I've dated my share of women. Sure, it was back before I had Charli, but I can remember bits and pieces. Puck bunnies—those women intent on snagging players for a night only, for the fame, the glory, the notch on their bedposts. We're guilty too, those who fall for it, but in the end, that's not what makes a woman attractive to me.

What's attractive to me looks suspiciously like Jocelyn Jones who, despite her buttoned up approach to business, is malleable beneath my hands, sensitive to my touches in unparalleled enthusiasm. She's incredible.

And I don't want to let her down.

I've already forgotten her question, and I think she has too because her hands come to clutch at my hips and pull me closer. I lower myself until I'm covering her with my body, balanced above her with my arms on either side of her shoulders.

Her hands caress the muscles taut along my biceps, testing the strength there. Her skin burns against mine, fingertips leaving scorching trails as she moves them lower, past my wrists, down to my stomach where she hooks a finger into the top of my jeans.

Though I'm itching to touch her, I surrender myself to the moment, let her explore for as long as she likes. The second her eyes flick to mine, however, I'm done for; it's my turn to take over.

My fingers run along the thin swatch of skin visible between her shorts and her tank top, and when I dip underneath, I brush against the smoothest bit of lingerie. I tense at the impact, she arches her hips upward, toward me, and it's everything I can do not to rip off her clothes.

Instead, I slide down and let my lips have their turn. The first kiss lands on the outside of her little shorts and on the inside of her thigh, but it's not enough, and she makes sure I know that. At the guidance of her hand, I slide the shorts from her legs and am left with the most delectable sight in all of this world.

A half-naked Jocelyn Jones.

Well, maybe it's only half of the most delectable sight in the world; a fully naked Jocelyn Jones would be ideal. In order for that to happen, I need to rid her of the rest of the pajamas, no matter how sexy they are.

However, there's a fair chance I might have a heart attack at the sight of her naked, so it's probably best if we take things slow.

The second kiss lands low on her stomach, just beyond the edge of her panties, heat radiating as I linger there, my fingers trailing a dance up the insides of her legs. This time, her words are laced with pleasure as she urges me for more.

I'm trying my best to be patient, to enjoy every moment—but another part of me is ready to combust. If I don't get my pants off shortly, I will be missing circulation to an essential member of my body. So I stand, remove my jeans and shirt, and return to the party, letting my kisses speak for me.

"I want you more than anything in this world," I grit out, holding her close. I let myself press against her, swallowing her groan of pleasure with a furious tangle of lips.

"But what . . ." she whispers, grinding her hips against me. "What about after?"

"After?"

"After . . ." She stills somewhat, her arms still wrapped around my neck. "If we do this?"

"Who cares?"

Immediately, I know that's the wrong response. I hate myself for it, but I wasn't thinking. I'm about to take off like a bottle rocket, and all of the blood that's supposed to be helping my brain is somewhere else entirely.

There's no way I'm capable of conversation right now, but that's not an excuse, either, and the worry that I've ruined everything hits me like a semi-truck.

"That's not what I meant," I say, watching as the lust in her eyes flickers, falters, and then begins to vanish. "I didn't mean *who cares*, I just meant that I want you so badly, I'll do anything . . ."

"No, you didn't do anything wrong," she says, but her voice is an icicle—thin, on the precipice of hurtling toward the ground to shatter for good. "I'm sorry, this is all my fault. I let you in, and I basically attacked you, and—"

"God, no. Joss, you didn't attack me. If anything, I'm the one who attacked you. I showed up without an invitation, without warning, and I invited myself in. I'm so sorry."

She slides out from underneath me, situating herself against the headboard. She pulls a pillow out from underneath her and clutches it to her chest. "You didn't do anything wrong, I'm just . . . I let myself get carried away."

I force myself to stand. This is an incredibly awkward conversation to be having with a raging boner. I'm trying to be contrite, but it's basically like pointing a loaded gun at her face while saying I'm sorry. It just doesn't work.

Not to mention, the way she's got her legs crossed and pulled into her body gives me an excellent view. Not one I am supposed to be appreciating right now, that's for sure.

"I feel horrible." I start talking and busy myself putting my pants back on so I don't have to meet her eyes. "For putting you in this position, and—"

"And I liked it." She looks up, a hint of a smile on her face. There's something in her eyes—a sadness that doesn't slip by me. "Please, Boxer, this is not your fault. I didn't mean to be a tease, or to let things get this far. I really did—*do*—want you. It's just complicated."

"I came over here to apologize for calling you beautiful earlier," I say, running a hand through my hair. "Well, not about the beautiful part, but to apologize for stepping past the line of business professional. And now look what I've done."

I can't help but notice that Jocelyn's eyes follow the ripple of muscle, the curves of my chest before they land on my hair. If I'm not mistaken, a shadow of lust returns, before finally, she shakes her head.

"Whatever this is . . ." she gestures between us. "It's a two-way street. One of us is not more at fault than the other."

"Well, I still think it's my fault, but whatever makes you feel better."

She laughs, a light sound that breaks some of the tension in the room.

"Look, I honestly didn't mean what I said a few minutes ago," I add. "About what happens after."

"I know, it was a stupid time for me to bring it up. Neither of us were thinking straight."

"Maybe I can get a second chance?"

"At what?"

"What I should have said is this . . ." I exhale, and begin again. "I like you, and I care about you, and I'm so damn attracted to you that I can't think. Which is why I say things that make me sound like a dumb teenager when I should be sounding like a grown-ass man."

Another smile lights her face, and I'm tempted to hope that maybe, just maybe, I can still recover from this.

"I probably shouldn't have started a serious conversation while you had your hand down my pants," she says, still grinning at me. "I didn't mean for it to be serious, I was just . . . I'm scared."

"Joss." I let myself fall onto the bed, the longing to wrap her in my arms too strong for words. So I let my body take over and pull her to me, guiding her head to rest on my shoulder. "You have no reason to be scared. What did I do or say to make you feel that way?"

"It's not you."

"Is there . . ." I freeze, a nightmare I hadn't imagined taking over. "Someone else?"

"No, no," she says quickly. "Of course not. Never . . . well, not for a very long time."

"Thank God."

We sit in silence, the only sound in the quiet room are the tiny puffs of air fluttering against my chest. My fingers trail lazy lines through her hair. I let my eyes close, basking in the all-encompassing sweetness of her scent.

"His name was Donovan," she says finally, and I feel my shoulders tense. "He was one of my clients, once upon a time."

I sense she's just gaining momentum, so I keep my mouth shut and continue stroking her hair.

"He was an up and coming player, and I was an up and coming agent," she says, her voice brittle. "It was a match made in heaven, or so we thought. And then I fell in love."

My heart aches for her, as if I know what's coming next. I don't. I've heard rumors, but I don't believe in rumors. I believe in learning the truth.

"I fell in love with him, and we kept our relationship secret for a long time. After six months or so, when we were starting to talk about moving in together, the media got wind of it. A flurry of articles, photos, paparazzi, everything brought it to the spotlight which, at the time, hadn't seemed like a big deal."

I vaguely remember the flurry of photos, but I hadn't followed the story. I don't make a habit of diving into others' personal lives, especially not their romantic business.

"A month after we went public, he out of the blue dropped me as his agent. He signed with Rumpert and stopped taking my calls. Then he met someone else, and ran away with her two months later. It was a disaster professionally, personally, and publicly."

"I'm sorry, Jocelyn," I tell her. It feels too generic to say, but I can't think of anything else to fill the silence. "It's not your fault. He's an idiot. A jerk."

"I was the idiot," she says. "I never should have mixed business with pleasure, but I did. And that's what happens. That's why I told myself I'd never do it again."

"And then . . ."

"Tonight," she says. "I've never broken my rule except for tonight."

"It's not your fault," I say again. "If I hadn't shown up here—"

"Stop," she says. "If I didn't like you so damn much, I wouldn't be frightened."

"I like you, too," I tell her. "A lot. I haven't dated since Charli was born much at all—a handful of times—but never anything with a spark. The dates were never worth the effort, the time away from Charli, the . . . everything. But with you, I don't have those thoughts. I enjoy every minute we're together. None of it feels like wasted time, like wasted effort—you're worth it. All of it. It's easy, and that has to mean something."

"Maybe, but I don't know what we can do about it."

"Well—"

"Besides sex," she says, with a roll of her eyes. "What comes after? You have Charli, and I have my job."

"Forget your job. I have enough money to support both of us if it comes to that."

"It's not like that," she says, a bit of sharpness in her voice. "I've worked my ass off to get where I am, and I won't throw it all away for a guy."

I blink, stunned into silence.

"I mean, I'm sorry, Boxer. I didn't mean it like that. I just—I can't yet. What if I'd given up my career to be with Donovan and he'd left me high and dry? I love my career, and I love what I do. I want to work."

"I shouldn't have said that in the first place," I say. "You're fantastic at what you do. But I'm not going to leave you like Donovan did."

"But what if we don't work out? What if you decide things aren't going well? What if *I* decide that? I don't have family to fall back on; I hardly have friends, Boxer. I have to take care of myself."

"Fine," I say, more quietly. "I understand that."

"Please don't be mad. It's nothing personal, but we just can't do this. Not right now."

"Okay." I stand, letting my hands slide off of her soft curves. "I won't pressure you into anything. That was never my intention."

"Boxer—"

At that moment, my phone rings, sparing us both further conversation. I turn my back to her and answer the familiar number. It's my brother.

"Hey, Charli's asking for you. I think she's sick," Steven says into the phone. "Where are you?"

"I'll be right there." I hang up and turn to find Jocelyn's eyes filled with tears. It kills me to leave her like this, but at the same time, she has made it clear she doesn't want me to stay. "I have to go."

"Charli?"

I nod.

"Is everything okay? Can I do something?"

I shake my head. "She's fine. It's nothing. I'll see you."

"Boxer—"

I stop in the doorway, then turn to face her. I spy my shirt on the floor and realize I probably need that before I hit the streets. I wait for her to speak as I retrieve the shirt and slip it over my head. She doesn't.

"Joss, you know how I feel about you," I say into the silence. Her eyes flash crystalline blue at me. "You know how badly I want you. If you change your mind, or your policies, come find me. Please."

"And in the meantime?"

I give her a tight smile. "I'll see you around."

I let myself out of the apartment, closing the door behind me before jogging to the car. I'm aching inside to turn around, to go back to her, but Charli needs me now. I only wish Jocelyn would follow.

I navigate home, turn into the driveway, and climb upstairs only to find my pink-cheeked girl smiling and faking sick. I let out a sigh of relief. I tuck her into bed and read her a story, which was her whole plan from the start. She could be an evil genius, I'm convinced.

However, once she's sleeping soundly, the threat of illness dispelled, I swing downstairs to find the bag of supplies on the counter. Charli's birthday party is this Saturday.

My heart soars. I just might be more excited about this party than Charli, which is ridiculous. But Jocelyn Jones strikes me as a woman of her word. And if that's the case, I'll be seeing her sooner than I imagined.

After all, she volunteered for cake duty.

CHAPTER 22

Jocelyn

"LOOK, IF IT'S not that big of a deal, then accept the date for lunch." Lindsay wipes sweat off of her brow. "Seriously, boss. He's a great guy. I swear on it."

It's barely six a.m. on Saturday, and Lindsay and I are just hopping off bikes at Spin Class. I don't particularly love sitting in one place and letting my legs pedal a hundred miles an hour to go nowhere, but Lindsay told me I've been uptight all week and needed to destress. Everyone knows how ineffective yoga is for my breathing routine, so we settled on bicycles instead.

"I'm not ready to date," I tell her. "This just happened."

"What, a kiss with Boxer?"

"More than a kiss. It was a full-on make out session, and almost more."

"You made out with a guy you found attractive. So what? You're almost thirty! You're allowed to do that whenever you like. Seriously, it's no big deal."

"It is when he's supposed to be my ringer client for the year."

"So what? You don't need him on your roster."

"I do."

"Why?"

"Because." I shrug, knowing I've backed myself into a corner. "I don't want to talk about it."

"Well, I don't believe you. Prove it to me."

"How?"

"Accept this lunch date."

"No."

"You promised you'd go on one date per month—and if you're not counting your lunch with Boxer as a date, then you owe me, girlfriend."

"I don't owe you, I just—"

"You promised. Don't break your promise."

"Speaking of promises, I have to pick up Charli's cake. I ordered it from Nadia's."

"Pulling out all the stops for this six-year-old, eh?"

"Nadia's is the best. I only buy from the best. It will change their lives."

"Sure. It'll also give you an excuse to see Boxer again."

"That's not why I'm doing it."

"Keep lying to yourself, boss."

"I made a promise, and I keep my promises."

"That's just what I wanted to hear." Lindsay gives me a smug smile as she wipes down her bike. "Keep your promise to me, then. Prove you're not interested in Boxer by going on a date with another guy. You don't have to kiss this dude, or bring him home. Just meet him."

"Fine," I say, a challenge in my voice. "But after I'm done setting up for the party. Make it a late lunch, we'll say two p.m."

"I will let him know," Lindsay says. "Two p.m. it is. I'll let him pick the place."

Despite winning this battle, she doesn't sound at all elated. It's almost as if she wanted me to turn her down flat. I've lost this sparring war, and I don't feel good about it, either.

I don't know why it's so difficult for me to admit what I want out of all this, but I can't seem to voice my thoughts. Maybe it's because they're not clear. Maybe it's because I don't truly know what I want. Maybe it's because I know exactly what I want, and it's that which I'm most afraid to admit.

We head toward the showers, rinsing off in near silence. My head is crowded with thoughts for the upcoming day: the cake, the party, the date. Only one part of it seems exciting, and that's the notion that I'll be seeing Boxer before the day is over.

My skin tingles with anticipation, my heart skipping beats until I have to shut off the shower and sit on the bench, breathing slowly to calm my nerves. Seeing Boxer. That's what has me twisted in knots.

"What do I say to him?" I ask Lindsay. The question comes out of the blue, but she must be thinking about it, too, because she fires back an instant response.

"What do you want to tell him?"

"I don't know."

"Come on, boss. For once, can you just be honest with me about how you feel?" Lindsay cranks her shower off. "I mean, seriously. It's obvious you have feelings for the guy. Why lie to me about it?"

"I'm not *trying* to. I'm still figuring things out."

"It's simple. If you *don't* want to be with him, fine—I get it. Then tell me that and be honest about it. We're not teenage girls; we are adult women. Just tell me how you feel. This guessing game is getting exhausting. What do you expect to come from all of this?"

Her tone is wildly out of character. Normally, she has miles of endless patience for me, but I must have used it all up. It makes me sit up a bit and pay attention.

Wrapping myself in a towel, I wait for Lindsay to do the same as we make our way toward the changing area. Where she's a free spirit in all her nakedness, I'm a bit more reserved, and I turn away as I slip into my undergarments.

"I like him," I say finally. "Because he makes me feel things I haven't felt in years."

"There's a start." Lindsay turns to face me, her towel resting on the bench. She fiddles around for her clothes, and not for the first time, I wish for half of her confidence. "Now keep going. Why do you like him? What things does he make you feel?"

"I don't know."

"Think about it."

"Safe," I say automatically. "Like he'd never say a word to hurt my feelings."

"That's good. A healthy thing for a relationship."

"I know, and I'm not used to it."

She makes a clucking sound under her breath, sliding a shirt over her head. "I know, and that's sad. But you have a type, and frankly, it's not a nice type."

"But it fits me. I'm not particularly nice."

"Sure you are!"

"No, I'm not. Look what I did to Andi and Ryan. Look how I run my business."

"That's business. You're smart and strong, and that's different than being mean."

"Andi and Ryan?"

"A mistake, and if you'll let me set you up with a stupid phone call, you can apologize. A mistake doesn't define you, just learn from it and move along. Ryan and Andi made it through, and I don't think they're sitting there thinking about it right this very second. Get back to the question. What does Boxer make you feel besides safe?"

"Happy." It's another automatic response, but as soon as it's out there on the table, I realize it's true. "He makes me laugh, makes me slow down and appreciate things like ice cream cones and cakes and sandwiches."

"That's all food, but it's a good start. And when you kissed? Was it good?"

I can't help the sigh. It comes out in a whoosh, so I just let it happen, my head falling back as I lean into the lockers. "So good. It's like he enjoys everything. Every little touch, every kiss. The whole thing was special. Like it wasn't some routine or checklist, or . . . I don't know."

"Boss, that's—" Lindsay shakes her head, wiggling into her jeans. "That's how it should be. If men are doing sex like a checklist, you run away just as fast as you can. Got it? That's not right."

"I just hadn't realized what I was missing."

"Now that you know you're missing it . . ."

"I want more of it," I whisper softly.

Lindsay nods, a look of sympathy scrawled on her face. "Yes, and it's impossible not to blame you for it. Sounds like you've finally got a man who likes you for the right reasons, and you're pushing him away just as hard as you can."

"Shit."

"Yep."

"What can I do? How can I fix it?"

"Well, are you willing to let business take a backseat in this relationship? Because it's probably a must."

I hesitate, knowing the answer on the inside, but finding it more difficult to admit than I should.

"Well, I can see the answer in your eyes, so I'll give you a pass on that. You're going to see him today, right?"

I nod.

"Make it clear how you feel."

"Clear how I feel," I echo. "I think I understand."

"Do you?"

"Yes."

"Great." Lindsay smiles. "Then don't be shy. Tell him how you feel. I'm guessing he's dying to hear it."

"I don't know how to do that."

"When the time is right, you'll just know."

We walk down the hallway, each lost in our own thoughts. Someone Lindsay knows waves to her, and she tells me goodbye before heading in the opposite direction to chat with her girlfriend.

"Remember what we talked about," she says. "Be honest."

I wave goodbye, and it's not until I'm halfway to Nadia's Cakes that I realize I've forgotten to cancel the date with Lindsay's friend. I make a note to text her later once I arrive.

But when I step into the cake shop, I find a series of errors waiting for me.

First, the cake features a horse instead of a unicorn.

Second, they've spelled her name wrong. I know, I asked Boxer to double check.

"Sorry, but where is the rainbow tail?" I ask the guy behind the counter. "And the sparkles? We need sprinkles that shine—glitter or whatever. And Charli is spelled with an *i*, no *e*. I hate to be rude, but I wrote it quite clearly on the form."

The poor kid behind the counter is barely sixteen years old, but I can't bring Charli a cake with a horse and her name spelled wrong. So, when he offers to redo it correctly, I agree and tell him I'll wait.

Thirty minutes later, the cake comes back as bright as a pile of unicorn vomit. I smile, tell him it looks very nice, and pay.

An hour later, I'm showered, changed, and on my way with the cake in hand—fresh out of the freezer—to see Boxer.

Charli. *Charli,* I correct myself. I'm going to see Charli.

CHAPTER 23

Boxer

"YOU CAME." MY voice sounds higher pitched than normal, so I clear my throat to try again. "You showed up."

Jocelyn, looking as beautiful as ever, tilts her head up, surprise glinting from her eyes. She's holding a cake, and underneath, I catch the edges of a sheaf of paper. "Of course I did! It's not a party without the cake."

As if to prove her point, she extends a box toward me. I leap to attention, retrieving the box and pulling it close. The familiar scent of sugary sweetness fills the air, and I'm tempted to believe it's coming from Jocelyn, rather than the cake in my hands. I wait to see if she'll hand over the papers, too, but instead she's tucking them out of the way in her purse.

I'd rather be holding Jocelyn, pulling her against my chest, but since that's not an option, I glance down and make some comments on the rainbow of a cake that's sure to make the girls hyper with energy.

"Come inside," I offer, standing back. "If you still have time."

"Of course I do."

She moves a little stiffer than normal, as if she's not quite comfortable here. Which is only natural, seeing how the last time we were together, I barged into her home and carried her off to the bedroom like a beast. I close my eyes for a moment, cringing internally with the memory.

It's been playing over and over again in my head, and it's damn close to the only thing I've been thinking about since it happened. If anything, the memories get clearer: my embarrassment, the inappropriateness of the action, the amazing way she felt underneath my hands. As much as I wish I hadn't made her uncomfortable—pushed her too far beyond her comfort zone—I'm not sorry she knows how I feel.

I care about her, truly, and if she doesn't want to get involved romantically, maybe we can make something work from a business standpoint. The way she's acting today, it's like she's walking on eggshells. It's probably best to let her take the lead on which direction she wants this to go.

"Where's Charli?" she asks, glancing around. "Is she here? I can get her braided up while you put the cake in the freezer and bring out all of the decorations."

"Charli," I echo, annoyed at myself for nearly forgetting the main reason Jocelyn's here in the first place. To make my daughter's birthday party a special one. "She's upstairs, let me call her."

It takes a few tries, but eventually, she hurtles downstairs, curly hair bouncing wildly out of control.

"Joss!" she squeals. "You're here!"

"Joss?" Jocelyn repeats, descending to her knees in order to catch Charli in a leaping hug. "I like the nickname. That's what my dad called me when I was little."

She giggles. "That's funny. It's what my dad calls you, too."

My cheeks are probably red, so I turn away and mutter something about melting unicorns, leaving the two ladies to snicker with each other. I hadn't realized the nickname I'd inadvertently given her—another notch in the personal column, a black mark in the business column. I'd never heard anyone call her Joss before, not even her assistant.

"Are you here on business?" Charli asks her. "Just like last time when we went to Monica's and then the park? That was fun."

I am being a major creeper, but I can't resist. I move so that I'm standing just behind the doorway, listening with unrivaled intensity for Jocelyn's response. When she speaks, it's quiet, and I have to lean forward to make out her words.

"Yes," she says. "Just business, I promise. I'm going to get you all set up for your party, and then I'll head out."

"You don't want to stay?"

"I have a lunch . . . meeting."

"Oh. With a friend?"

"Yes."

Jocelyn's voice is thin, and I sense she's uncomfortable. I should stop Charli before she turns all Spanish Inquisition on Jocelyn, so I round the corner and force a smile on my face. Either I'm making up things, or Jocelyn's expression is strained.

"Hey, what's all the jabbering about? Why don't you go put on your dress, Charli?" I say. "We've got some work to do down here."

"Okay!" Charli twirls around and sprints up the stairs.

"We bought a princess dress," I tell Jocelyn. "It's pink."

"I'm sure it'll look great on her." She stands, stepping toward me with a hesitant look in her eyes. "Boxer, I was meaning to talk to you about—"

"We don't have to talk about it." I raise a hand, giving her the pass she most likely wants. I hadn't realized it when I'd been eavesdropping on their conversation, but now everything is clear. Jocelyn's lunch meeting isn't a meeting—it's a date. That must be the reason she's uncomfortable. She didn't know how to tell me.

"Let's leave it in the past. Forget it happened."

"Forget it happened?" She sounds surprised.

"Absolutely." I nod, though it kills me to dismiss the moment like this. I'm still convinced there's something special, but it has to be a two-way street. If Jocelyn isn't interested, I have to let her go. "Business partners?"

"Business," she says, giving a somewhat bewildered nod. "Sure."

"Great." My voice rings hollow. "Thank you again for coming today. Instruct me around, direct me, whatever you need me to do."

"Why don't you . . ." She trails off, as if distracted. It takes a long second for her eyes to focus on the bags of streamers, party favors, and poppers I've unearthed from the closet. "Right. Streamers. Can you hang this from the ceiling? Drape them something like this."

She takes a roll of pink crepe paper and weaves her way through the kitchen until she finds the dining room. I follow, watching as she leans up to hook the roll of paper over the light fixture.

I may be a man, but I know how to hang a damn streamer. I don't tell her this, however, because the view I have is too good to pass up. It's not every day I get to admire the curve of her body as she leans on her tiptoes, her long legs peeking out from underneath a uniform of black.

Today her legs are bare instead of covered by the usual nylons she wears. This discovery has me so distracted I completely miss her question the first time around.

Her face turns pink as I flinch and ask her to repeat the question. She tugs her dress down. Clearly, she's caught me staring. "I said, does that make sense?"

"Yeah, um. Yeah."

Had I not just decided that we'd be business partners? Now

less than a minute later, I'm staring at her thighs, imagining a hand sliding underneath to feel her soft skin, the brush of my fingers against her satin undergarments, and . . . *Shit.* I'm doing it again.

"Sorry, what?" I ask.

"I said, can you hang these so I can take care of Charli's hair?"

"Sure."

She tosses me the roll, and I miss it completely. It thunks against my chest and drops through my arms to the floor where I'm stuck staring at it like a moron.

I fumble for an excuse, but there's not much to say. I'm supposed to be an athlete. Athletes are supposed to be graceful. Then, there's me—even though it's not *my* fault the second she tossed it, she bent over to retrieve another roll.

Thankfully, this gets a laugh from her, and instead of throwing the next roll, she walks over and hands me the bag. We both pretend her fingers don't brush against mine. I pretend I'm not wishing this moment turned into a kiss.

Before I embarrass us with another attempt to turn things awkward, I spin away from her and start throwing streamers in every direction. A vase clatters to the floor and shatters.

She clears her throat.

"What?" I growl. "Am I doing it wrong?"

"Oh, um . . ." She looks up, and I follow her gaze.

There are streamers in every direction. X's, O's, circles, tangles. It's a big knot of mess and broken glass.

"I can fix it," she says. "Why don't you, uh . . . go outside and rake leaves."

"Rake?"

"Or change your clothes?"

I look down, realizing I've got on lounge clothes—long shorts and a t-shirt. Not party material.

"Yeah, good idea."

"What do you think?" Charli whizzes down the staircase, twirling and twirling in her pretty pink dress. "I used the makeup Uncle Steve gave me."

"Oh—" I suck in a breath as she stops twirling for long enough to give us a glimpse of her face. "Oh, honey. What did you *do*?"

"You look beautiful!" Jocelyn saves the day with a smile that almost manages not to look fake. "You did that all yourself? My, you are a natural."

"I know." Charli curtseys, but the effect is ruined by the make-up. Pounds of it caked across her face. "It's pretty."

I don't even know what or how she managed it, but she's got enough junk on her eyelids that she can hardly open them. Her lips are three shades of purple and pink, and there's a blue line across her cheek. I have no clue what that's all about.

"How about we go upstairs to do your hair," Jocelyn suggests gently, "and I can add a little of my makeup, too?"

"You have makeup?"

"It's very fancy," Jocelyn says. "But we might have to wash up first before hair. It's easier to braid that way."

I'm pretty much frozen in place. Makeup hasn't entered the equation yet, and I hadn't expected it to until Charli was what . . . twenty-five? When do women start wearing makeup? I don't want my baby to wear makeup or talk to boys or any of it. But something needs to be done, *stat*, because she looks like a drugged-up clown.

"Thank you," I mouth to Jocelyn over Charli's head. "I'll do the streamers."

Jocelyn can barely hold back a laugh, but her smile is kind as she takes Charli by the hand and leads her upstairs. The water starts running moments later, and it's not long after that I hear them laughing and yammering away.

I climb upstairs after cleaning up the vase, pleasantly surprised to find that I can spy on the pair easily from the staircase. Jocelyn left the door wide open, and together, they're joking while Charli sits on the edge of the tub wrapped in a robe, and Jocelyn carefully peels back the makeup from her face with a washcloth.

I'm enamored watching it. I don't understand it, what's happening, but it's some sort of girl bonding—and it's something Charli's never had before. Not in any meaningful way. She's never met one of my dates for more than a few minutes at a time, and usually they're busy sucking up to her with gifts.

My heart is full.

I thought I could be Mr. Mom. I thought I could do it all.

As much as Marie has been there for Charli all these years, she still goes home at the end of the night. She has a family of her own, kids of her own, and it's too much to expect her to play mother, or grandmother, to my little girl, too.

As full as my heart may be, it cracks at the realization that after everything I've done, after all the times I've watched YouTube videos on braiding hair or played dress up with a crown and jewels on my head, I can never be both a mother and a father.

And that breaks my heart.

CHAPTER 24

Jocelyn

I'M ALMOST AFRAID to admit how much fun I'm having.

Braiding hair, little dabs of sparkly lip gloss, bright streamers and party favors everywhere—it's been a long time since I've had any excuse to play princess with a little girl. And Charli makes for an excellent partner in crime.

Once we've completed our beauty ritual, it's time for me to go downstairs and make sure Boxer hasn't set the rest of the house on fire or shredded the streamers out of frustration. I leave Charli to inspect her French braid in the mirror, pleased to see that her eyes are wide with excitement, her lips plastered in a huge grin.

"It's okay?" I ask Charli before I leave. "Are you happy with it?"

"I love it so much." Charli's hands skim over her tightly woven locks. "When my dad tries to braid my hair, he just twists it until it hurts."

"Well, your dad does a lot of things great," I tell her. "We can't expect him to be perfect."

Charli turns to me, her lower lip stuck out. "Yeah. You're right."

The moment blows over, and I'm relieved Charli didn't catch my blatant admiration of her dad, or the fact that I used the word *we.* I'm so relieved to have escaped discovery that I barely hear her calling to me.

"Do you like my dad?" she repeats. She doesn't turn away from the mirror, but her eyes reflect off of it and meet mine. "Are you going to take him out on a date?"

I lean against the doorframe, measuring my words. "No, honey, we're working on business together."

"So you're just my friend? You're not his friend, right? That's business. Just mine."

"Yes," I say. "We're friends."

"Okay." She grins at me. "I'm not going to share you."

This time when I leave, she's fastening a little tiara onto her head and waving in the mirror like Miss Universe. I make my way shakily downstairs, frustrated that I let a newly minted six-year-old rattle my nerves . . . and my resolve.

I'd come here meaning to tell Boxer how I felt. How I wanted him to be more than a business acquaintance, more than a friend. How I'd been wrong to push him away the other night.

But when Charli had cornered me earlier, I'd chickened out. The look on her face had me backtracking in seconds, and I wanted nothing more than to promise her wide blue eyes that I wouldn't take her father away.

So I'd said that I wasn't here for any reason except business, and Boxer had heard. Apparently, he agreed with me, which *should* be a relief. Even so, it doesn't feel like it.

I step onto the first floor, debating pulling him aside to clarify what I'd meant earlier, what he'd overheard in my conversation with Charli. However, he whisks out of the kitchen, a frenzied look on his face. Now is not the time. We've got an hour until the party starts, and the place is a disaster. If ever there's a time to focus on business, it's now.

"This isn't working." Boxer pokes his head out from the kitchen. "Do you know how this works?"

I follow him into the kitchen, discovering he's tried to use the feather boas I'd bought as party favors like streamers. "Why don't you hang the piñata," I suggest. "I'll do the rest."

"Thank you," he groans. "Stupid feathers everywhere."

"Hey, everything is going to be okay," I say, resting a hand on his shoulder. I shouldn't have done it, shouldn't have reached out and closed the gap, but it felt natural. Underneath his gruff exterior, he's tense, and if things were different, I would've pulled him in for a hug, a bit of a neck rub or a back massage. "Why are you so nervous?"

"I'm not nervous."

"Sorr-ry," I say, dragging the word out. "What's going on, then?"

He turns to me, apology in his eyes. "The girls are coming in an hour. I have yet to shower. The piñata's not hung. Do the parents stay? I forgot what Marie said. Am I supposed to do something for the parents? What about Charli—I haven't seen her in what—an hour? Is she still dressed like a clown?"

"Slow down," I tell him, "and relax. Everything is under control. You focus on hanging the piñata and taking a shower. I'll do the rest."

"How do you have time to do the rest before your date?"

"My what?" I've completely forgotten about Lindsay's plan to set me up with someone. "Oh, crap."

A light in his eyes dims, as if he'd been hoping for me to deny it wasn't a date. And, as much as I want to, at this point it'd just sound fake. I should never have mentioned it in the first place; it just popped out of my mouth. Things have a tendency to do that around Boxer and Charli, things I'd never intended to say in the first place.

"So, you have a date." He says it like a statement. "You should get going. Where's the paperwork? Let me sign it in case you need to leave before I'm out of the shower."

"Paperwork?"

"I thought you needed me to sign something for the endorsement deal."

"Don't worry about that. Today's not about business."

"Not about . . ." He shakes his head. "Then what the hell is it about?"

"What's got you so cranky?" I ask him. "I'm here because I like Charli, and I'm trying to help her have a nice birthday party. If you don't want me here, I'll leave."

I've never had an outburst like this around Boxer before, and it leaves both of us struggling for air like fish out of water. With clients, I'm always professional. No matter what. No matter how childish, rude, stupid, or inconsiderate they might act at times, I always control my emotions.

That was an emotional outburst, and I don't like that I've let myself slip. It came from inside, from a place my brain has no power to control. I can sense Boxer is upset at something beneath the surface, and he's taking it out on me. If it weren't for Charli, I'd leave, but she's who this is all about. Leaving now would only serve to hurt Charli.

"I'm sorry," Boxer says, turning away. "Thank you for your help."

I debate going after him, but the clock chirps on the hour, reminding me that time is ticking. Instead, I go into the kitchen and begin unwinding the feather boas from the lampshade. Feathers are flying everywhere. I'll have to sweep before the kids arrive, but I don't mind; it's calming.

Pulling out my phone, I send Lindsay a text: CANCEL DATE. Lindsay's text back is immediate: YAY!!!!!

It takes me a second to decipher what she means. Then, it hits me. This was all a test.

I peek out into the living room, but Boxer is nowhere to be seen. Either he's upstairs with Charli or in the shower, so I use the moment of silence to call my assistant.

"Was there even a real date?" I hiss into the phone. "Or were you just playing games?"

"I wasn't playing games," Lindsay says, the clatter of a restaurant behind her. "I was just inviting you out for lunch if you were sad after meeting with Boxer. With me."

"Let me get this straight. You set me up on a date with yourself?"

"Sort of," she says. "But it's okay, I'm just going to take my order to go."

"Why would you do that?"

"Because! You're acting a little blind, boss. You like the guy, right?"

"Not at the moment. He's annoying."

"Right, whatever. I figured that if you had a serious date to look forward to, it'd push you toward a decision. Do you *really* want to languish in the dating world longer?"

"As opposed to?"

"Telling Boxer how you feel! Or, better yet, showing him. Sounds like the attraction is mutual."

"Well, it's not."

"Trouble in paradise?"

"He's acting like he's annoyed I'm here!"

"Huh. Any idea why?"

I shift uncomfortably. "Maybe."

"Boss! What'd you do?"

"He might've overheard me telling his daughter that I was here on business only, and had a lunch meeting. He guessed it was a date."

"Aha."

"So, I ruined it. I came to take two steps forward, and took ten backwards instead."

"Don't be dumb. You're looking for an excuse to get out of telling him how you feel."

"I am not."

"Talk to him! It's a pretty damn easy fix, if you ask me."

"You think?"

"No, I *know*."

"Well, what should I—"

I'm interrupted by Boxer tearing into the kitchen like the house is collapsing around him. He pulls up in a dead stop upon seeing me on the phone, apologizing before backing slowly out of the room.

"Wait," I call to him, holding up a finger. "Sorry, gotta go, Linds."

"Duh."

I hang up, an amused smile still perched on my face. "What's wrong now?"

"Wrong? Nothing's wrong, I just wanted your help to see if the piñata was straight."

I follow him to where it's hung incredibly lopsided from the swing set outside. "It's perfect," I tell him. "I think we're almost ready. I'll just set up the table, and that won't take long. Have you seen Charli?"

"Me?" A small voice squeaks from the top of the staircase. The girl responsible for it bounds down seconds later. "I'm here."

"Well, it wouldn't be a birthday party without a present," I tell her. "Would it?"

"No, of course not!"

"Charli," her dad warns, but I wave him off.

"Here," I say, handing her a big envelope. "Go ahead and open it before everyone else gets here."

She reads her name on the outside of the card, a tiny finger drawing over the cursive lines. Unceremoniously, she digs into the paper and rips it to shreds, fits of giggles erupting as the card bursts into song as it's opened.

"What do you say?" her dad asks. "Cool card, huh?"

"There's something here." Charli glances at her feet as two stiff slips of paper flutter to the ground. "Notes?"

"Something like that," I say, holding my breath as she bends over to scoop them up. "I hope you'll like it."

When I'd bought the tickets to Six Flags, it'd been right after I'd botched our lunch date by bringing Barbie along. I'd been trying to win over Boxer's heart through his daughter, but now I couldn't care less what he thinks. I just want her to be happy.

"Dad! Dad! Dad!" She's a jumping bean, flying toward her father. "Two tickets to Six Flags! Can we go? Today? Now?"

"What?" He looks exasperated. "After all this work to plan a party, and you would've been just as happy if I'd taken you to an amusement park?"

"Nope," Charli corrects. "More happy."

Boxer face palms his forehead, and I can see the frustration building. "You *asked* for a party," he says. "I told you we could go somewhere just the two of us instead, but *no* . . . you *demanded* we throw you a party for all the girls in your class and—"

"And now you get to do both!" I clap my hands. "Is this better than a Barbie?"

"Oh, thank you, thank you." Charli clasps her arms around the back of my knees, and fireworks of happiness bloom through my chest. "This is the best present ever."

"I'm so glad," I say, finding it a little hard to speak over the lump in my throat. "No more Barbies."

What is wrong with me? It's not a particularly emotional gift—it's a pass to get wired on sugar and scream bloody murder on roller coasters. It has nothing to do with me, and yet, I'm quite pleased with her reaction.

Boxer, meanwhile, is staring at me. Blatantly staring. When he doesn't stop, it begins to make me uncomfortable.

"What?" I finally ask. Then it hits me. "Oh, *shit*. I should've asked you first. Right? I'm sorry. I totally didn't think about that—"

Charli tugs on her dad's pants. "Dad, she said shit."

"I'm sorry!" I clap a hand over my mouth before I can ruin the day further. "I should get going. Let me set up the table and get out of here before I make somebody cry."

"Ruin the day?" he says, his voice an echo, the rough edges of his face softening as he tilts his head and speaks quietly. "You haven't ruined anything. I haven't seen Charli this happy in a long time."

We're all frozen there, Charli staring at her tickets, Boxer looking into my eyes while I can't turn away. It's special, private, and there's nothing businesslike about it.

He sways toward me, as if he wants to reach out and touch me, maybe, but before anything happens, the doorbell rings.

Charli shrieks with excitement. "The party is here!"

Boxer looks down at his athletic gear. "It's half an hour before the start time! I haven't even showered."

I spin him around, a hand on either of his shoulders, and push him in the direction of the staircase. "Go. Relax. Take your time. I'll handle the next thirty minutes."

He moves like a robot toward the staircase. I watch him go, admiring the shape of him from behind. Then he jerks to a rigid stop. "You have a date. Really, Joss, you should get going. I'm such an idiot."

"It wasn't a date." I wave a hand at him. "It was a meeting, and I cancelled it."

There's one extended moment between us, tension blended with hope, a longing to close the distance between us and put to rest this tension once and for all. I have a mind to follow him upstairs, slide into the shower behind him, and let the water wash away our inhibitions . . .

Until the moment is shattered as Charli flings the front door open and a second little girl's voice joins the screeches.

"Go," I tell Boxer, hurrying to join Charli and greet the parents. "I'll be here."

CHAPTER 25

Jocelyn

THE TOTAL IS five.

Five little girls running around by the time Boxer returns to the party. To my surprise, all of the mothers have stayed. Maybe this is normal, or maybe they don't trust a strange lady opening the door to watch their kids. Probably the latter.

I turn from organizing cookies at the snack table at the sound of Boxer's low, rumbling laughter. It's infectious, and I'm already grinning when I look up to find him climbing down the staircase.

My hands freeze and my body stills, but my heart doesn't get the memo. It's racing, pounding out of control at the sight of him there. Fresh from the shower, his hair still damp and a little mussed, as if he'd only run a hand through it after toweling off.

Then, there's the rest of him. He's dressed to impress today, and it is a stunning sight. As I look closer, I realize it's not his clothes, per say, but the way he's wearing them. I've gone on dates with men whose suits cost more than my mortgage, but they were nothing compared to this.

Dark jeans hug his legs, moving with his tall figure. A button down shirt sits on top, accenting his broad chest, the sturdy arms through the tapered waist. All of it complimented by blue eyes that shine like the frosting of the cookie I've just dropped onto my plate.

I glance down, hurriedly moving the cookie back to the platter, and guiltily steal one last look at Boxer before backing away. I'm not the only woman who's noticed him, either, and that gives me a shot of jealousy that I'm not exactly proud to admit.

I fight it back, pretending it's a jolt of annoyance as the women migrate toward Boxer from all directions. It's like he's a magnet, sucking paperclips to his person by simply being in the room.

Ducking into the kitchen, I pour a glass of water from the fridge. Cold water. Then I add a few ice cubes and slurp it down until I have a brain freeze. *Get a grip, Joss.* I'm sure they're just making friendly parental small talk.

However, I find a most peculiar thing in the kitchen. Six cakes sitting out. Homemade cakes. Which doesn't even make sense because there are only five guests here. Did someone bring two cakes? Surely that can't be normal.

I pretend this is a reason that I need to talk to Boxer. To find out how he wants me to handle the extra cakes.

As I navigate through a group of giggling girls, I find nearly all of the parents surrounding Boxer. It's looking like I'll have to hack my way through to get his attention.

There's only one problem. I'm not used to caring so much. Usually, I'd just go after what I want. I'd walk right up to him and tell him exactly what's on my mind, but for some reason, my mind isn't working right today.

I sort of hover near the edges, waiting my turn, lingering and listening as the other women speak with him. After all, I'm the extra one today, just here to help. For Charli. The cakes can wait, and so can I.

As I take a step back toward the kitchen, however, his eyes raise to meet mine, holding there for a long second. The woman he's speaking to continues to talk, but it's as if Boxer isn't listening to a word she's saying.

The connection feels surprisingly intimate, and if I were in the mood to admit something crazy, I'd say it made me feel special. I'm not used to feeling special. Intimidating, maybe, or competent—after all, I'm great at my job. I'm comfortable in that zone. As Lindsay says, I'm married to it, and that's a relationship that works for me.

This—whatever this relationship is between Boxer and me—is not comfortable. Far from it. This isn't like anything I've ever known, and it brings a blush to my cheeks and a shiver of excitement.

Eventually, the woman speaking to Boxer realizes that he's not entirely listening, and she trails off, her gaze following his line of sight until it lands on me. She flashes a murderous glare toward me, and I'm jolted back to reality, sucked out of my warm and happy daydream.

Luckily, the doorbell rings then, and I make some excuse under my breath and hustle off to answer it. On my way there, my brain's working double time to figure out what just happened. The murderous glare, the swarm around Boxer, the number of home baked goods in the kitchen—and suddenly it makes sense.

Landon Boxer is in high demand.

I don't know why it didn't hit me before, but Landon Boxer is a unicorn. Even amongst a party of unicorns. A hot, successful single dad who openly adores his daughter, his career, and nothing much else except for ice cream. Frankly, I understand the appeal.

I push the thought out of my head, a little overwhelmed by the interest in Boxer. I hadn't realized he was such a hot commodity. Not that it changes how I feel about him, it just makes me feel a little more . . . insecure. These women all have children. I don't.

Boxer does. It's a big thing, and I'm at a disadvantage.

I don't like being at a disadvantage. That's how I run my business, and until now, my life. I don't go into business meetings without knowing the possible outcomes—all of them, good or bad. But Boxer is a wild card. I most certainly hadn't anticipated the turn of events, and quite frankly, it's cause for alarm.

"Hello?" The door knob twists from the outside and a male voice announces himself to the room. "Anyone home? Do we have a birthday girl in here?"

"Uncle Steve!" A speeding bullet in the form of Charli comes racing around the corner, hurtling herself into his open embrace. "You're back!"

"Of course I'm back. You gave me an invitation, so I came. How are you, dude?"

"Good, dude." Charli pulls back and grins at the man standing before her. "Uncle Steve, want to meet my friend Jocelyn?"

"Would I ever?" His eyes, bitter blue, look over at me. They're the same shade as Boxer's, just a bit more pale. "I most certainly would. Name's Steve. I'm Danny's older brother."

"He gets the nickname from you, then?" I shake his hand and grin. "Jocelyn. Pleasure to meet you."

It's a firm handshake, his fingers slim, narrower than Boxer's. It's difficult to see the pair as brothers. If Charli hadn't made introductions, I'd have thought this man had the wrong house.

Where Boxer is all tall muscle, his sheer form an intimidating presence in the room, Steve is a bit shorter, thinner, and ganglier. His hair is long, down to his shoulders, a goofy smile spread across his face.

I get the impression he has a sense of humor. There's a vibe about him that has me a little confused, though, and I can't quite figure out if he's a brilliant professor or an unemployed stoner. It could really go either way.

"Danny got the looks, I got the brains," Steve says, still holding my hand. Then he leans in and winks. "I'm kidding. Mostly. I got the looks."

I can't help but laugh as the new Boxer turns and playfully loops Charli into a hug, making her giggle as he whispers something into her ear. Then, he produces a present that earns him a squeal from his niece, and this turns his eyes into shades of blue that are almost exactly the same as Landon's. The effect is almost eerie.

"So, do we have any punch here?" Steve stands, sending Charli back to play with the kids. "Which one is yours?"

The two questions have me confused for a minute, only until I realize his eyes are scanning the playing children before us.

"Oh," I laugh. "None of them. Punch, however, is this way."

"None of them?"

"Nope." We enter the kitchen, and I scoop some punch into a cup for him. I make a move to bring the punchbowl to the other room. "I should set this out."

"Are you the new nanny?" He extends a hand to stop me from leaving, continuing the conversation. "Sorry, but I'm the nosy brother. You'll have to forgive me."

That goofy smile is back, and I relax slightly. Unlike with Boxer, there's no tension between us, no half-told stories. Steve's blunt, and that's perfect because I can handle blunt.

"Oh, no. I'm working with Boxer."

"On business?" Steve looks skeptical. "I still don't understand why you're helping at a kid's birthday party. Sounds like punishment to me, and I love my niece."

"I volunteered to help. Marie's out of town, so Landon could use a hand."

"Landon . . ." He tries out the name. "I called him Danny

when he was little, and it's one of those nicknames that just stuck. Landon was always too formal."

"Are you in town just for the party?"

"Mostly. I'm a researcher, came into town to speak at an event, and I'll stay through tomorrow. Danny doesn't know it, but I'm crashing in his guest room tonight." He leans in and faux-whispers to me. "Don't spill the beans. My plan is to drink too much of the punch, and then he can't let me drive anywhere."

I point at his glass. "The punch isn't spiked."

"We can pretend." He winks. "Also, I know where he stores the better beverages."

"Ah."

"So what's it like working with my brother?"

"Well, maybe I was a bit premature. I'm trying to get his business."

"Hold on, you're the agent."

"That's me."

"Miss Jones?"

"Jocelyn."

"Jocelyn. I've heard great things about you."

"Really?"

"Charli said you took them out for a business lunch, and she couldn't stop talking about you. Pretty good, considering you gave her a Barbie."

I cringe. "I didn't realize."

He waves a hand. "Presents are overrated. I used to just put newspaper around a box for Charli and stuff it with bubble wrap for Christmas. It worked until she was about four years old."

"Bubble wrap is underestimated for its entertainment value."

"Touché." Steve finishes up his punch. "So, is it just business between you and Danny?"

I'm caught off guard by the question, especially coming from Steve. I have no clue what Boxer has told him about me—if he complained about the other night when I basically made out with his face the second he opened the door.

"Yes, hopefully," I say with a smile. "We'll see if he enjoys working with me."

"I don't see how he couldn't." Steve grins and takes a step closer to me. "You seem very nice, and I'm familiar with your work."

"You are?"

"I had to Google you after Charli's speech the other day. You are quite impressive."

"I don't know about that—"

"Hello, Steve." Boxer's voice breaks the silence. "Found the punch, I see?"

"And the prettiest woman here." Steve winks at me from across the table. It's playful enough to make me laugh, but that seems to annoy Boxer even further. "Hope you're planning to sign with this one. Even Charli loves her, and you know she's the toughest critic of us all."

"You don't say." Boxer moves until he's behind me and, to my surprise, rests an arm on my shoulder. "We agree then. Joss is the best."

"Joss?" Steve raises his eyebrows at me. "Business?"

My cheeks are flaming now, and I can't tell if it's because of the brothers' banter, or if it's the close proximity to Boxer. The man smells heavenly. His whole body is warm, and if I curled into him, I could feel safe for eternity. Strong arms would clasp around my back, hold me to his chest. Before I realize what I'm doing, I sink toward him.

Boxer doesn't disappoint. His arm squeezes my shoulder, holding me closer and closer with each passing second. Steve's eyes watch, critical as a hawk, before turning his gaze back to Boxer for a brotherly stare down.

"Come upstairs with me for a minute, Steve," Boxer says finally. "Let's have a chat."

CHAPTER 26

Boxer

I'M FURIOUS, STOMPING up the staircase at my own daughter's birthday party, all thanks to my brother, Steve. Stupid Steve.

We barely have the door closed to my bedroom when I whirl on him. "What the hell was that?"

"What?" Steve doesn't look as dumbfounded as he should.

"Don't play stupid, Steve."

"Stupid Steve?"

"Don't show up at my daughter's party and then mack on all my guests!"

"Mack on all your guests?" Steve's holding back a laugh, and that pisses me off further. "I talked to one woman. I didn't *mack* on anyone; I held a pleasant conversation over the punch bowl."

"You mauled her. She could hardly breathe."

"Seriously, Danny. Calm down."

He's right, which makes me even more angry at myself. There's no reason for me to fly off the handle at my brother. He didn't do anything wrong except show up and make conversation with a guest.

I'm the only one who's being a jerk here today, and I should probably apologize to Steve and Jocelyn before I scare away the only two people who are here solely for Charli.

"I thought it was just business."

My fists clench and unclench. "Is that what she said?"

"It's what both of you told me. You told me just the other night, remember?"

Of course I'd told Steve about Jocelyn. It'd come up as an accident at first, probably because she'd been on my mind exclusively for the past few weeks. I didn't have all that much to talk about—everything else paled in comparison.

"Both of you lied," Steve adds.

"Lied about what?"

"Stop being an idiot."

"She only wants a business relationship, so that's what I'm giving her."

"Right. And would you have punched me in the face if I talked to Duke over the punch bowl?"

My jaw works slowly, clenching and unclenching as I measure my response.

"I've never seen you this interested in a woman. Ever."

The gravity of Steve's statement sinks in as he holds my gaze steady. Lauren flickers into my mind for a brief moment, a twinge of guilt along with it. What she and I had felt like love at the time, but in retrospect, was nothing more than a burst of chemistry in a world that requires a long-burning flame.

"Yeah, well, Joss doesn't want a relationship," I say again. "So, I'm giving her time."

"Coward."

"Shut the hell up, Steve. You don't know what you're talking about."

"Maybe not." My brother takes a step closer to me. "But if you don't ask her out, then I'm going to do it. You've got a week."

I'm itching to clock him a solid one to the nose. It wouldn't be the first time my brother and I have fallen to punches, but it *would* be the first time we've fought over a woman. We have different tastes. Lucky for him, curiosity holds me back. "Why would you do that?"

"Because you can't handle the competition." Steve leans in, pokes me in the chest. "And I'll let hell freeze over before I watch you walk away from the first woman you've cared about in years. So pull your head out of your ass, and go after her."

"You're an asshole," I say, for lack of a better retort.

"You're a bigger asshole, and I'm sleeping on your couch tonight."

CHAPTER 27

Boxer

"I DON'T KNOW how to thank you for everything today."

Jocelyn wipes a hand across her forehead. "Well, you threw one helluva unicorn party. Heckuva party," she corrects with a glance at Charli. "Sorry."

But Charli's too busy stomping on bubble wrap from Uncle Steve to notice. Steve thinks that's the most clever present of all. Then again, it's the only thing Charli's still playing with, so maybe he's onto something.

"You didn't have to stay all day. It means a lot."

Her cheeks blossom to a light pink. "I hadn't realized it would be ovary central. You're in high demand, Boxer."

"Ovary central?"

"Six homemade cakes from the first five guests?" She raises an eyebrow. "You're a hot commodity. My store-bought thing pales in comparison, sorry."

"Stop that." I hesitantly reach up, squeezing her shoulders in my palms. "I'm the one who needs to be apologizing for stealing your day. Without you, the party would've been rotten."

"Did Charli have fun?"

"What do you think?"

I steer Jocelyn so she, too, can see Charli dancing around on fat little bubbles, squealing when they pop beneath her toes. Jocelyn smiles and leans against me, which is the whole reason I've tucked her there in the first place. If I could extend this moment and not make things awkward, I'd do it. It feels right.

She sighs, a light, whispering sound that eases from her lips like a breeze from the ocean. Her head tilts, coming to rest against my shoulder, and I freeze.

Maybe she's feeling it too—the way we fit together in this moment. I hardly know the woman, yet she's given up half of her weekend to throw my daughter a birthday party.

Look, I'm not blind. I realize that a handful of the women lingered today because of me and not my daughter. I might not have graduated Valedictorian of my class, but I could tell you the one thing they all had in common, and it's that they were the single mothers. Most of which have been on the prowl for as long as I've known them.

I don't blame them one bit. I suppose I'm on the prowl too, but I have a target in my sights. Strangely, this house feels a little bit more complete with the three of us here—Charli, Joss, and myself.

"Dad!" Charli tires of exploding bits of plastic and pops her head up. "Guess what?"

Her bright blue eyes are a jolt of electricity as Jocelyn and I straighten. She pulls her head from my shoulder, stepping back and adjusting her clothes as I put a hand on my hip, clear my throat, and get my bearings. "What's that?"

"It's almost time for birthday movie night!" She twirls, then lands facing Jocelyn. "Are you going to stay?"

"Oh, I couldn't—" Jocelyn starts.

"But we watch one movie every year on my birthday." Charli has an argument ready. "Last year we watched Beauty and the

Beast."

"And the year before that," I add. "And the year before that. The agenda never changes."

"Well, of course not." Jocelyn turns to me in mock horror. "Beauty and the Beast is the best pick out there."

"It's your favorite, too?" Charli asks this like it's an interview question.

"Most definitely."

"Then you must stay," I tell her. "I insist."

"It's already late—"

"So a little later won't hurt."

She gives me a complicated expression, almost exasperated at my persistence. It's not like I can justify it. I just don't particularly want her to leave yet.

"Twist my arm," she says finally. "Do we get an extra slice of cake?"

I instruct the girls to get cozy on the couch. This movie is our birthday tradition, and it's the first thing Charli sets out in the morning.

I pop it into the DVD player and grab the fluffy blanket Marie keeps tucked in the closet. When I return, Charli has picked a seat on the couch next to Jocelyn. There's no space for me in my usual seat.

"Where am I supposed to sit?" I tease, tossing the blanket over the pair of girls. "You took my spot, Charli."

"Should I move?" Joss's neck jerks up. "Did I steal your spot? I can move."

"No." Charli rests a hand on her knee. "Stay."

Joss raises her eyebrows at me, her lips quirked into a smile. "Yes, ma'am."

Since the ladies don't seem to miss me, I beg off to put together a plate of food. Both women had a list of snack requests longer than my CVS receipt. And CVS receipts are the longest receipts I've ever seen. Like, three feet long.

I pause for a moment, watching the back of their heads in the doorway as popcorn pops in the background. I hit the lights as the movie comes on, but it doesn't pause Charli's jabbering for even a second.

It does, however, catch Jocelyn's attention, and she glances over my daughter's head to find me staring back at her. This time, she doesn't blush. She hardly looks uncomfortable. If anything, she belongs here.

"Cute," a voice says from behind, startling me. "They seem to get along well."

"What the hell, Steve? Stop creeping around."

"I'm your guest. Aren't I allowed to pop into the kitchen for a bite to eat?"

Because he's my brother, and he's the only option I have for company at the moment, I pull open the fridge and grab two beers.

Steve gives an approving nod, retrieving the bottle opener from the drawer nearest him and sending it sailing across the table. "You going to tell her tonight?"

"What?"

"How you feel?"

I sip my beer. I don't respond; I don't know what to say.

"Grow a pair," Steve says. "One week, *hermano*."

"I *have* a pair," I retort. "It's more complicated than that."

He takes a step back and raises his hands. I've always been bigger than Steve, and he's always been smarter than me. Normally, we didn't capitalize on the other's weakness, but sometimes it just happened. Apparently, when I'm angry, I'm intimidating.

"Relax," he tells me. "I'm trying to help."

"Shut up."

"You want to talk, obviously."

"Yeah, but I don't want your opinions."

"I'm shutting up." Steve takes another step back. "How is this situation so complicated?"

"I'm a package deal. Me and Charli, we come together. When a woman dates me, she dates my daughter, too. If things get serious, it changes for our family. I have more to consider than myself."

"Would you have already slept with her if it weren't for Charli?"

"This isn't about sleeping together."

"You care about her?"

"I can't stop thinking about her," I snarl. "If I could, would I be sitting here talking to you about it?"

Steve shrugs. "I'm just here for the beer. And the cake."

"Next time, bring a real present."

"She played with the bubble wrap longer than anything else, didn't she?"

"That's not the point." I take another swig and slam the bottle onto the island. I'm looking for reasons to be pissed now; I know that. It feels good. But it doesn't accomplish anything, and that ticks me off more. "What would you do?"

"Me? I'd ask her out," Steve says. "She'd turn me down, but I don't mind trying."

The note of ambivalence in Steve's voice is enough to calm me down. I know he'd like to find a woman to balance him out, a family, a soul mate, but he's had horrible luck with women. Where they tend to flock around me at times—thanks to my name and my career—they tend to overlook my brother. Which sucks because he's a great guy.

And now, I feel even worse for complaining to him. "Steve, you're going to find a great girl—"

"I'm not looking for sympathy," Steve says. "But you've gotta admit there's a logic to my reasoning. The worst she'll say is no, right?"

I make a show of gathering a variety of snacks onto the tray and dumping the popcorn into a bowl. Before we part ways, I grab a second beer and hand it to my brother.

"Thanks for coming," I say. "Feel like watching a movie?"

"Not really. But I'll be here if you decide to drive your friend home and need some time alone, away from the house."

I meet his gaze for a long second. "Thanks. For the record, I meant it, too. You'll find someone."

"You're getting sappy in your old age."

"You're just getting old."

"Night, asshole."

"Sweet dreams, buttercup," I call, a smirk on my face as we part ways and I head toward the living room. I begin an announcement to the crowd of ladies there. "Food's ready . . ."

I trail off at the sight of two heads tilted against one another, two sets of light snores reaching my ears. I take a step backward, slowly retreating from the room until I can set the tray back onto the kitchen counter. Then, I take tiny steps into the living room and situate myself in the big fat armchair.

It's there that I alternate between watching the end of Beauty and the Beast and the two women on the couch. There are similarities between the two ladies, the hinted smile on their lips, even in sleep. The blonde hair—one set of locks curled into spirals, the second straight as my hockey stick. Long, gorgeous lashes resting against perfectly rosy cheeks. If I didn't know better, I'd think they might be related.

When I start to feel awkward watching Jocelyn take shallow breaths, I turn my attention back to the television and watch the beast transform into a prince. I sympathize with the guy, today of all days. Sometimes it's easier to be the beast than a prince.

I let the credits roll for some time before I stand and rest my fingers on Jocelyn's shoulder. She squirms closer to me, nuzzling against the heat of my skin as I lean in to whisper against her ear. "Let me drive you home."

"Mmm," she murmurs against the couch pillow.

"You're welcome to sleep here," I say, my heart racing. "Let me get you a blanket."

"Blanket . . ." She snuggles closer into the couch, and Charli sighs and eases closer to her, too.

I pull the blankets up higher onto their chests, wrangling limbs into position to prevent stiffness in the morning. I try to lift Charli into my arms, but she's having none of it. She moans, groans, and swipes at me in her half sleepy state as I try to pull her off the couch until finally, I give up.

Instead, I plant a kiss on each of their foreheads, grab a second blanket for myself, and stretch out on the La-Z-Boy.

Tonight has turned into one huge sleepover, and I have Beauty and the Beast to thank.

CHAPTER 28

Jocelyn

THE MORNING ARRIVES like a fog, slow and steady, enveloping me whole. One minute I'm dreaming of Boxer's lips pressed to my forehead, and the next I find myself shaking off stiffness and finding a little girl drooling on my arm.

Confusion strikes first. It takes me a long moment to remember how I got here—and where *here* actually is. That's when I hear the low tones of someone humming, a distinctly male voice coming from the kitchen, and everything crashes into clarity.

I slept over at Landon Boxer's house. A potential client. An almost lover. A man that has my stomach twisted in knots every time he enters the room.

Worse, I hadn't even asked permission. I'd just zoned out and started drooling on the couch. *Had I drooled?* God, I hope not. I quickly check the couch, but it is free of wet spots, thank goodness.

I close my eyes, wanting to slap a hand over my face as panic sets in after confusion, but I don't want to risk waking Charli. A sleepover. At a *potential client's house!* What was I thinking?

My knee cracks as I attempt to straighten my leg, and the slight sound is enough to stop the humming radiating from the kitchen. I pause, debating whether I should pretend to sleep or face my fears, when a figure pops into the doorway, and all thought pauses entirely.

It's Landon Boxer. And he's wearing an apron.

It's not a tough, manly sort of *I'm Grilling* apron. No, it's got a line of purple ruffles around the bottom and puffy painted words across the front that say *World's Greatest Dad*. I have one guess as to who put them there.

I'm torn between laughing and melting into the couch at its adorableness, so I choose the safer option and giggle.

He looks down, grins, and then meets my gaze again, not the slightest bit embarrassed. "Last year's Father's Day gift," he says in explanation. "By the way, good morning."

"Good morning," I mouth back. "I'm a little trapped here."

"Sorry about that. She's an aggressive sleeper."

Landon approaches the couch, a hint of a smile on his face. He reaches down to scoop Charli up, but I press a hand to his wrist.

"Don't wake her," I say. "I can sit here; I don't mind. It's cozy."

He gives a soft laugh. "Watch this—it's a magic trick."

Swooping her into his arms, Charli's head falls onto his shoulder with an unceremonious droop. Her legs dangle, arms flopping all over, and save for a cute miniature snore, she doesn't show any signs of waking.

"She can sleep through anything," he says, repositioning her on the other end of the couch. "Come on, let me get you a cup of coffee."

Coffee sounds incredible, so I follow him into the kitchen, the scent of freshly ground beans enough to make me weak at the knees. Either that, or it's the incredible sight before me—a man confident enough to wear a frilly apron while cooking what looks like sprinkle-encrusted pancakes in a skillet.

Then again, he has every reason to be confident. He lifts the coffee pot and pours it into a gigantic sky-blue mug while I stand gazing at his arms tense with lean muscle, every vein defined. He's back in athletic shorts and an old t-shirt, the fabric so worn I can see hints of skin through it.

I don't know what's wrong with me, peeping at his body when I should be explaining myself. Maybe it's the lack of coffee putting me into a deep, lusty stupor because I can't hardly remember how to say *thank you* as he passes me the mug. I splutter something that I hope sounds like gratitude, and take a slurp of the piping hot liquid.

"How is it?" He looks genuinely concerned.

"It's delicious."

"Steve got me hooked on his fancy hipster coffee." He gestures to a machine that looks more like a beaker than a coffee pot. "I hate that I love it."

"I don't blame you for it." I smile, watching as he deposits the grinds into the trashcan. "I think it helps that you wear the apron when you make it."

His eyes flick once more to the fabric covering his waist, and he shrugs. "Charli made me wear it so often when she first gave it to me that I just got in the habit of putting it on when I make breakfast. It's really the only meal I cook. Marie cooks almost all of our meals during the week, but Charli and I like to do our own breakfasts."

"She does, huh?" I raise my eyebrows at the sleeping body curled on the couch. "Great teamwork."

"She's six going on sixteen, I swear," he says with a shake of his head. Then, almost to himself, he murmurs, "It goes too fast."

"It does," I agree. Then I realize I don't have children, so it sounds a little fake that I'm responding. "Time, in general, I mean."

"Do you have siblings?"

"Me? No," I say. "Not really."

"Not really?"

I force a smile. "Is Steve your only brother?"

"He's more than enough."

"He seems nice!"

"There's more to him than meets the eye." Boxer leans forward, holding the spatula before him like a weapon. There's a teasing glint to his eye. "Don't fall for his innocent act."

I raise my hands. "Never."

"Did you sleep well?"

"I did. I managed to snooze and shower all in one go." When Boxer looks confused, I laugh, holding a hand up to show the light outline of drool on my wrist. "Charli is an active sleeper."

"Here, I'm so sorry about that." Boxer runs a cloth under warm sink water, squeezes it out, and then approaches me slowly. "May I?"

I can only nod, moving to sit on one of the kitchen stools for balance.

One of his hands has encircled mine, the other gently sponging away the mark on my arm. It's everything I can do not to shiver under his touch. The way he moves is soft, gentle, and I force my mind to stop thinking of other ways he might touch me.

"Is that better?" Boxer pulls the washcloth from my arm.

I nod.

Instead of letting go, he squeezes my hand tighter, takes a step closer, and lets his fingers trail up my arm. His eyes come up to meet mine. "Sorry about that, Joss."

"I'm not sorry at all." I blink, shocking myself. "I mean, about . . . this."

"Me neither," he says, his hand sliding the rest of the way up my arm until it's at my shoulder, then my back.

His touch trickles across my neck sending fireworks

throughout my body. I'm nearly quivering under his touch—pathetic, really, but I can't help it. He has everything I never knew I wanted. A heart big enough for two. Goals. Desires. Generosity and kindness born naturally to him.

This life—*his* life—it's not mine, but suddenly, I want it all.

That's why I lean into him, brushing against his chest as he lowers to meet me. The air sizzles between us, crackling with long anticipated tension. We were cut off the other night at the peak of our desires, and I'm relieved to know it's not just me who's still frustrated.

"I'm glad you stayed," he murmurs against my cheek. "Thank you for being here."

It's me who should be thanking him, not the other way around. I let my fingers press into his shoulders and pull him to me. He moves both arms behind my back so he's holding me entirely.

Lifting me off the stool, he makes it seem like I weigh no more than the spatula he wielded seconds ago. In my place, he sits down and balances me on his lap, wrapping his arms around my waist until his fingers situate on my hips.

I can feel him beneath me, and it's enough to make my breathing turn ragged. The moment our kiss begins is peppered by sunlight. Bits of it streak through the room, dancing across his face as we linger just centimeters from one another. My lower body may be trembling with desire, but up here, between us, there's only caution.

Until he inhales a deep breath and the caution flies into the wind. His hands slide down until they're cupping my backside, holding me against him as his tongue slips between my lips. He tastes of fresh coffee and sugar, and it's invigorating.

My hands find his face, my palms pressing against his cheeks as I forfeit any sense of self control. I forget that he's wearing an apron. I forget his child is sleeping in the next room over, just out of sight behind the wall. I forget that his brother is upstairs. I'm lost in every one of his low groans of need, his roving fingers pleading for more as he holds me against his lap.

He's taut with desire, and I'm burning up inside. It's not enough anymore, this game we're playing. Two steps forward, one step back. Business or pleasure? Passionate lust or responsible adults?

"Why can't it be both?" I murmur in a moment fogged with desire. "Business and pleasure?"

"Whatever you want," he says back. "So long as I'm next to you."

These words, this hint that we could be something more than two adults wanting each other from afar, never quite giving in, is enough to push me past all logical reason.

"Do you still want me?" I manage, though it's a gasp.

"More than anything." It's low, husky. "God, I've wanted you for weeks."

"We're both adults, what if we . . ." I remember what the ladies at the bar said the other night, about being adults, the value of taking Boxer home, if even for a night. "What if we get this out of our system?"

"Out of our system?" His eyes darken, and I can see conflict written there. "What do you mean out of our system?"

I could argue with him, but we're in no position to at the moment, so instead, I show him. I grind my hips against his lap, the friction causing his eyes to close and a low curse to sigh from his lips.

"I want you, too," I whisper. "Maybe if we just let ourselves have a night together, we can move on and focus on business."

"What if I don't want to move on afterward? What if I want

you for more than one night?"

I rest a finger against his lips. It'll never work between us, I know that. I'm not the type of woman he deserves. He deserves someone motherly, someone peppy and perky who'll join PTA meetings and stay at home and raise a happy houseful of kids. I know I'm not that person, and he'll figure it out soon enough.

"Let's start with one night," I say. "No strings attached. We can go from there."

"Be open to it."

"What?"

His eyes are begging me as he leans in, pausing to kiss my cheek, behind my ear, across my collarbone. "Don't push me away after a night," he murmurs as he dusts his lips against the top of my chest. "I'll give you one night, if you give me the potential for more."

"When?"

He looks up at me, my confirmation everything he needs. Instead of an answer, he stands, bringing me with him, my legs locking around his waist. One of his hands reaches to the wall over my shoulder as my arms cling to his neck.

I'm pressed firmly against him, wishing for my clothes to vanish. It's irresponsible, irrational, and I'm well aware my desire is wreaking havoc on my ability to make thoughtful, adult decisions, but I can't help it.

"I don't want to wait until tonight," he says, "I want you now. Let me drive you home—Steve can babysit, the pancakes will wait. We can take our time."

"Not now," I say, but my body says differently. It arches to meet his, and he responds.

He moves so my back is pressed against the wall, his hard chest against mine. We connect until the spiral of kissing drives us into a frenzy, and it's only when movement sounds in the other room that we both freeze entirely.

"Drop me!" I hiss at him, poking his shoulder. "Boxer!"

He does as I command, and it's lucky I've taken yoga classes because I somehow manage to land on my feet. I think it's called Tree position. Or maybe Standing Human. I don't really pay attention in yoga, but whatever it's called, it works.

Boxer raises an arm, scratching behind his head in an awkward motion as he spins around, closes his eyes, and takes a few deep breaths.

"I'll check on her," I say, straightening my attire. "You might want to, uh . . . fix your apron."

He looks down to where the frills of the apron are all off kilter, protruding in ways they weren't ever intended to be worn, and the image strikes me as funny. I never thought I'd make out with a man in an apron.

I laugh, hating that I sound like a hyena, but loving it all the same. I haven't been this giddy in years. I take a second to gather myself, pull my hair together and my shirt all the way down, and then make my way out to the couch.

"Good morning, birthday girl," I tell a still sleepy Charli. "How does it feel to be six?"

"Are there pancakes?" she asks. "We have pancakes on my birthday."

"Sure are," I tell her. "We'll just give them a second to, uh, cool off."

Luckily, Charli had wild dreams, so we spend a good twenty minutes discussing them. Charli has a way of telling stories that goes on, and on, and finally, sometime between a dinosaur eating her cheese, and a mouse chasing her around the yard, we are called into the kitchen for breakfast.

With twenty minutes to have calmed down, Boxer once again looks at ease in his kitchen. He has a few pancakes still sizzling on the skillet, and a plate stacked halfway to the ceiling with the rest of them.

Charli moves about the kitchen with a dedicated role, pulling out the syrup first, hoisting it to the table with both hands. She then makes her way toward the silverware drawer and withdraws two forks, mumbling to herself as she makes her way back to the table.

At the last second, she glances up, catches sight of me, and shines a shy smile. Still yammering to herself under her breath, she hurries back to the drawer and retrieves a third utensil.

"Is there anything I can do to help?" I ask.

Boxer waits for his daughter to respond.

Charli looks to her father for guidance but when he raises his eyebrows, she puffs up her chest and answers. "No, you're our guest."

"What can I get you . . ." Boxer prompts.

"What can I get you to drink?" Charli interrupts excitedly. "Water? Wine? Beer?"

Boxer stares at her. "Where'd you learn that?"

"Uncle Steve always wants wine or beer," she says.

"Uncle Steve doesn't want wine or beer at ten o'clock on a Sunday morning," Boxer grumbles. "Coffee?"

"Thanks," I say. "And thank you," I tell Charli as she worms her way in front of me to set the table. "Everything looks delicious."

It tastes delicious, too. And smells delicious and feels delicious and everything about the morning is entirely delicious. Charli struggles to pour syrup for her dad, finally drowning his plate in a pool of maple sugar. Golden butter melts onto the top of the warm, brightly colored sprinkle-pancakes. Boxer even adds a candle and a scoop of ice cream to Charli's, and we sing one more round of happy birthday to her.

"But it's not your birthday anymore!" I tease once we're finished. "That's not fair; I want ice cream too."

Boxer gives me a scoop of ice cream and Charli insists we sing another round for me, even though it's not my birthday for another few weeks. I realize with a twinge of surprise that it's the first time someone's sung happy birthday to me in a long while. I told everyone at my office to ignore my birthday and, save for Lindsay, they pretty much do. Lindsay will slip me a card and a cake, but she doesn't make a big deal out of it.

What's more surprising is that I don't mind the attention when it's coming from the two sitting across from me. We're all being silly, squirting whipped cream straight from the can into each other's mouths and pouring rainbows of sprinkles over our ice cream, and it's fun.

We laugh as Charli tells us jokes that make zero sense whatsoever, and we listen as she rambles on and on about her exotic dreams. I've never had a dream about a dinosaur before, but the way Charli tells the story, I feel like I'm missing out.

The whole thing is easy. Fun and light and sparkling with sunlight through the wide kitchen windows. Boxer has propped a window above the sink open, and a fresh breeze washes over us. He keeps my coffee cup filled with piping hot liquid, the taste warm and welcome after our sweet choice of food.

I haven't felt this elated since my childhood. I can't put my finger on exactly what it is, but everything feels right. I haven't checked my phone once in the last twelve hours or so, which is beyond rare. For all I know, it might be dead. Nearly twenty-four hours have gone by in which I haven't sent a single email. That didn't even happen the day I had my appendix removed.

Boxer and Charli are in the middle of a conversation about

what sort of cereal to buy for the upcoming week, and it's pleasing to simply sit back, listen, and enjoy being here. It won't last, that's for sure, since as soon as this spell is broken, I'll be back to work. Tomorrow is Monday.

Monday. It rings like a curse word in the bright Sunday morning, so I push it out of sight and focus on the party at hand. Boxer, however, must sense my change in mood because he shifts Charli to his lap, snuggles her for a long moment, and then sets her on the floor.

"Go upstairs and get dressed," he says. "Wash your face because you smell like syrup, and brush your teeth."

"Why?" she moans. "I don't want to go."

"We're going grocery shopping today since Marie can't come back until Tuesday, now."

"To the store?"

"Where else do you buy groceries?" he asks. "Of course the store."

"Does that mean we can stop by Gabe's?"

"You just had ice cream."

"But it's Gabe's," she pouts. "He says to stop by more often."

"I can't argue with her logic," he says to me. "It is Gabe's."

"So we can go?" Charli asks.

"We'll see," he says. "We're not going anywhere if you still smell like syrup in fifteen minutes."

She's gone in a flash, and suddenly the easy chatter that's filled the kitchen falls to silence. It's not uncomfortable, not really. It's uncertain.

"Thanks for feeding me," I say finally. "Everything was delicious."

Boxer doesn't answer, instead retrieving the coffee pot for one last refill. I murmur a word of thanks, but I have the feeling he's not listening as he pulls the apron off and tosses it onto the counter. When he returns to his seat, he's got a contemplative look on his face.

"There's something between us," he says finally. "Wouldn't you agree?"

I shift in my seat, the memories of earlier, in this very kitchen, resurfacing. "Yes."

"I have a proposal for you," he says. "It came to me while I was cooking."

"What sort of proposal?"

"The sort of proposal that I hope you'll listen to."

"I'm listening."

He folds his hands and rests them on the table before him. Our fingers are inches apart, not quite touching, and I wait to see where this is going before I move one way or the other.

"You want to get *this* out of our systems." He gestures between us. "But I don't think that'll work. It's *not* a one-time thing."

"How do you know that?"

"Come on, Joss. I'm not a one night sort of guy, and you're not a one night sort of girl."

"How do you know what sort of girl I am?" He's right, mostly, but I've always hated when people tell me what I am or what I'm not. So, naturally, my shackles come up.

"I don't, but I'm guessing," he says gently. "You can tell me if I'm wrong."

He's not wrong, so I sit back and cross my arms over my chest.

"New York is in two months—the endorsement deal. I talked to Steve last night, and he's happy to stay here with Charli for that weekend. What do you say we spend the next two months getting to know each other . . . with one catch."

"I see where this is going."

"No sex," he says. "Before we complicate things, let's see if this—us—works. Let me take you out on a few dates. Spend some more time with me and Charli." He gestures his hand in circles, signaling the passing of time. "Then, if we still want one another after two months, we'll have New York. Alone for the entire weekend."

Listening to him talk has my nerves in a spiral. First, my heart sank, then rose, and now I have chills thinking about a weekend alone with Boxer.

"I need more from you than one night," Boxer says. "I'm not asking you to marry me. I'm not even asking you to be my girlfriend. But I don't want to get you out of my system, Joss, and I refuse to ever pretend I do. If we're going to act on this, we're going to give it a fair shot."

I swallow, stalling, trying to come up with something to say. "But what if you're wrong?"

"Wrong about what?"

"Us? What if we'd be better off just putting to bed the tension and forgetting it ever existed? Then we can go on and be business partners like planned."

He closes his eyes and rubs his hands across his eyebrows. "Is that what you want? Really?"

I blink, looking up to the ceiling. "It would be easier."

"Maybe," he agrees, eyes still closed. "If you want to take the easy route."

"I never take the easy route."

"Then why the hell are you taking it now?"

"I'm not, I'm just suggesting—"

"That I'm not worth investing your heart into. Right? Because surely, I'll break it?"

"No, Boxer, that's not what I'm trying to say—"

"That's what it sounds like."

"Wait!" The word emerges like the sharp crack of the whip. In that moment, a flood of information crashes through my brain, drowning me in a pool of confusion. My talks with Lindsay, my past relationships, Mr. Hot Shot who didn't bother to know my last name. "No, that's not what I'm trying to say."

Boxer opens his eyes, then his hands, and gives me time, space to talk. The only problem is that I don't know what to say.

"I'm listening," he says.

"I don't think I'm right for you. Long term. But I do care about Charli, and I'm trying to avoid hurting her feelings. That's why it might be better to just wrap up this weird kissing thing we keep doing."

"Don't you think I know my daughter better than you do?"

"Well, yes, but—"

"Then let me protect her. I'll decide what's good and bad for her—what I want her exposed to and what I want to shelter her from."

"Fine."

"Why would you say something like that in the first place, though?" His brow furrows in genuine confusion. "Shouldn't I be the one to decide whether or not you're right for me?"

"Yes, but I'm just trying to be realistic."

He stands abruptly, his chair shooting back as he leaves the table. Feet pound on the stairs as he climbs them, the low murmur of conversation filtering back. It sounds like he's first talking to Charli, her high-pitched squeals signaling good news. Then, the responses turn lower, more annoyed. Steve.

Boxer returns downstairs, changed into jeans and a long-sleeved shirt that looks soft enough to sleep in, and extends his hand. "Do you have a few minutes? I'd like to go for a walk."

"Oh, um . . ." I scrunch up my sleep hair and push my coffee away. "Maybe I could use the restroom quick?"

"Why? You look great."

"Well, I still need to use the restroom."

"Oh." He actually blushes, and it's adorable. "Of course, sorry. I'll be waiting outside."

I ease into the bathroom to take care of business and wash up. Before I leave, I pause in front of the mirror. I dig in my purse for remnants of barely-functional mascara, and do the best I can to touch up the mess that is my now makeup-free face.

Even then, I'm still not ready to face him. I take a few deep breaths, wondering where Boxer came up with this idea of dating for two months. I still don't know what to think about it.

I'm not used to the idea of men turning down an offer of a no strings attached relationship. Not that I've ever offered it to someone before, but I just figured the answer would be an easy one.

Then again, Boxer's surprised me from day one, and I have a feeling that's not about to stop anytime soon.

CHAPTER 29

Boxer

"HOW DOES THE beach sound?" I ask, and she nods in agreement.

I pull her hand into mine. It's small, warm and gentle as she squeezes back.

There's a short path between my house and the sandy shoreline, and the area is mostly private property. On a Sunday morning, it'll be deserted.

I don't know why I feel compelled to bring her here. Outside, away from others, out of the stifling kitchen in my own home. When I am in a room with Jocelyn Jones, the air becomes more difficult to breathe, and maybe being outdoors will give us the space to talk as we need.

We're quiet as we make our way to the beach; the only sound along the way is our footprints grating sand against the path. It's one of those perfect mornings, the ones made for the happiest moments in life.

The sun is shining brightly, the breeze carrying a hint of coolness to combat the warmth of its rays. The world is not yet bustling with movement for the day, the busyness not yet taking over the pleasant stillness of morning.

The weight of Jocelyn's hand in mine, however, tells me this might not be the happiest moment. There's something there, something she's harboring inside that's causing her to keep me at arm's length. Maybe that's why I wanted to take her here, to see if she'd share the burden.

"It's beautiful." Her face tips up toward mine, cherubic and sweet without her normal makeup. "So peaceful."

"It is."

But I'm not talking about the landscape; I'm talking about the way we are together. Dewy lashes blink up at me, and she's brilliant in the stilted sunlight through the clouds. Her hair shines with a light all of its own, and her eyes, bluer than the water and so perfectly unique, watch me with a hint of curiosity.

"I had so much fun spending the day with you and Charli," she adds. "Thanks again."

"What did you mean at breakfast?" I turn to her, unable to resist a moment longer. We've reached a large boulder with a perfect ledge for sitting, and I nudge her toward it. "That we wouldn't work out long term?"

She climbs onto the rock easily, folding her legs under her bottom and situating herself just out of the spray from the waves crashing below. If she extended her foot, her toes would dangle into the water.

She considers her words carefully. "We're very different people."

"Different people can make for a great relationship. Keeps things interesting."

"Yes, true, but we're extremes. Our lifestyles, our priorities. Our goals."

"How do you know what's most important to me?"

"I suppose . . ." She clears her throat. "Maybe I assumed."

"Take a guess," I offer. "I'll tell you if you're right."

"Why don't you tell me?"

"Take a guess."

"Okay, then. Your first priority is Charli," she says, her eyes fixed on something above and beyond the ocean in the distance. "I think that one's obvious."

"Lucky guess," I say, which makes her laugh. I like making her laugh. It's not something she does often, so when the sound rings through the morning, my heart thumps a little bit louder. "What's next?"

She scoots back on the rock as a large wave sprinkles our legs with mist. I've climbed up next to her, and I like that her adjustments bring her closer to me. We're touching at the hip and nowhere else. It's incredibly intimate.

"Your career is second," she says. "Then ice cream."

"You're not all that far off. Pretty good."

"What am I missing?"

"Missing?"

"You said I'm not all that far off," she says. "That means I'm not exactly correct. What haven't you told me?"

"Nothing."

"If you expect me to be honest, you'd damn well better be honest, too."

I survey her through a side-eyed view. "You're correct about my current goals. I had one other goal, but it's expired."

"There's no such thing," she says. "No goal ever expires. It might change, or adapt, but it's not dead."

"Maybe not."

"What did you want, Landon?"

Her words are soothing. Nobody calls me Landon—I'm Boxer to everyone except my brother, and to him it's Danny. Somehow, though, when she says my given name, it's fitting. Selfishly, I like that it's unique to her, that it's only between us. Then her hand reaches for mine, finds it, and squeezes, which draws me another inch out of my shell.

"I wanted a family. I wanted so badly to make us a family," I say. "And I failed."

"Lauren?" she murmurs.

I nod. "I asked her to marry me three times. Before Charli, after Charli was born, and again on the day she left us."

"Did you love her?"

"I thought so, initially. Maybe I did, but it wasn't true, lasting love. When she left, she told me that she'd never loved me. Never had been in love with me. She didn't cry, she didn't call, she didn't send letters. She just erased us like a blip in her book, an error while balancing the checkbook."

"I'm so sorry," she says again. "I can't even imagine what that must've felt like."

"I don't feel much about it anymore."

It's true. My heart feels like stone now. I don't get emotional—not angry, not upset, not frustrated. If anything, there's just a deep sense of loss. Disappointment, maybe, and sadness for Charli. She's the one who loses most in this situation.

"It's not your fault," Jocelyn says. "You tried the best you could; you gave an incredible effort. Love, relationships, families—all of those are a two-way street. Group efforts."

"Maybe if I'd done something differently, or been more of the flashy hockey star she thought she'd fallen for—maybe she wouldn't have left."

"But that's not you." Jocelyn's tone is fierce, defensive. "Relationships are about compromise, sure, but not about changing who you are. Plus, you had a beautiful baby girl—naturally some of the glamour and parties and everything else would take a backseat to her. At least for awhile."

"I never did the parties. I went a few times, and that's where we met. I'm afraid she had a distorted idea of what my life looked like, and she couldn't get out until it was too late."

"Not too late." Her voice is still quiet, but determined. "Charli is perfect. Whatever happened between you and Lauren, a very good thing—a very incredible little girl—came from it. That's hard to regret."

The fact that Jocelyn understands, that she would care enough to put herself in my shoes and understand means everything to me. Another woman might've been petty, or badmouthed Lauren—it would be easy enough to default to name calling. Not Jocelyn. All I can do is squeeze her hand.

"You're wonderful at doing it all, you know," she says, leaning her head against me. "I know I'm just the outsider here, but what you have in the Boxer household is so, so special. Don't think for a minute that the two of you aren't a whole family. In my mind, you already achieved your goal."

I bring her to me, my lips pressing a long kiss against her forehead. I stroke her hair as the breeze whips around us, the salt thick in the strands of her hair. She smells fresh and wonderful, and in this moment, I'm happy. We fit together, and it all makes sense.

If only I can make her see it, too.

"Why did you say you wouldn't be good for me long—"

"Because of everything you just said." She interrupts me before I can continue speaking. "You have a beautiful family already, Boxer. You don't need me to be a part of it to be complete. I've made certain choices in life that put my priorities in different places than yours."

"Like what, work?"

"It's my life," she says. "I live it, breathe it."

"Not yesterday, not today."

"Excuse me?"

I let my arm slide around her shoulders. I'm not willing to let her run away from this conversation—mentally, physically, or emotionally. We're here, and we're going to hash things out.

I don't believe she has to choose between a life, a career, and a family. I have it. It might not be perfect, but it's wonderful. She can have it too, and that's what I need to make her understand.

"You didn't look at your phone," I tell her. "It was on the counter all day. I saw it. Did the world crash and burn without you?"

"I don't know if the world is still alive, since I haven't checked my phone."

"I'll tell you, the world survived. Even if you have missed messages, guess what? You can check them on Monday."

"But—"

"Your clients can wait. We have lives, too. We understand. And anyone who doesn't shouldn't deserve your time anyway."

"Fine, but that was for one day," she says. "And besides, more importantly, I'm not *mother* material. Have you heard what people call me?"

"I have," I say softly. "But they're wrong. They call you cold because they're intimidated. Women call you certain names because you're gorgeous and determined. Men call you other names because you are intelligent and beautiful and, frankly, it's enough to make an insecure man wet his pants to find himself in a meeting with you."

This eeks a tiny smile from her lips.

I shake my head. "You're the sexiest woman I've ever met. You're also the most determined and the most intelligent, and you can do whatever you want to, Joss. If you want to change the world, you can do it. If you want a family, you'll have the best family. You're an incredible person."

She blinks, and it looks suspiciously like the verge of crying. To diffuse the moment, I pull her fully onto my lap so she's cradled there, her head on my chest as I wrap her into a firm embrace.

The wind continues to simmer over us, the waves churning beneath. The world continues to spin, yet we sit, perfectly still, for what feels like an eternity.

"I don't understand family," she whispers. "It's been a long time."

"What are you talking about?"

"My parents died when I was seven," she says. "We had a family, and everything was perfect. Then it was ripped away, and now I'm alone. I don't want children, Boxer, because I can't ever do that to them."

My heart breaks. Hearing her thin words chiming against the wind, the shudder of her chest as she sinks against my body, malleable and completely exposed in my arms. I hover around her, determined to protect her not only from the elements, but from whatever she's been fighting alone all of these years.

"I'm so sorry," I whisper into her hair. "I'm so sorry about everything."

"It's okay, really." She doesn't sound as if she's crying, but my shirt is stained wet, and when I steal a glance at her face, her cheeks shine with emotion. "It was a long time ago."

"What happened after?"

"A few foster homes until I was old enough to take care of myself," she says, a wry smile turning her lips upward. "Believe me, I learned quickly."

The names she's been called in locker rooms return to me, and my blood is boiling underneath the surface. I'm trying to stay calm for her benefit, but my arms are shaking. To mask the tremors, I pull her closer, so tight we can hardly breathe, but she doesn't resist.

I might've been guilty for wondering about her before, in the past. One can't help but wonder—almost admire—a woman so successful in a wildly male-dominated industry. But I'm ashamed that anyone could judge her success with names that have scarred her so deeply.

"I've been alone for so long, it's just easier that way," she says. "I'm not good with kids—I don't spend much time around them, and I don't want to subject my own to what I've been through."

"What if things were different?"

She blinks. "Things aren't different. I don't survive on dreams; I survive on hard work and reality."

"Jocelyn, you have so much to give. I watched you with Charli all weekend, and she adores you," I tell her. "I'm not saying you have to have kids—that's your choice, obviously. But if you want them, don't be afraid of something that might never happen. It's horrible what happened to your parents, but you can't let it prevent you from living your own life."

She forces a smile.

"I'm not just saying that." I hold her shoulders, pulling her far enough back so that we can make eye contact. "If you were married, settled into a little family, would you want children?"

She bites her lip. "I haven't thought much about it. I just assumed I'd be horrible at raising them."

"Well, you're not. You wouldn't be. You made the newest six-year-old very happy yesterday. I think you'd make an incredible mother."

I'm not sure what has me so convinced, or why I'm so determined to change her mind on the matter. It's a feeling. I just know, the same way I *know* that Jocelyn Jones is full of love. She so clearly has enough of it to spill over into the world, to a family, to a child of her own. It's heart wrenching to realize that she can't see it.

My fury melts at the sound of her gasp for air, the way she twists around, turning her face away from me and struggling for breath. A tear falls onto my knee, the first of many, and I can feel her shoulders shaking as she tries to stifle the sound.

"It's okay, honey," I murmur, moving my hand over her back in quiet circles. "You're allowed to cry."

"I h-hate to cry."

"But out here, nobody can hear you. Let it out."

She hiccups, her arms wrapped around her own body as I continue to hold her. She's faced away from me, staring out to sea, the sound of the waves swallowing her ragged breaths. We're alone, completely alone, and I wouldn't have it any other way.

She mumbles something, and I lean in closer to hear.

"You can," she says again in an echo. "You can hear me."

"Yeah, but I'm just me. Who cares what I think?"

Then, in a voice barely audible, she whispers. "I do."

"You shouldn't."

She turns back around to face me.

"Why shouldn't I care?"

"Because I'm a human, you're a human, we're all just humans. What do you care what other people think?" I run a hand through her hair. "We're all here just doing our best. So long as we're not hurting anyone, what's the problem?"

"I never cry. Not in front of players, coworkers, business partners, at least. It's a weakness."

"So what?"

"It's a weakness! I don't show signs of weakness in my job. I can't."

"You're not weak, Joss. You're one of the strongest people I've ever met." I lean in close and brush a kiss on one cheek, then the other. If only I could kiss away the pain and hurt that caused those tears to fall. She's stopped crying, but salt is still dusted on her cheeks. "Even the strongest ones cry."

"Do you?"

"I have."

"You're strong, you know." She squeezes her arms tight around me. "You're so strong. You're perfect."

I'm touched, but it's not true. "I'm far from perfect."

"No. You know exactly what you want, and you know how to get it. You know what's right and what's wrong, and you never doubt yourself." She shifts over to sit next to me, her hand resting on my leg. "I don't know any of those things."

"No."

"No, what?"

"I don't know how to get what I want."

"What are you talking about? When we talked about contracts—"

"I'm not talking about business," I say, sharper than intended. I wait until her eyes meet mine, and then I hold onto her gaze a second longer. I need the weight of my words to mean something to her. "I want you, and I'm not sure how to get you."

"You want me? But you just said you wanted to wait."

"I don't want you for the night, for the day, for the week," I tell her, the words coming from somewhere deep within me, somewhere so sure I have no doubts they're true. "I have a feeling that if we begin something, it won't ever end."

"How can you know that?"

"It's a gut feeling." I run a hand through my hair and expel a sigh. "But that's what worries me, Joss. If it were just me, I'd have taken you to bed weeks ago and worked out the details later—but it's not that simple anymore. I have to consider Charli, and if I give my heart to you, and she opens hers . . . it's a risk. It's a risk I'm more than willing to take, but I won't go into it if you've no intention of giving us a real chance."

"A real chance."

"I'm not asking for marriage. If you don't fall in love with me, if things don't work out, so be it."

"But if they do—"

"If you fall so madly in love with me that you can't be without me, without us," I tell her. "Then I need to know you'll marry me. That you'll be open to it. Because if you come to bed with me, if you tell me you want to make this work, there's a very real chance we'll become a family of three. It's a lot to ask, I know."

"No." She looks up through eyes brightened by tears. "You have a great family, and anyone would be lucky to join it."

"What do you think about New York?" I ask her. "Two months. Time to get to know each other, to see how things play out. No pressure. You get bored of me before then, and no hard feelings."

"What about . . ." She hesitates. "I'm sorry, I don't want to turn this to business, but I need to know where we stand on all fronts."

"Let's see how it plays out," I say. "Two months, and then we'll make a decision. About us, about business, and we can go from there."

"Should I continue to try and win you over?"

I laugh, her lips quirking up in a smile. "Why don't you relax? Let me woo you."

CHAPTER 30

Jocelyn

I DON'T KNOW where Landon Boxer learned to woo a woman, but he does a *fine* job of it. In fact, over the next few weeks, he *wooed* me as if it were his one and only job.

First came a picnic lunch at the park, Charli running about like a madwoman, the day filled with sweet strawberries and laughter and freshly cut grass.

The second date was nothing more than a quick afternoon walk to grab coffee across the street from my office. Boxer came fresh from practice, and I snuck out between meetings. It was the best cappuccino I'd ever had, though I wondered if the company didn't have something to do with it. That was just the first week.

The second week consisted of more of the same, plus an additional night out watching Boxer play. The LA Lightning looked to be going far this year, and with playoffs approaching quickly, there was a noticeable lift in both optimism and tension in the air.

While their record spoke for itself, mistakes could be made and the team could choke. Boxer's schedule would most certainly be crazed until one of two things happened: his team was eliminated from the playoffs, or they won the Cup.

Weeks three and four grew in intensity, each date more special, more tantalizing than the last. True to form, we never progressed more than a steamy make out session, but by now, we were both feeling the tension looming over our heads. Everywhere we went, it followed. All at once, it was both promising and hellish, but we stuck to our plan.

Week five was torture. I wasn't able to see him at all due to travel on his side. Week six brought slushies all around and a trip to the movie theater for a Disney flick.

Week seven was another travel week for Boxer, which led us to the edge of week eight, our final week before New York.

Specifically, Friday. We leave a week from tomorrow.

"Seven days!?" Lindsay calls the second I step foot into the office the morning before the weekend begins. She's made one of those countdown chains like children make in school before Christmas. She tears a ring off every time I step into the room and tosses it into the air. Then she picks it up off the floor just as quickly because she's too nice to leave it for the janitor. "Diana called again. She wanted to know if you had an update on Boxer yet."

"Freaking Diana," I tell her. "I am never available for an interview. Can you tell her to shove off? You know, in nicer terms. Like you always do."

"I've told her you hate interviews."

"Well, tell her again. I never do interviews."

"You got it, boss. Anyway, how are you feeling about my chain?" She waves it back and forth. "Pretty exciting, huh?"

I wave her off, but it's half-hearted. I don't mind that she's almost as invested in this countdown as I am—it's fun. We're like giddy kids, rushing into the office every day to put our heads together and whisper, gossip, theorize about boys. Her relationship with Mark Greggs is taking off, and my relationship with Boxer is—if nothing else—keeping me on my toes.

We've been taking things slow as promised, with only scorching kisses to tide us over these last two months. Though he and I haven't explicitly talked about New York, it's fairly clear what we're both expecting to happen there.

And I can't wait.

"So . . ." she says with a dramatic flourish. "What's on the agenda for this week? Chocolate dipped strawberries? Sharing a romantic ice cream cone? A little stroll through the park?"

I spin and move into my office—excitement might be rampant in the air, but there's still work to be done. "It's a surprise. He hasn't told me where he's taking me!"

"Surely you have a guess!?"

"Did you cancel my meeting this morning?" I call through our open doors. "My calendar is open."

"I didn't cancel it, Andrea cancelled it. Luke's assistant. She said they'll reschedule later, but I wouldn't hold my breath."

I tap my pen against the desk. I had a day booked solid with meetings, and I had been looking forward to the full schedule. A day driven by work left me no time to think about my status with Boxer, and that's exactly what I need. After all, we left off our last date with him saying he'd call me, and I have yet to hear from him.

Not that I'm counting, but it's been exactly four days and twelve hours since that promise was made, and I haven't heard a peep.

"He's been busy," Lindsay says, leaning against the door. "Relax—I can see you stressing. Should I order some breakfast?"

"No, I'm not hungry," I tell her. "Unless you want something. Otherwise, I'll just pop down and grab a cappuccino—"

"No—" she says too quickly. "Let me. I have to stretch my legs."

"Stretch your legs?" I watch her hustle out of the room like her seat is on fire. It's eight thirty in the morning on a Friday. Nobody needs to stretch their legs before nine a.m. on a Friday morning.

I settle into my office, set my purse in its place, and boot up my computer. I'm logging on when someone calls a *hello* from the front door.

"Come in," I call out, letting my eyes glance over the calendar on my screen. I blink and do a double take. It looks like my meetings have all been cancelled. For a moment, I panic. All of my meetings cancelled? It must be a mistake. Maybe Lindsay moved some things around thinking I'd be stressed. That's got to be the explanation.

I'm pulling out my phone to text her when heavy footsteps pass through the lobby, then continue toward my office. I recognize those footsteps.

Slowly, heart sailing a hundred miles an hour, I look up from my desk and stare over my computer screen. "Boxer?"

He grins. "I have something for you."

I'm too shocked at finding him standing here to respond. He looks great in his jeans and a black t-shirt that shows off a set of beautiful arms I've been dreaming of for weeks—longing to have them wrapped around me, holding me late into the night and into the next morning.

True to his word, he's never pushed things past a kiss. Much to my dismay.

"Do you want to see what it is?" A smile sparkles beneath his blue eyes, his expression warm and excited. "It's homemade."

"I haven't heard from you . . ."

"I'm sorry," he says, face falling. "I should've called first, but I wanted this to be a surprise. I didn't trust myself to talk to you on the phone because I'm terrible at secrets."

"A surprise?" I feel like an incredibly stupid parrot just repeating phrases of his sentences. "For me?"

"Yes, for you!" He laughs. "I'm glad we caught you off guard. This took a lot of planning and coordination"

"We?"

"Are you going to take this or not?"

"Oh, of course." I reach for the envelope in his hand. The outside is papered with stickers, and I have a strong suspicion that Charli had a hand in its decorating. "It's beautiful."

"Team effort," he says.

I laugh at the unicorn prancing across the flap and do my best not to rip the paper as I tear it open. Holding my breath, I slide out a handmade thank-you card. It's signed by both Charli and Boxer and lists seventeen different reasons they were grateful for my help at her birthday party. The cake. The Target run. The party favors. The tickets.

The whole thing is so sweet, and I can't help but feel strangely touched by it, even as I wonder why this is relevant two months after the fact. I clear my throat and murmur a thank you back. "You didn't have to hand deliver this."

"I did," he says. "Flip it over and read the back."

I shoot him a skeptical glance and do as he says. There, on the back, is a whole new set of firework stickers. Underneath all of the explosions is a handwritten invitation from Charli:

Dear Jocelyn,
Please come with us to 6 Flags. I'm bringing a friend, and dad needs a ride buddy. We have your ticket already. You're his best friend besides me.
From,
Charli

If I found it difficult to hide my surprise before, it's nearly impossible now. It's all I can manage to squeak out a question. "Six Flags, huh? When?"

He leans forward, the scent of him spiraling toward me, bringing me back to earlier nights of shared whispers, close embraces, and moonlight kisses outside of one of our homes as we prolonged an evening of wonder together.

"It's a get out of jail free card," he says, pointing to the date at the bottom. "Please excuse Miss Jones from work."

In Charli's handwriting. "She gave me a hall pass for 6 Flags?"

"I hope you don't mind, but I coordinated with your assistant so you could play hooky today."

"Lindsay's in on this?!" Suddenly, her disappearance makes sense. "Oh, that little sneak."

"I begged her to let me do it," he says. "I asked her weeks ago."

"Weeks ago?!" The door cranks open in the lobby, hesitant footsteps tiptoeing across the carpet. "Lindsay?! Get in here!"

She walks in, three cappuccinos in a carrier tray. "Sorry, boss," she says. "You get the day off."

"I don't take days off."

"It's true," Lindsay tells Boxer as she hands him a coffee. "Not once since I've been hired. She barely leaves the office early for doctor appointments, and she always works from home after to make it up. She's nuts, I tell ya—nuts!"

"You're nuts, thinking you could keep this a secret from me!" I tell her, eyebrows raised. "I can't believe it."

She pauses, inches forward and drops the cappuccino on my desk. "I did keep it a secret. You're surprised, right? Mission accomplished."

"I thought we were friends," I tell her. "Best friends tell each other everything."

"Except surprise parties," she says. "I've cleared all your meetings from the calendar—they were moved weeks ago. Nothing was last minute. I just didn't tell you about it because I knew you'd get suspicious."

"Well, yes. What about the meeting with Marc?"

"Monday at nine a.m."

"Mr. Waters?"

"Tuesday afternoon at three, he'll swing by the office."

I raise my eyebrows at her. "You took care of everything for me?"

"He did most of the work," Lindsay says, pointing an elbow at Boxer. "I just played Tetris with your calendar."

"It sounds like you have no excuse not to come with us," Boxer says. "Like Charli said, I need a ride buddy."

"Jocelyn gets sick on the Tilt a Whirl," Lindsay says with a shudder. "Tried to take her once awhile back. My advice: Don't."

Boxer extends a hand for mine. I place my fingers in his and allow him to pull me to my feet. The next thing I know, I've said goodbye to Lindsay, set up my auto responder to show *Out of Office* for the first time in ages, and ditched my job for a day at the amusement park.

Who would've thought? Almost thirty years old, and I'm finally becoming a rebel.

CHAPTER 31

Jocelyn

HE ADORES HIS daughter; there's no other way to describe it. And the feeling is mutual. The way Charli looks at her dad, it's like there are beacons of light shining from her eyes.

When she's old enough to get married, men everywhere are going to have their work cut out for them. They say women marry men like their father—I hope that's true, for Charli's sake.

"What do you say, one more ride?" Boxer asks. "Then we'll call it quits."

"Ten more rides!" Charli screams.

My stomach goes queasy with the thought. Thankfully, Charli's friend, Abby, is looking peaked too, and it's with a firm shake of his head that Boxer says no. "One more. That's final."

Charli, smart cookie that she is, picks the ride with the longest wait time ever. The ride itself is a rollercoaster, the biggest one in the park that they're tall enough to go on, and it's the one everyone wants to hit one last time before leaving.

"She picked this one on purpose," I tell Boxer. "She doesn't want to leave."

"I don't mind," he says as the girls inch forward, leaning on the railing as they watch cart after cart take off, waving wildly to each one. "Hard to complain about a little more time next to you."

He inches his hand onto my lower back, his thumb tucking beneath the fabric of my shorts. Luckily, we swung past my place so I could change out of my heels and dress clothes before spending a day at the park.

The girls are oblivious to us, and I'm suddenly grateful for the long line. Boxer moves me in front of him, wrapping his arms around my shoulders and pressing a spine-tingling kiss to my neck. It's just tender enough to make me shiver, just hot enough to make me melt back into him.

He groans as my backside presses to him. I clear my throat and stand straight, but he growls his disapproval. "Where do you think you're going?"

"We're in public!"

"It's dark outside. Park's almost closing."

Despite his argument, he moves to stand next to me and lets his hand meander back toward my waistband. All day we've been acting like high schoolers, waiting for the girls to get distracted so we could have a moment of privacy. Boxer hasn't told Charli about us being anything but business partners yet, though she must be picking up on something—judging by the note in her handmade invitation.

Best friend, I think, leaning against his shoulder and watching as the first legs of starlight dance upon Charli's hair. I like that. Best friend.

I slip my hand through his and raise onto my tiptoes to whisper in his ear. "Thank you for an amazing day."

"Girls," he says, guiding me forward with a hand to my back as he leans down to Charli's level. "How do you feel about being responsible?"

Charli gives him a rightfully confused expression. "Meh."

"Why don't you and Abby ride by yourselves, and Jocelyn and I will wait right over here near the exit?"

Charli surveys the scene. We don't have that much further until the front of the line, and we can see each other the entire way. The exit pops out right next to the entrance, so it's next to impossible for them to get lost.

"That's cool," she says, sounding much older than her years. "We can do that."

We wait with the girls until they're safely buckled into the ride, and then step off the platform and perch ourselves near the exit. There's a little offshoot that's quite empty, a vantage point from which we can watch the girls and maintain some semblance of privacy.

"Not feeling well?" I tease, my breath catching in my throat as he boxes me in against the railing with one arm on either side of my body.

"Sure," he says, nuzzling against my neck. "Whatever you want to believe."

I laugh softly, cherishing the warmth of his arms against the chill of the night air. The ride takes off, and we separate for a moment, waving to the girls before they round the corner and shrieks carry them into the darkness.

"I needed this, needed it so badly," he says, his arms landing on my shoulders and spinning me to face him. "Going four days without talking to you was too long."

"I know. I missed you."

His lips meet mine, starving for this moment. There's no time to be tender, no slow build to fuel. We're on fire. He presses against me as he clasps my face in his hands and deepens the kiss.

My arms are around his neck, dragging him under with me. I can't breathe, can't see, can't think; I need him. To be apart from him is an ache impossible to ease.

These last weeks, we've been testing boundaries, pushing our limits. If New York wasn't looming, I'd insist he come home with me tonight.

"This was a horrible idea," he murmurs, breaking just long enough in his pause to pepper my cheek with kisses. "I just want you more, now. I don't know if I can wait."

"I know." I grin, then squeeze him into a hug to get the smile back on his face. "Just think, though, the anticipation will all be worth it."

"Are you ready?" he asks, his eyes landing on mine. Our bodies are still lined against one another, but the heat has faded to a cool burn. "Are you ready for New York?"

"Yes." I meet his gaze head on and supplement my response with a nod. "Are you?"

"More than anything, sweetheart. But you know what it means—when we sleep together, when I introduce you to Charli as my girlfriend—"

I silence him with the softest kiss I can muster. "I know," I tell him. "I want everything. You. Charli. Whatever that entails."

"Come home with me tonight." He's got me pressed against him again, and it's intoxicating. "I need you, Joss."

"Tonight's not the right time," I tell him, gritting my teeth as I try to convince myself. I can feel his need, and my own desire is streaking through me. "One week."

As if to prove my point, the ride comes to a stop and we're forced to break apart. He gives me one last kiss, fast and hard to the lips, his hands covering my body in a way that has me feeling like I belong. To him. To the here and now.

"Fine," he says, as the park employees start letting children off the ride. He glances over my shoulder for the girls, then turns his gaze on me for one fiery moment. "But don't make any plans for New York because you're all mine. All weekend."

I barely manage to nod.

"The week after, and the week after that, too," he says, brushing a kiss against my forehead. "For as long as you'll have me."

The moment is broken as the girls hop down the exit ramp, and we move to the gate to greet them. But as we drive home, I find myself sitting in silence, Charli's recap of the day falling on deaf ears as I think about what's to come.

Later in the night, as I toss and turn in bed, my stomach twisting in knots, I realize that I'm nervous. I'm nervous for the week ahead, the anticipated stay in New York. Our first night together, what it will be like—and what it might not. I worry about the future—what I will lose if everything falls apart.

Then I worry about my heart because somehow, I've fallen in love—so deeply and desperately in love that the mere thought of it brings an ache to my chest, and I hadn't even seen it coming.

CHAPTER 32

Boxer

THIS IS STUPID. I've never seen underwear so stupid.

I can't believe they're paying me a stupid sum of money just to wear these and smile for the camera. If it weren't for Jocelyn, I'd probably tell them where to shove their underwear and get on a plane back home—forget about the money.

But I won't do that because I'm too excited to see her tonight. All night. Every inch of her. It might've been my idea to wait for New York, to hold off until we could be alone and uninterrupted, and until we'd gotten to know each other before jumping into bed.

Except now, at the end of eight torturous weeks, I'm feeling pretty stupid for that being my idea.

This is going to be the most awkward photoshoot ever if I don't stay focused. Two months of making out with Jocelyn Jones and not having much in the way of closure would be enough to drive most men insane. Add on the daydreams that've been plaguing my mind, and I'm in trouble.

The makeup lady knocks on the door, and I throw on sweatpants and a sweatshirt. "Come in," I tell her.

As she sits me down and begins work on my face, I'm left with nothing to do but think. I can't think about tonight, however, for reasons already stated. If I daydream too much, I'll be poking the crew in the face.

But my mind won't stay away from her, and I realize that maybe the two month wait was worth it. In the long run, it's a blip on the spectrum of life. A mere breath in the passing of time.

The woman drives me crazy, and she doesn't even realize it. I act irrational around her, break all my rules, forget all the promises I made to myself when Lauren left us years ago.

Charli. She's the reason for the two month fast. The delayed gratification. Going into tonight, I have no doubts. It's not only right, it's necessary. Whatever comes afterward, so be it. I need Jocelyn in every way, and I can only hope she needs me back. Needs us in her life. My greatest hope and greatest fear, all mixed into one.

"There you are," Jocelyn says, pushing the door open. "How are you feeling?"

"Go away," I tell her. "Please."

Her eyebrows furrow in confusion. "Sorry?"

"Just a second. I'll be right there."

She closes the door without another word.

I feel bad sending Jocelyn away, especially since we didn't fly out here together, so this is our first meeting in New York. I flew with Charli up to San Francisco where my parents were tickled pink to watch her over the weekend—my mother's words, not mine. Steve had initially planned on it, but something for work had come up, so I'd made the flight out here from SFO while Joss had jumped on a plane from LAX.

Now, I'd sent her off without a proper hello. But really, it was for safety reasons. I last saw her at Six Flags a week ago, and that damn kiss is still imprinted on my mind—the second she walks into the room, the memories are sure to come flooding back.

I rush the makeup artist through whatever she's doing with her brush. When she finally declares me all done and tucks her brushes into her belt, I breathe a sigh of relief and pull the door open.

"There you are." I find Joss standing outside, examining her nails while pretending to not be annoyed. "Come inside."

"Hello to you too," she says with a crispness to her words as she enters the room. "Quite busy, I see?"

"Joss." I let my hands trail through her hair. "I'm sorry."

"You don't have to apologize."

I examine the back of her in the mirror, the curve of her hips in tight black pants, the bright blue tank top that brings out her eyes, the little jacket that doesn't quite reach her waist. She's stunning.

"I couldn't let you in here," I say with a small smile. "Because I knew this would happen."

"What?"

I lean in for a kiss, grasping her arms in my hands. There's a buzz of excitement in the air, the tension thick as butter. She's surprised, I can feel it in the stiffness of her limbs, just like I sense the second she relaxes and urges her body toward mine.

"Oh, my God," she giggles, feeling the weight of me press against her. "We can't have this happening during the photoshoot."

"No kidding."

"I'm sorry."

"Don't apologize," I tell her. "I just wanted to give you a proper hello."

She grins back. "Well, I missed you, too."

"This week has been excruciating."

Because we've been waiting for this moment for so long, the next seconds seem important, essential. Underneath the rampant desire electrifying the room, there's a note of nervousness in the air.

These past few months we'd been running on excitement, on intensity so strong it raced through us like kindling. We'd kept ourselves safe, protected from rushing into things too quickly by setting up shields and precautions. Now, we'd run out of excuses. If we were going to continue this song and dance, we were going to finish it, once and for all.

I inch toward her for another kiss, but she gives the slightest shake of her head.

"The others," she murmurs. "The staff."

"Private dressing room. We're alone."

"God, then yes."

I inhale her words, clipping the end of her response. Her hands slide behind my back, her fingers cool against my skin. Goose bumps prickle my body in anticipation.

She tastes like buttercream cupcakes, all bright and delectable. A treat to be savored, and savor I do. Long, slow kisses until I can't handle the wait any longer.

"How do you look so beautiful after traveling all day?" I lift her onto the dressing table, her arms still swung around my neck. She opens to let me stand between her legs and nuzzle in against the soft skin of her neck. "This weekend took too long; I need you so badly."

"I need you too."

I'm treated to a view of her back in the mirror, and the only thing wrong with it is her clothes. There are too many of them. Hair swishes in golden lines, her figure outlined like the silhouette of an hourglass as I gently remove the leather jacket.

Bare flashes of skin from her shoulders appear, and I brush my fingers there, closing my eyes at the shot of lust it sends spinning through my veins. She points her chin upward, eyes closed, and initiates a hungry kiss.

She parts her lips, teasing me with a taste. Her legs rise to wrap around my waist and her arms tug me toward her until I'm forced to rest an arm on the mirror so as not to bowl us both over.

She pauses, her hands trickling down my sides. "Your body is out of this world."

The tips of her fingers against my bare skin make me flinch. Apparently, I have a sensitive rib cage.

"Am I tickling you?" A grin breaks onto her face, and she moves her fingers faster, toying with me, until it's too much. Her eyes light up with the question, and it's adorable.

Adorable, never a word I thought I'd use to describe Jocelyn Jones. When she looks at me through those gorgeous eyelashes, the light blue underneath so bright, I can't help but want to tuck her into a special place in my heart and keep her, protect her, for all of infinity.

Instead, I tease her back, nipping at her neck, behind her ear, until she squirms closer against me, her shoulders shaking with laughter. I'm pleased to realize her pants are made of some flimsy material, leggings almost, and my hands have full access to her figure.

"Are you sure you want to do this shoot?" she murmurs against my neck, once the teasing subsides and the threat of more hovers over us. "We could go back to the hotel. I mean, underwear is overrated, right?"

She reaches down to toy with the band around my waist, but on the way her knuckles brush against my stomach, and I stiffen. If I needed her before, I was wrong.

The feel of her hands against me is enough to bring out animal instincts that've been dormant for ages. This time, when I pull her close, it's no longer a gentle exploration.

"Screw underwear," I tell her. "Let's go to the hotel."

"But—"

Her argument is interrupted by a knock on the door.

"One minute," I growl to the intruder, sounding almost murderous. I take the ensuing silence to hold Jocelyn's chin in my hand and tilt it toward me. "Don't think this conversation is over."

The moment is broken by a second knock, and I reluctantly let her go. She straightens herself out, pulls the door open and slips outside. Jocelyn makes a disgruntled noise of surprise, and I poke my head out a second later.

"Andy?" I frown at the man standing there. "What are you doing here?"

CHAPTER 33

Boxer

"WHAT DO YOU want?" I ask, closing the door behind him as Jocelyn eases away. "I didn't expect to see you here."

"I know the producers," he says vaguely. "Since I was in town, I thought I'd stop by and see you."

"Oh. Why?"

"Are you free for dinner tonight?"

"No."

"Ah, I see." He casts a casual glance over his shoulder, his eyes following the same path Jocelyn took on her exit. "You're busy."

"I have plans," I tell him, trying to keep my voice even. "I'm getting dinner with friends."

"I see." Andy shoves his hands in the pockets of his expensive suit, sounding just as oily as his slimy hair gel. "Which friends?"

He moves to stand in front of the dressing table. While he's waiting for a response, his eyes flick up to where there are distinct fingerprints against the mirror. Under my breath, I curse. He's putting things together.

"An old girlfriend lives here," I blurt out. I'm practically bellowing at him, trying to draw his attention away from the fingerprinted mirror. "We have plans tonight, if you catch my drift."

"Good man." Andy turns around, claps me on the shoulder. "I hope she's worth it."

"She is."

I must answer too sharply because he turns to me and watches my eyes.

"Interesting," he murmurs finally. "Are you free for lunch tomorrow?"

I narrow my eyes at him. He may be a piece of slime, but he's smart enough to have succeeded so far. If he links Jocelyn and I together, the person who'll be hurt most is her. It's because of this that I agree to lunch.

"Have a car pick me up," I say grudgingly.

"Which hotel?"

I give him the name and address, and he nods, then takes his overdue leave.

It's good, I tell myself, turning back to the mirror. I'll have time to meet with Rumpert tomorrow, squash out whatever weasly little idea he's got brewing, and get on the plane home. Jocelyn won't have to be any the wiser.

When the sound of Rumpert's footsteps fade in the distance, I stand and slam the door behind him, the echo bouncing off the walls, the ceiling, and back to me. Then, I yank the door right back open.

"Hey," I call down the hallway to whoever's listening. "Can we get this thing going? I have plans tonight."

CHAPTER 34

Jocelyn

DURING THE SHOOT, I'd stood in the wings and watched, alternating between a keen interest in what was happening on camera, and biting my nails wondering what had drawn Andy Rumpert cross country to bother us here.

Surely, if he guessed at a relationship between myself and Boxer, he'd feed it to the wolves. I can only imagine the headlines: *Ice Queen Melts for Star Recruit!*

My heart thuds at the idea that Andy Rumpert could turn something so good, so promising into a weapon. If I wasn't so upset, I'd be downright livid. For now, I'm somewhere in between.

By the time the shoot has wrapped, I've vowed to push thoughts of Andy out of my head. I can't do anything about him now, and I've waited so long for this evening that I won't let Rumpert ruin it; I'm stubborn, and I refuse to give him the satisfaction.

Boxer showers, changes, and joins me in front of the studio. Keeping things chaste with a kiss to my forehead, he follows me as I direct him to a waiting car and issue the driver instructions to bring us to our hotel.

Our hotel.

It still sounds so strange. For a hot second, I had debated

getting a room of my own just in case, but Boxer had put the kibosh on that. Which leaves us with one room. One night. Eight weeks of torturous build up.

"You did great." I squeeze Boxer's hand as the cab pulls away from the curb and heads down the street. "Congrats! It will make for a perfect campaign."

"Why'd they ask if I skipped a dentist appointment?" Boxer asks so quickly that I must look dumbfounded at the change in subject. "The producers asked me about my tooth, and I had no clue what they were talking about."

I lower my gaze to my hands. "Oh."

"So, you do know about it."

"When I first got the gig for you," I began with a sigh, "the producers suggested I look into getting your tooth fixed. This was months ago."

Boxer doesn't respond but I can see him running his tongue over his front teeth.

"I just . . . . I didn't follow through. I should've told them, I'm sorry."

"Why didn't you tell me about it?"

"I don't really know."

He cocks his head to the side, surveying me. "If we weren't dating, would you have forced me to make an appointment? Be honest."

I don't need to think for long. "Yes. I mean, I wouldn't have *forced* you, but I would've strongly recommended it."

"What changed?"

It's been so long since I've paused to actually think. About anything, really. I reach out, my fingers grazing down his chin, but he doesn't pull his lips into a smile, so I retract my hand.

"I couldn't ask you to change, even something so little. Because there's nothing wrong with you."

Boxer's hand grasps mine. Once it's in his clutch, he doesn't let go, pressing a soft kiss to my palm before guiding it to rest on his leg. Then he raises his eyes.

"I'm not perfect," he says, meeting my gaze. "I'm a mess, Joss. Even my teeth can't manage to stay unbroken. I'm bruised and chipped and whatever else, but this is all I have to offer. I wish there were more for me to give."

I swallow, but it's a challenge.

"Don't ever apologize to me for that." I shake my head.

"I'm broken, too," I tell him. "I was shifted from one foster home to the next until I found myself on my own. Nobody wanted me."

He brings his hand to my cheek, rests it there, and pulls me in for a kiss, though it can hardly be called that. It's light as mist, almost a curiosity, and when he finally pulls away, I'm left wondering if it happened at all.

"Puzzles start out whole," he begins. "Then they're broken. But the thing about puzzles is that when the right person comes along, they can put all the pieces back together again."

"Do you want to pick up the pieces of me?" I'm more hopeful than I want to admit. My breath stills in my throat.

"That's not what I meant." He gives me a sardonic sort of smile. "You've already put me back together."

I smile, reach for his hand, and wait out the rest of cab ride in a test of self-restraint.

I moderately pass the test, but Boxer fails in a glorious fashion. His hand creeps up, again and again, higher and higher onto my thigh until I am forced to move it back to my knee. I don't care if the apocalypse comes tonight, I'm letting Landon Boxer take me to bed if it's the last thing I do.

Boxer finally forfeits with the hand thing and instead slips his arm over my shoulders. He settles for a lazy kiss, a precursor for the rest of the evening. If the appetizer is any signal about the main course, then I'm in for a treat.

When the driver announces that we've arrived at our hotel, we're both startled. Boxer stumbles through an overzealous tip before we continue his stumbling through the front door, past the front desk, and into the elevator.

I had stopped by the hotel after arriving in town today, checking in and retrieving the key before ever going to the studio. Boxer's luggage had already arrived here, shuffled over by a PA from the set. We had nothing left to worry about except each other.

As soon as the elevator doors close, with only the pair of us inside, Boxer takes charge, pressing me against the wall and covering my body with his own. He's magnificent—his long torso toned by years of intense athletic training—and it's a joy to run my fingers over his shoulders, down his chest, to the lip of his pants. He's taut with muscle everywhere, hard and lean and tough.

His lips, however, are everything but. Soft and sensual, when his tongue slips between my lips, exploring, teasing, the taste of what's to come, it's enough to make me molten lava in his arms.

It's been so long since I've let passion take over, since I've been recklessly in love, and it's exhilarating. I'd bet that if I jumped off a building tonight, I just might fly.

We're on the verge of spontaneous combustion by the time we reach the door to our room. Boxer hastily attempts to slide the key into the slot, and on the third try, he gets it unlocked.

"This is nice," I say out of formality, surveying a suite that would impress royalty. My eyes still land on the most incredible thing in the room—him. I sigh and brush my sweaty palms against my pants. "So, how are we going to do this?"

For a long moment, he stares at me with a completely blank expression.

I clap a hand over my mouth. "I'm so sorry, I didn't mean it like . . ." I give up, letting a hand clasp against my forehead. I close my eyes. "It's been awhile for me, if you can't tell. I'm rusty."

At this, Boxer unfreezes and throws his head back to laugh.

The tension has broken, and the remaining silence is an easy one—a pleasant, contented silence. Until his eyes flash from periwinkle bright to something darker, and the air inherits a sense of urgency.

"In answer to your question . . ." He steps toward me, suddenly commanding. Amusement lines his words, but there's something primal underneath. "I'm going to hold you, kiss you, and now, if it's okay by you, I'd like to bring you to the bedroom and relish every inch of you."

My heart is racing. My breath—I'm not even sure if it's there.

He pulls me into his arms and lands a tempting kiss just on the edge of my mouth. "I'm going to savor every moment with you. Every touch, every word, every look."

He scoops me into his arms, carrying me from the living area to the bedroom, bringing alive a playful mix of exploratory kisses and joyful caresses. Of sweet touches and weighty glances. Of sizzling tension and lazy enjoyment.

He eases me out of my jacket one arm at a time. He inhales sharply as it falls to the floor.

"Let me see you," he says, spinning me around like a slow dance. When I come to a stop and rest against his chest, our eyes lock and hold. "More," he says gruffly.

I help with my top, but he manages to slide my pants down all on his own, leaving me in a state of undress that precious few men have ever seen. I've dated plenty of men; I haven't gone home with most of them. Sex complicates things. I'm not a fan of complications.

Tonight is different. He's different. *We're* different together.

"You're beautiful," he says, his eyes roving over my skin. "Perfection."

Framed by the elegant hotel room, modern black lining every surface and trimmed by deep mahogany on the desks and furnishings, he looks like he's stepped into a scene from a movie. His shirt has vanished, leaving me with a delicious view of his chest—wide and muscled, his arms sturdy to lift me like a pencil.

This is the stuff fantasies are made of, I think, as he lowers his mouth to mine. Except for one thing—this, here, is my reality. It *must* be reality because it's better than anything I could've possibly dreamed.

"Your pants," I murmur, as he deepens the kiss. "They're still on."

I'm not eloquent, but it does the trick. We struggle together to get his slacks off, and it's a show of teamwork to accomplish this without someone toppling over. We each sigh as they fall, discarded with the rest of our orphaned clothes on the ground.

Finally free, he covers my body with his. I'm blanketed by his sheer, delicious mass, and I don't care if I ever breathe again. This is perfection, even if he's slowly relieving me of all the breath in my lungs.

My hands come around to his back, my nails digging in as he shelters me, warms me from all sides. I find his hair, my fingers locking tight as I lean to him. "I'm nervous."

"About what?" he murmurs. "Am I hurting you?"

"I want you more than I've ever wanted anyone," I say, holding him close even as he attempts to pull away. "I've never dreamed I'd find this sort of relationship. It's too intense."

"I did," he says bluntly. "I wanted to find love so badly that I was willing to sacrifice everything for the wrong person."

"I don't *want* you anymore, I need you. When I'm not with you, I think of you all the time. Life feels half lived when you're not next to me."

"I know," he whispers, those blue eyes so achingly gentle. "You ruined me a long time ago, Jocelyn Jones. I was just waiting for your heart to catch up."

"Well," I choke out a half-laugh. "It has."

He watches the rainbow of emotions pass over my face like a storm. "Are you crying? Don't cry. This is supposed to be a happy night."

"I'm not crying," I say. "I hate crying."

"Joss," he whispers. "You don't need to be scared. I'm not going anywhere."

I gasp as he lowers his head to my neck; the conversation is over. He warms me in a trail of kisses that lead past my throat and down to my collarbone, then my chest.

His hands work the whole while, skimming down my sides, tracing my curves like a map. I sink into the moment, trying to remember every touch, every movement, though it's impossible. He moves in a well-orchestrated symphony that can't be separated into pieces.

When his mouth ravages mine, hot and aggressive, it turns into a war between us, a war to hold back words, emotions, every last bit of self-control—if we have any left. Should one or both of us collapse, it'll change everything. We'll collapse into something that's joined and united, together. My hips raise, his hand sliding underneath to hold me against him. Chest to chest, core to core.

"Joss." He holds me tight against him, pulling his face away just enough to speak. "I can't . . ."

"Can't what?"

"I can't wait a second longer." He's lined up against me, every curve of his body matching mine. "I love you."

My eyes fly open. I'm lost for a moment, blurry from battle, when I realize that I, too, have already fallen. I've fallen, and yet I'm still fighting to hold back, trying to keep some semblance of control over this whole thing.

"You don't have to say anything back," he whispers, "In fact, I don't want you to. Say it when you want—*if* you want. Only if and when you mean it."

"But—"

"No," he says, and that ends it.

I swallow, the darkening in his eyes begging me to wait. To let this moment belong to him, to the start of us.

"Okay," I tell him, my hands coming to surround his face. The quietest kiss seals the moment into a time capsule, one I want to remember when I am old and gray.

A groan slips out of Boxer's mouth as I arch against him, one hand slipping behind my back to ease my bra off. He drinks in the view for a long moment, and it's only when I shiver under his gaze that he blinks back to reality. Lowering his mouth to my breast, he offers a murmur of appreciation, a caress, a taste.

My stomach tightens and my eyes close, my hips lifting of their own accord as he begins to explore everywhere. He takes advantage of my raised body to remove the last bit of lingerie, leaving it on the floor with the rest.

He moves downward, descending in patient bursts and showering every inch of my body with attention, just as he has promised. When he reaches my stomach, he peppers kisses in a line from my center down to my inner thighs, teasing, toying, skipping over all the places that need it most. Then he gives me a look with his eyebrow raised and a cheeky smile.

"Please don't stop," I tell him. "You're evil."

He issues a soft laugh, but it's enough of an encouragement. First his hand, then his mouth. Gentle, giving—utterly selfless.

Working in harmony once more, he circles me, pulls me higher until I'm crying out at the first waves of pleasure. My fingers find his hair, holding on as he drives me to new heights, only to guide me crashing to the depths below.

By the time I'm able to feel, to see, to comprehend, he's moved next to me and wrapped me in his arms. He holds me tight, the scent of us together swirling into one. I'm breathing in ragged breaths, and his match mine.

I roll over, face him, a shy smile turning up my lips. "Wow."

"Yeah?"

"Oh, yeah."

He laughs, runs a hand through my hair. "Good. We're just getting started."

"Well, of course." I reach lower, between us, and run a hand over him.

He closes his eyes and groans, burying himself into me—save for the fabric of his boxers. I sit up, but he stops me in the process. "No. Not tonight."

"But, you just—"

"And I can't wait a second longer." His voice sounds strangled. "Please don't make me wait longer. I need you. All of you."

I dodge his hand, sitting up more fully, and work off his boxers until he's a free man. An impressive one, at that, and I pretend not to stare. Landon Boxer, in all his naked glory. More impressive than I could've ever imagined, and most certainly the most beautiful man I've ever seen. Possibly the only man I've ever loved.

I plant a series of kisses down his chest that have his hands fisting in my hair. He pulls tight against my scalp, and the tension has me on fire for more, to drive this man wild, to make him lose control.

I reach his waist with my treasure trail of kisses and, despite his flimsy arguments, I circle him with my mouth. A string of hissed curses is enough of a confirmation that I'm doing something right. His head falls back to the pillow, eyes shut. When I rest a hand on his chest moments later, his heart is racing.

"Joss," he growls. "Wait."

Before I can argue, he pulls me up and onto his chest. We're both naked, breathing heavily, and he presses into my stomach. This moment, this brief respite is the calm before the storm. His fingers skim my back and my head rests against his chest. It's more intimate than anything yet.

He dips his head into a long, languid kiss. The sort of kiss that brings tears to the eyes and has one wondering how they've survived so long without it, and how they could ever survive without it again.

"Landon." I blink, but one droplet escapes onto my cheek. "I love you. I love you, too."

"God, I've been waiting so long to hear that."

He brings me into his arms and rolls us so that he's perched over me, my face cradled in his palm. His eyes turn almost savage, possessive.

"I've waited so long to have you." From somewhere, he's rolled on a condom, and there's nothing but the weight of him against me now. "I need you, Joss."

We hold there, the last moment before everything crashes into a wild spiral. When he pushes inside me for the first time, our eyes are both open, locked on one another, his gaze surveying mine. I let him drink all of it in—the fireworks most certainly lighting in my eyes, my desperate gasp as the pressure intensifies, my clenched fists grasping at the sheets—until I can't possibly keep my eyes open.

I reach to feel him. I'm greeted with smooth skin, strong arms, and I latch on as he shifts and increases the friction between us. One thrust, and then another. He fits me—a perfect match.

His lips meet my neck, suckling as he presses against me, raising my body so my back curves to a new angle. He drives harder, faster, murmuring sweet encouragement against my neck.

"Stop thinking so much," he says as I mumble nonsense. "And just feel."

Finally, I forfeit and let myself go completely over the edge and into his arms. We move together, and it's no longer two of us, it's one—a single rhythm, melody, racing toward an inevitable conclusion.

Together we reach the edge, the precipice, and pause for one moment, trembling on top of the world, before he slides in one final time, and we crumble together into pieces. His release comes seconds after mine, and when he says my name, it drags out every last sensation in my body. Each and every wave until the pulsing subsides, and calmness settles.

One of his arms drapes over my body, snuggling me close. My back is pressed to his chest, his lips resting near my ear. We don't speak, don't move; we simply savor the closeness. The closeness turns into a dream, and for the first time in a long while, my dream can never be better than my reality.

If this is what love is, then I want it. No matter the cost. Forever.

CHAPTER 35

Boxer

I'VE BEEN AWAKE since seven this morning, and I'm too afraid to move for fear of scaring the shit out of Jocelyn. I want to hold her tighter, but I'm afraid I'll stab her with my current state of affairs down below.

I want our first morning of being together to be romantic. Memorable. Perfect.

Poking her in the back with my boner probably isn't the way to get things started.

Instead, I'd like to hold her, wake her with kisses, and, yes, make love to her all day long. Cancel our flights, forget about the world, and get lost in one another for hours on end.

Unfortunately, it's almost nine a.m. . I've been awake for two painful hours, watching the rise and fall of her chest, following the subtle curves of her body from head to toe with my gaze—looking, not touching. Her hair is spread out on the pillow like a gorgeous mosaic while sweet smelling perfume drifts from her sleeping figure.

My hand reaches out of its own accord and lands on her shoulder, trailing down over her pale skin, making a happy little path down her arm. She shudders slightly, but doesn't wake.

My fingers land at her waist. She's still gloriously naked, the both of us having made love two or three times throughout the night, one of us waking the other, then switching, until we'd both been completely satiated and exhausted.

Yet here I am, just hours later, in a state of agony waiting to see if she'll wake up in time for us to make love once more. She shivers as my fingers trace small circles on her hip, and I have a sudden thought. A distraction from my single-minded focus on her body.

My stomach growls, and if I were home, I'd be cooking her a homemade breakfast: eggs, bacon, English muffins, the works. We're not at home, so instead I slink out of bed and move to the living area. It's a ritzy hotel; Jocelyn booked it on the underwear company's dime, and she spared no expense.

I quietly place an order for a widespread array of breakfast items, realizing I don't know what she prefers to eat in the morning. Better to order everything and let her choose. After all, with the amount of calories I burned last night, I'll be able to finish everything she doesn't. I'm ravenous. For food, yes, but first, for something—someone—else, too.

A murmur sounds from the bedroom, and I make quick work of slipping back under the covers. She's wrapped in my arms and pressed to me before her eyes open.

"Good morning, gorgeous," I whisper, along with a nibble on her ear. "How'd you sleep?"

She shivers, a faint sleepy giggle coming from her throat as she throws an arm over her head and stretches. That long torso of hers is on perfect display as she turns to me, and I try to focus on her face, but her breasts are too distracting.

I've been trying to hold back for two hours. I deserve an award for my restraint. And that reward is a long, unobstructed stare.

"Enjoying the view?"

I snap my head up and catch her grinning at me. "You're like an art display."

"Then, you'd better look and not touch."

"Is that right?" I long to reach out, cup her in my palm, feel the warmth of her in my hands, but this game is suddenly sexy, and I don't mind her taking the lead. "You never answered my question."

"I slept just fine," she says, her voice low, husky. "But it wasn't the sleeping that was the highlight for me."

I groan as she pulls herself to her knees and pushes me back on the bed. She has me flat on my back, her hands on my shoulders. Leaning down, she relishes in a tantalizing kiss, a smoking hot slip of her tongue driving me more insane than ever.

I'd slid into a fresh pair of boxers when I got up to order breakfast, and as she reaches for them, I grab her wrist to pull her toward me. She broke the kiss, but I'm not finished yet.

"No," she says sharply, just a hint of a smile in her eyes. "Look, but don't touch, remember?"

I close my eyes, hissing a breath between my teeth as she presses my wrists to the bed. This is new. A new confidence that wasn't there last night. Not the first time, nor the second, and even on the third round of loving that lasted until the earliest hours of the morning. Maybe it's the threat of a looming goodbye that gives her a new urgency.

"Oh, my," she says, her hand running down my abs, coming to rest on my length. "You're raring to go."

"I've been ready half the damn morning."

"Impressive."

She laughs, then bats her eyes flirtatiously before lowering her hands to the waist of my boxers. She pulls them down, inch by inch, until I spring free. I'm burning inside, itching to wrap my fingers around her waist and dig my fingers into the soft skin of her bottom, but every time I so much as flinch, she presses me back to the bed.

"If you move," she says, lowering her head. "I'll stop."

I have a retort ready to go, but the second her lips surround me, I'm done for. My eyes shut, blackness swallowing me as she teases with every touch, every swirl of her tongue. She pulls me further and further down a path I never knew existed. As if the black and white world has turned colorful, the feelings and sensations more intense than ever.

I can hardly hold back, but I refuse to let go this early. We've barely gotten started, and I need more. I need her, and I need us together.

The doorbell rings. "Room service!"

Her head shoots up, eyes wide. "Did you order breakfast?"

"Oh, *shit.*" I sit up and yell at the door. "Come back later!"

"Room service, we've got breakfast!"

"Just leave it outside," I yell again, wrapping a towel around my waist as I waddle toward the door like an awkward penguin. "We're busy."

Thankfully, the guy gets the picture. Footsteps sound in the hallway, and I waste no time returning to the bed. Jocelyn's laying there, like a beautiful cake on a platter—her cheeks pink, eyes blue, hair blonde—the picture of pretty.

"When did you order breakfast?" she asks. "I thought you were sleeping."

"Doesn't matter," I growl. "Where were we?!"

Her eyes flash dark as I drop the towel, and she takes one look below my waist. She sucks in the slightest of breaths, and it's enough to turn me to steel.

"Forget it," I say, climbing onto the bed. She's trapped beneath me, and I have no plans of letting up. "Let's start over."

"I don't want to start over," she says. "Let's pick up where we left off."

I lower my mouth, kissing her until we both lose our breath. I slide my hand down, pressing it to her stomach, then lower and lower until I can dip a finger inside of her. The moans coming out of her mouth have me on edge already.

We stay there, melded together until she's gasping for more. I roll on a condom and press against her, waiting there, teasing her as she had done to me earlier.

Her fingers raise, press against my back to push me inside of her, but I hold steady. "Look," I say gently. "But don't touch."

"Don't be difficult."

I laugh, but her lips find mine before I can respond, the heat of the moment too much to handle. If I don't have her now, I might die.

So I press into her, and together we sigh in relief. We're lost in this moment, this basic need as our bodies fall in line and move together in sync. There's a flow to this dance that's entirely natural, as if the two of us are made for one another.

Her hips tilt up at the exact angle that drives me wild, and I curse at the sensations because I know there's no going back. When she cries my name, I let everything go and release, entirely and completely, until the world is black and I'm seeing bursts of sunlight that have me wondering if this is a stroke.

But a stroke can't possibly feel so damn good.

When the waves between us subside, Jocelyn's breathing slowing to somewhat regular bursts of air, I roll off of her, bringing her with me into a warm bundle on the bed.

I kiss her neck, her hair, her back, feeling myself getting turned on all over again minutes later.

"Really?" she asks.

"Look, this hasn't happened before," I tell her, a little frustrated at my own stamina. "Which means it's not me, it's you."

She laughs, climbing out of bed and pulling on a robe. "Well, lucky for me, I hear there's room service outside. I'm starving. And I need a shower."

"I think you look beautiful. Skip the shower and come to bed."

She rolls her eyes, then disappears for a moment. When she returns, she's wheeling a cart back with all sorts of breakfast rolls, meats, and eggs. It smells heavenly, but it's nothing compared to the goddess behind the tray. Long blonde hair tumbling over her shoulders, the robe revealing milky white skin that's desperate to be touched. I can't decide which I want to devour first—Jocelyn, or the food.

Jocelyn reaches for a roll, so I follow suit.

She smacks my hand away, and I give her a questioning glance.

"Look, but don't touch," she says with a beaming smile. "We're still playing our game. This is all for me."

"Oh, I don't think so." I reach for her and tug her to bed. She barely manages to set the roll down before I have her pinned to the sheets and my lips to her breasts. She's writhing and shrieking with laughter as I take her into my mouth.

"Please!" she gasps playfully. "I just want a bagel."

"You're lucky I love you," I tell her, pulling my head up and nuzzling against her neck. "You can have all the bagels."

"Because I love you," she says, reaching for the cream cheese. "I'll share."

CHAPTER 36

Jocelyn

THE SHOWER SINGS over my shoulders, warm gusts of water washing away years of stiffness, frustration, hurt—solitude. Landon Boxer changed me last night, this morning. He broke open a dam I'd been keeping safe all this time, locking in the sunshine, the laughter, the tiny shred of Jocelyn Jones that used to know how to be silly. Fun. Outgoing and bright.

We'd teased, laughed, made love, held each other until the sun began to rise. The whole evening to night to morning had been the stuff of magic. But now, we had to say goodbye. It might be only for a short while, but it was still too long. Especially now. Today. After all of this.

Boxer would take a separate flight up to San Fran to spend tonight with his family, then back to LA to prepare for his first playoff game this upcoming Friday night. It'd be an intense week for him, and he'd already told me not to expect to see him. Though the frown when he'd told me this had made the news slightly easier to digest.

I blush thinking of what he'd said next, something about making up for lost time after Friday, and as I towel off and slip into a new dress, I think that Friday night can't come soon enough. Win or lose for the Lightning, I'm pretty sure I'll score.

I survey myself in the mirror and almost cry out of embarrassment at the sight there. I had let Lindsay take me shopping. She picked out a pink dress.

Violent pink.

I've never worn pink in my life, and I feel like a carnation standing here, twirling around. Like I belong in somebody's wedding as the flower girl.

Yet even so, there's a small part of me that I've kept shielded from hundreds of days spent wearing nothing but black dress after black dress that admits it's cute. Fun. Flirty. All things that Jocelyn Jones is most certainly not.

However, this morning, I suddenly feel like flirting. I feel like grabbing Landon Boxer's hand and traipsing down the street for a coffee before taking off on my flight, showing the whole world just how colorful Jocelyn Jones can be.

With the burst of confidence, I pull myself away from the mirror and step out of the bathroom. Boxer's waiting in the bedroom with his back to me. He's dressed in jeans and a button up shirt, hair still damp from his shower. As usual, he looks perfect.

When he turns, I watch his eyes closely. They begin at my legs, my feet specifically, which I've slipped into a pair of slick black pumps. I can't go all pink, not yet. I'm not that brave.

Then his eyes travel up to the hem of my dress which floats just above my knees, and then further up still until he's at the neckline, which just barely shows a hint of cleavage. He lands on my face, his eyes coals of fire blue.

"Pink," he says, with a shake of his head. "I never thought I'd see the day."

"I knew it would be too much." I clap a hand to my forehead. "I'm such a dork. Ignore me, and pretend you never saw this."

"What? Wait!" Boxer's long legs cross the room in four steps. He catches me, one arm around the waist, and pulls me back from the bathroom. "Where are you going?"

"We both know I look ridiculous in this getup. Something some teen girl might wear, and I'm a grown woman."

"You're nuts."

"What?"

"Nuts. Absolutely insane." He twirls me into his arms, our eyes locking on one another. "I wasn't criticizing you."

"Then what were you doing?"

"I was trying not to peel your dress right back off. Pink? It suits you."

His arms slide down from my back until they're at my waist, his fingers pressing into either side of my body, holding me against him. I can feel him, even through his jeans, and I have no doubt that if we didn't have flights leaving shortly, we'd be discarding the pink for a shade of nude that'd make us both quite pleased.

"Joss." He exhales, and it sounds painful as he curls around me, his hand inching down further and further still, until he sneaks a feel underneath the hem of my dress. "You're wearing lace."

"Shall we cancel our flights?"

He looks at me, a note of seriousness in his gaze. "If I weren't meeting . . ."

"Charli?" I finish.

"Right. Charli." He clears his throat and looks away. "I have to meet her."

"Of course, hey—" I give him a squeeze around the shoulders. "Your daughter comes first. I was just teasing."

He recovers from whatever clouded his eyes moments before and buries my hand in his. "Do you have time for an ice cream before I drop you off?"

"Of course I do."

We swing through the lobby, our bags waiting for us behind the counter. Hand in hand, we stroll along the streets, the springtime sun bursting bright on our faces. Boxer slides a pair of sunglasses over his eyes while I settle for squinting. If anything, they make him even more handsome, a shade more mysterious, and I take my time ogling him as he orders for both of us.

"Would you like a lick?" He offers me his cone, eyes glinting.

"I'll trade you." I extend my cone, but he shakes his head.

"I have something else in mind," he whispers in my ear, smelling of sugar and vanilla, his breath a tickle against my skin. "How long do we have before your flight?"

I steal his cone. "You're insatiable, you know?"

We make our way outside the shop, his arms encircling me from behind. We waddle down the sidewalk, stumbling over one another as we kiss, taste, enjoy the last moments of our perfect weekend. It's been incredible.

By the time we reach the car, I'm ready to cry tears of frustration for the sole reason that I don't want this moment to end. Ever. If I could stay here, I'd be perfectly happy for life.

Just as happy as I'd been on my sixth birthday, minus the bittersweet aftertaste.

"Call me tonight if you have time," I tell him. "But if you're busy with Charli, that's fine. Promise you'll think of me."

"I don't have to promise that," he says, swooping me into an embrace. "That's a fact of life, these days. I'll give you a call before bed."

"After Rapunzel?"

"After Rapunzel."

"Boxer." I rest both of my hands on his shoulders, the aftertaste of mint ice cream fresh on my lips. "Thank you for everything.

This weekend, the way you talk to me and hold me and treat me."

He presses a series of kisses along my jawbone. "Don't thank me for those things."

"But—"

"Those are the perks of being in love." He tips my chin upward. "And I have fallen for you."

"Me too."

We circle there, in the middle of the sidewalk, my feet barely touching the ground as he molds his mouth to mine. The kiss is long, luxurious, neither of us wanting it to end.

When it finally does come to a close, Boxer punctuates it with a twirl that has my dress spinning like a tutu around me. It's more than I'd ever dared to dream.

A day filled with joy. Love. Pink.

I sigh when Boxer tucks me into the car, waving goodbye as the driver peels away from the curb. He stands, watches me go, and a bit of my heart is left with him.

Then again, as I face forward, I realize that I wouldn't want things to be any other way.

CHAPTER 37

Boxer

"WHAT DO YOU want?"

"Cappuccino? Coffee? Jack and coke?" Andy Rumpert pulls the menu down from in front of his face, an eyebrow raised. "Why are we rushing things?"

"Why did you come to New York?" I pull out a chair at a rickety old table that's supposed to look antique, but to me, looks like a flimsy set of toothpicks just waiting to collapse under my weight. "I know it wasn't to visit friends."

"Is that right?"

"A guy like you doesn't have friends."

"Take a seat," he urges. "Stay awhile. I promise you'll want to hear what I have to say."

"No, I don't think I will." I'm perched at the edge of the table, my knuckles white. "Say whatever you want quickly because I've got a flight to catch."

He sighs, as if this is the greatest chore in the world. "You're acting like a child."

"Last chance, Rumpert."

"If you hadn't gotten tangled up with Jocelyn Jones—"

Whatever he'd intended to say never got the chance to exit his lips. I took two steps around the table and towered over the guy. He might look smooth and slick to most people who weren't well over six feet tall and built, but to me, he looked like a shiny little beetle from up here, and I am in a beetle-squashing mood today.

"Get to the point, and leave the lady out of this."

"I would, see, but she's the whole reason we're here today." The flash of fear in his eyes that had given me a glimpse of satisfaction, vanishes as he pulls something out of his pocket. "Alas, here she is."

He splays a set of photographs onto the table, flipping them right side up before I can do it myself. My hand comes down, clenching around Rumpert's shoulder as I lean over him. My stomach tenses as I catch a glimpse.

A bitter taste forms in my mouth, next. Lips curling, I survey the series of photos starring Jocelyn and myself. She's wearing her pink dress, and my hand is on her waist in the first one. The second, I'm kissing her. The third, I have her tucked into my body as I lean in, hungry for the rest of her. The chemistry between us sizzles, and there's no way anyone is mistaking these photos for anything other than what it is—a relationship. Romance.

"Where'd you get these?" The question sounds stupid, but I already know the answer to *when*. This morning—the only time I've ever seen Jocelyn dress in a color besides black. "How the fuck did you get these?"

"With a camera. It's not like my *friend*," he pauses to enunciate the word, "had to work hard to capture them. It seems neither of you care to be discreet."

"I don't care who sees us together."

Rumpert shakes his head. Sighs. "So it is love."

I grit my teeth together and remain silent.

"What about her?" he asks. "I'll bet she cares. I'll bet she cares a great deal."

I stay silent. He's egging me on, just begging me to get mad enough to cause a scene. That'll make for an even better story than what he's got now, but I won't fall prey to his tricks. Even if my blood is boiling and my fist is itching to say hello to his little jaw. *Not* because I'm a hero of any sort, but because Jocelyn doesn't deserve it. This. Any of it.

"I see you're following my train of thought," Rumpert says. "So, if you've decided not to go caveman and knock me unconscious over your new girlfriend, why don't you sit down so we can discuss terms and conditions like two businessmen?"

"You're not a businessman," I tell him. "You're scum."

"One and the same, isn't it?"

A few heads have turned our direction and, as much as I hate the attention, people do recognize me on the street now and again. I have to be careful now that someone else—someone I love—is involved.

I sit and order a coffee like a good little boy, all while battling back the lava burning inside of me. No wonder the weasel wanted to meet in a public place. He didn't want to risk being an asshole in private where we could handle this like two men—*no*, he wants the drama. It's disgusting.

"Great, there we go," Rumpert says, his smile growing in wattage. "Now we're getting somewhere."

I sit back, arms folded across my chest. "I've got a flight."

"Straight to the point, then. Here's my contract. Sign with me, and we'll keep these photos quiet."

"Why do I care about the photos?" I don't think he'll take my bluff, but it's worth a shot. I already gave myself away when I debated clocking his head. "I love her, so what? Let the world see it. You going to sell these to a tabloid somewhere?"

"The two of your names mashed into one article will raise some eyebrows in our industry," Andy says. "I know Miss Jones better than you might think—we've been colleagues of sorts for years."

"Right. Colleagues," I add sarcastically.

"She's worked for how long to build up a name and reputation for herself? An article like this—rumors that she might be sleeping with a potential recruit—get circulated, she'll be ruined. At least, her credibility."

"She's not sleeping with me to get my business."

"I don't care all that much what you two are actually doing; I care what this looks like. And it looks like she's wooing you by opening her legs—"

I stand up, my fists slammed to the table. "Shut up, Rumpert. Another word, and I don't care who sees, I'm going to smack you into tomorrow."

That flash of fear appears again, giving me the smallest blip of satisfaction before he gathers himself. "Sorry, man, I'm just telling you how it looks."

"No, you're telling me how you're going to spin the story when you sell it to the media."

"I'm not spinning anything, just . . . offering photos. Really, they speak for themselves."

My eyes are drawn to the photos again, and if they hadn't been captured in such a creepy, secretive sort of way, they might be beautiful. Mementos or keepsakes of our trip together. But the fact that Rumpert, or one of his buddies, had followed us around in the hopes of blackmailing us has me seeing red. This morning had been perfect, beautiful. And now it's blemished.

"How do you know that's not what she's doing, anyway?" Rumpert asks, leaning over, his voice syrupy sweet with suggestion.

"How do you know she's not playing with your heart to get your business?"

"She wouldn't." I respond before I can think about it. Even so, I take another look at the photos, and a flash of doubt streaks through my mind. That's how this whole thing had started, wasn't it? As a ploy to earn my affections as a friend, and then a trusted business partner. When had things changed?

"How well do you know her?" he asks, narrowing in on my hesitation. "She's a ruthless business woman. She'll do anything for the job."

"I know her well enough."

I clear my throat and push the photos back, annoyed and angry at myself for letting his vile suggestions spend even a second in my mind. He hadn't been there last night, hadn't kissed tears off Jocelyn's cheeks or seen the way she smiled this morning, sweet and innocent in that pink dress of hers, as if this were the first time she'd fallen in love.

Maybe it was. It certainly is the first time I've fallen so hard for another. Because of this, I know I'll protect her, no matter the cost.

"If I sign with you, these photos get burned?" I ask, tapping the contract.

"Take them with you, frame them for all I care," Rumpert says. "I don't have copies."

My mind flicks to the idea of grabbing these, ripping them to shreds, and then leaving here for good.

"If you really do love each other, there'll be more where they came from," Andy says with an easy shrug. "Take them and run. I never figured you for a runner, though. I always thought you'd stand and fight."

"This contract is for five years. Make it one," I tell him. "We'll go from there."

Rumpert grins. "Thought you might say that. Here."

He withdraws a second contract with slightly better terms. I pick up the proffered pen. "I should have my lawyer look at this."

"You should," he offers. "Or you can trust that everything's there. I'm not trying to pull any funny business on the contract. I do truly want to work with you—in fact, I want to work with you so badly, I had my friend play paparazzi for the day. I don't do that for just anyone."

"I'm flattered."

"Great. Then sign here."

I pick up the pen, sign it, fold the paper in half, and then hand it to him just as the coffee comes. "These are mine?"

He pushes the photos toward me. "Have a ball. There's a great frame shop in Santa Monica. I have a guy there, if you need a recommendation."

"Shut up, Rumpert."

"Glad to be working with you, Boxer. We'll talk back in Los Angeles. Safe flight, have fun visiting your daughter."

My fingers flex at his ability to know seemingly endless amounts of information. One of these days, I think, I'm going to let my hand do as it may. I have a feeling it won't end pretty.

I tuck the photos into my pocket and stomp back toward the car. I growl out the name of the airport and grouch my way through security. It's not until Charli calls me five minutes before take off that my blood pressure notches down a bit.

"I love you, daddy," she says after updating me on her latest dream, a story that takes no less than twenty minutes to tell in a rambling fashion. "Is your best friend coming too?"

"No, Jocelyn's on her way back to LA. We'll see her soon though."

"Okay. I miss you. And her."

"Me too, honey. Me too." I sigh as we begin boarding, and I'm forced to hang up with Charli. One night away, and everything turns into a disaster. This is why I can't have nice things.

As I buckle my seatbelt on the plane, I fashion a few messages to Jocelyn. None of them sound just right, and I can't manage to put my thoughts into a coherent text that doesn't sound absolutely nuts. She's still in the air, so calling is out of the question.

Finally, I settle on a simple message:

Joss, I miss you. Please call me tonight. Would love to chat.

It's simple, to the point, and hopefully doesn't send up too many alarm bells. But, if I know the way the world works, she'll hear the news before she lands.

Rumpert is a jerk, but he knows what he's doing, and he'll make sure Jocelyn knows, too. I sigh again, fumbling to type out a second message when the stewardess asks us to put our phones in Airplane mode.

"Missing someone?" the woman says, kindly watching me switch my phone off with a reluctant glance upward.

"You could say that."

She pats my shoulder and moves onward.

Missing someone doesn't even cut it. My gut aches, I have a headache, and I'm lost not being able to talk to Jocelyn, to see her face to face. Everything happened so fast, and now I have six hours of no cell service to stew in my own thoughts.

It ain't gonna be pretty.

CHAPTER 38

Jocelyn

I PEEL THE mask off my face, smiling at the world. I haven't been able to sleep on a plane in years. Usually I'm so tense I leave the cabin with a knot in my shoulders the size of a softball, but not today.

Today, the cabin smells fresh and floral, and my neighbors—a young couple with a baby—seem adorable, and not at all annoying, despite the thirty minutes of straight screaming from the child.

I suppose that's what a night of falling in love will do to a woman—it changes her, and turns the world just a few more shades of pink. Love, or maybe it was the marathon of delicious, toe-curling sex. That probably didn't hurt.

All these years of yoga, I think, and I'd been doing it all wrong. I didn't need any of that deep breathing crap or stretching business, I just needed a few solid orgasms with a magnificent specimen of male.

"Fun weekend?" The harried mom asks next to me, bouncing her baby up and down. "You look so refreshed and carefree."

"Oh, yes." I grin. "It was incredible."

"New love?" She leans against her husband's arm, who's too busy staring out the window to notice. "It's written on your face," she whispers. "I remember those days. So great."

"It is!" I fan myself. I've never been one to make many girl-friends, not besides Lindsay, at least—and I pay her to be involved in my life. That sort of means she has to be my friend. "He's the most incredible guy in the world."

"I'm so happy for you. Enjoy it."

"Thank you," I say, smiling as the baby smiles back at me. "What about you? Does it ever fade?"

"It doesn't fade," she says, again tossing a grin over her shoulder. "It just changes. No glamorous weekends in New York for us, at least not now. But that's okay because we have something more important than ever . . . don't we, Charlie?"

"His name is Charlie?" I ask, sticking out a finger until he latches on. "He's so sweet."

"We think so too!" She uses a high-pitched baby voice. "Six months tomorrow, isn't that right, buddy?"

"I can't imagine how you do it all. Do you stay home with him?"

"Nope, I'm a teacher."

My eyes widen in surprise. "How?!"

She laughs. "You sort of just do it. Priorities fall in order—sometimes they change or adjust, but it's doable. Plenty of women do it. Do you want kids?"

My smile grows fainter. "I'm not actually sure."

"They're great. A lot of work, but we think we'll keep this guy, don't we, Charlie?"

The baby giggles, as if he understands the joke.

We gear up for landing, and the mother becomes engrossed in keeping the baby from crying. I can't help but wonder if I'd be any good at it—if that's even the life for me.

Boxer already has a child. I love Boxer, and if we stay in love, the next logical step—sometime in the future—is marriage. That would make me a mother of sorts, and the thought sends a shiver down my spine.

I want to be good at it—to have the soft touches like the woman next to me, the goofy voices that make her son smile, but it doesn't come natural to me. Charli deserves the best mother the world can provide, but what if I'm not good enough for her?

"How'd you know when you were ready?" I ask the woman as we land. "To have kids."

"You're never ready," she says. "You just jump in and figure it out from there. Don't overthink it too much. Things fall into place."

"Thanks," I say, gathering my things as the doors to the plane open. "It was really nice meeting you and Charlie. You have a beautiful family."

"Enjoy your young love," she calls, winking after me. "He's a lucky guy."

I'm so distracted by this family, my new friend who's name I'll never know, that I forget to turn my phone on until I hop into a taxi. Once there, I finally power up my cell, give the driver my home address, and sit back as the messages roll in.

The first one is from Lindsay.

Scratch that, the first three are from my assistant.

Lindsay: Nice weekend?! Deets, please!

Lindsay: What happened with Boxer?!

Lindsay: Boss! Are you flying? What happened with Rumpert?

Lindsay: Call me, boss.

Boxer: Joss, I miss you. Please call me tonight. Would love to chat.

Confused, I hit speed dial to Lindsay. "What's going on?" I say the second she answers. "Why all the urgent texts?"

"Why didn't you tell me?" Lindsay says, her voice high pitched. "Boxer signed with Rumpert?!"

"What?"

She hesitates. "You didn't know."

"That can't be," I tell her, sounding more confident than I feel. "Trust me, this weekend was . . . incredible."

"That's great, boss, but I think you should swing by."

"Your apartment?"

"You remember the address?"

"Yes, of course."

"Seriously," she says. "Swing by."

I update the address to the driver, who makes a sharp left at the next light. Meanwhile, I hover my finger over Boxer's message, but I don't click into it. He's still flying, so it'd do no good to respond. And there's the small fact that I don't even know what I'm responding about.

All I know is that my pink dress seems suddenly pale, and I feel like an idiot for wearing it. It'd seemed like such a fun idea this morning, so new and fresh, marking the start of something just as new and fresh between Boxer and myself.

But now Rumpert . . . of course Rumpert weaseled his way into this.

I just need to find out what stunt he pulled this time.

CHAPTER 39

Jocelyn

"GOT ANY PLANS tonight?" Lindsay opens the door to her apartment with a bottle of wine in hand. "Because this is for you."

She pushes it into my arms before relieving me of my suitcase and pulling it inside behind me.

"That bad, huh?" I ask, taking a look around her apartment. I've been here a few times, not so much for socializing, but for late night conferences or tough decisions made easier over a glass of wine.

Her place is cute and adorable—all things my expensive, somewhat cold condo will never be. She's got throw pillows the color of Skittles decorating her couch and warm glowing lights lining her living area. It's the grown up version of a college dorm room, and one can't help but feel warm and welcomed inside.

"I'll drive you home," Lindsay says. She leaves the suitcase and my carry-on in the middle of the entryway and stalks toward the kitchen. The ankle-length skirt she's wearing swishes around her bare feet, and she's got somewhat of a flower-child vibe going on. "In exchange, you can pay me in news. Tell me about your weekend."

"Why did you call me over here?" I slide off my heels and plod, also barefoot, into the kitchen. "Sounds urgent."

"Tell me about your weekend, first. Because there's a chance I'm dumb and confused."

"Nope." We slide onto bar stools, and I clink my glass against hers. "You're definitely not dumb."

"Confused, then."

"Probably not that either, but I am," I admit. "I can't figure out what happened between my taking off and my landing that has everyone in an uproar."

"Everyone?" She raises her eyebrows.

I shrug. "Okay, you are everyone."

She lets out a laugh, shaking her head as she takes a healthy sip of wine. "Just one glass for me, then I'm driving. What happened? I'm not asking again, so 'fess up."

"It was . . ." I feel a rush of excitement returning as the memories flood back. The hot kiss in his dressing room, the feel of his body against mine, soft sheets shrouding us, the bursts of laughter that made even the most tender, sensual moments something filled with happiness. "Amazing."

"So, you slept with him?"

I hold up a few fingers to demonstrate exactly how many times.

Her jaw falls open. "Damn, woman! You were only in town, what—twenty-four hours? You've been busy."

"But he's so . . ." I pause, debating which word to use first. He's so many things, and I can't possibly pick between generous, kind, sexy, romantic. "He's incredible. God, I sound like a teenager over here."

"You're in love! Did you tell each other?!"

I grin, wait for a suspended second, and then nod.

"Ohmigod."

"I know! I didn't plan on it. I most certainly didn't prepare anything, and I never dreamed it would happen—especially not this weekend, so soon. But everything just felt right. I wasn't an idiot, was I?"

"No, you're not."

I frown. "That doesn't sound nearly as convincing as I hoped it would. What did I do wrong? Is there some dating taboo I'm not aware of that I broke? He said it first, so I figured it wasn't too soon."

"I'm just confused at one piece of the equation," Lindsay says, eyebrows furrowing. Her glass of wine is forgotten on the counter as she leans in nearer to me. "If you both are madly in love, then why the hell did Boxer sign a contract with Andy Rumpert?"

I blink. "He didn't."

She sits back, fingernails tapping against the counter. "Then color me confused."

"Who did you hear this from?"

"Andy."

"What?!"

"He called my cell—my cell phone, and I don't even know how he has that number—to congratulate you. Through me. It was bizarre."

"Congratulate me on what?"

She clears her throat. "Your relationship."

"Why would he do that without telling me, without saying anything?"

"You had no clue about this whole thing?"

My face colors, and it doesn't escape Lindsay.

"What am I missing?" she says. "Tell me what you left out."

"Andy showed up in New York," I tell her. "Out of the blue. From what I can tell, Boxer was completely surprised too. At least, it seemed like it—I'm not so sure anymore. We never talked about it."

"Where? Why?"

The details here are all hot and fuzzy, and a flush of warmth to my stomach has me blushing again as I recall the details. "Rumpert visited the shoot Saturday afternoon and surprised us both."

Lindsay's barely holding back a smile. "And?"

I roll my eyes and lower my voice, as if someone's listening. "We were making out in Boxer's dressing room, and things were getting all steamy when Rumpert knocked on the door and inter-rupted everything."

Lindsay leans forward, her face in her arms, clearly stifling laughter. "I'm trying not to be insensitive."

I groan, the images coming back to me in droves. Boxer pressed against me, his hand on the mirror, holding me in his arms as we spiraled into an abyss of desire. "The fingerprints."

"Fingerprints?"

I explain a few more of the details and Lindsay eats it right up, wearing a look of surprise and an odd smile on her face.

"I didn't give you enough credit, boss," she says. "That sounds like a fantastic make out session."

"It was," I tell her. Even at a time like this, I can't deny it, nor can I wipe the satisfied smirk off my face. Until I remember the evidence. "But I'll bet you anything Rumpert connected the dots. It's not like Boxer was wearing a ton of clothes, and I was probably all flustered, and with everything else . . ."

"What does it matter if he put everything together or not?" Lindsay shrugs. "It's your business who you make out with and where."

I give her a look. "It's Andy."

"Right."

"Where there's a will, he'll find a way to ruin things."

"Boxer didn't say anything about meeting with him?"

"No, he . . ." I pause, flicking through memories of this morning when he'd begun to say something about meeting someone, and I'd filled in Charli. "He didn't volunteer anything."

"Maybe he was trying to keep you out of it?"

"Maybe," I say. "Any thoughts on where Rumpert is now?"

She shrugs. "I've got his number, since he just phoned."

"What do you say about calling him back?"

She clicks dial. "Should I talk, or do you want to?"

I push the wine glass away. "I'll handle this one."

CHAPTER 40

Jocelyn

"I'LL WAIT HERE," Lindsay says as she pulls up in front of Andy's office building. "I figure you want privacy on this one."

"Probably best," I say, climbing out of the car. "Thanks again for the ride. I don't know what I'd do without you."

"Me neither," she says on a laugh. "But I guess you've been hiding some things from me."

"Hiding things?" I frown, turning back to glance through the window. "What do you mean?"

"Here I thought you were all buttoned up and proper, and it turns out you're macking on hockey stars in their dressing rooms!"

I roll my eyes, standing and waving her off with my free hand.

"Show him who's boss in there, alright?"

I give her a thumbs up and hike my purse higher onto my arm before striding inside. He's working on a Sunday—go figure. My phone call with him had been brief, and I'd all but demanded an invitation to wherever he was hiding out.

It wasn't a far jaunt to reach him. In fact, he'd sounded prepared for my phone call, even though it'd come from Lindsay's number. Clearly, he'd been coaxing me on, planting the breadcrumbs I'd been eating up every step of the way.

Even as I can't bring myself to regret a moment of my weekend with Boxer, I feel soft, vulnerable and exposed as I march into Andy's building. I summon a faux cloud of confidence around me, but it's weakened; I'm weakened. Because now I have something that's more important than my job, and that puts me at a disadvantage.

Despite the mask of confidence, I'm aching inside. Hurt by Boxer's hesitation to confide in me, to give me even the slightest inkling what he was thinking on the matter of an agent. Whether or not he signed with me, it didn't matter. What hurt worse is that he hadn't talked to me about his decision at all, not a word. Not even a text to let me know before Rumpert blindsided me with his shiny news that'd be sure to make the rounds by tomorrow morning.

"Ah, lovely seeing you here," Andy says, as I bypass the lobby and open his office door without knocking. "It's been so long."

"What's going on?" I don't mince words even as he scans me, head to toe. "Rumpert, eyes on my face."

His gaze lingers at the hem of my dress, a bit of curiosity there, more than anything. As if wondering what's underneath, what's behind the curtain.

The stupid pink curtain.

I shouldn't have worn pink—this is why I never veer from my standard black uniform. On the one day that I do, I have to face my nemesis down wearing cotton candy colors and flushed cheeks from a night spent thinking about everything but work.

A wave of stupidity rolls over me. All these years of hardening myself, preparing myself for the worst—never letting a crack, a fissure weaken my spine of steel. So what if I'd earned horrid nicknames? At least I'd been consistent. Stable. Reliable.

Now, it feels as if everything I've worked for all of these years has faded to nothing. A wave of embarrassment racks over me as

I stand before the one man I desire more than anything to beat. To win. I don't even know the game we're playing, but I hate that I'm losing.

"Nice color," Rumpert says. "It looks good on you."

"What'd you pull on Boxer?"

"Pull? Nothing. We had a lovely chat."

"When?"

"Oh, he didn't share?" Rumpert sits back in his chair, arms folded behind his head. "We set up our little meeting on Saturday afternoon. We had a nice breakfast today."

"What makes you think he'd tell me that?" I shake off the jolt of surprise—it had been pre-planned? I'd been assuming that something had happened behind Boxer's back, or last minute, or that there is some logical explanation for everything. "We're acquaintances. He's allowed to meet with whomever he wants."

"Don't play that game with me."

"I don't know what game we're playing here, Andy. I'd love a little clarity."

"Love, funny word, isn't it?" Rumpert eases forward and pushes a small stack of papers near me. "Boxer signed with me for a year this morning in New York."

I blink, staring down at the papers. Sure enough, there's a signature scribbled on the lines, and the rest of the contract looks to be standard and in order.

I wish I had a smart retort, a comeback of sorts, but I have nothing. My energy is draining slowly, surely through my limbs, seeping out every pore. In seconds, I fear I'll collapse.

"He loves you, I'll give him that." Rumpert raises an eyebrow. "So, if we're playing the game of love, sure, you win. But the rest of the game, the most important game of all . . . I win."

"Your priorities are not in order," I tell him as he taps Boxer's name on the signature line. "If you think that's what's most important."

"You wouldn't be so upset if it didn't bother you."

"I'm upset because you're playing dirty. How did you get him to agree to this?"

"I'm persuasive." He waves his hand, then returns it behind his head. The room is filled with flashy, showy bits of trophies, plaques, and other paraphernalia blaring his name. "I'm good at my job."

"Humor me. How'd you do it?"

"Let's just say I gave Boxer a keepsake of his stay in New York."

"Keepsake?"

"Don't worry, I saved one for you." He reaches into his desk drawer and removes a photograph, then slides it across to me. "This is the last copy. I promised him I'd handed them all over, but I kept this one for you."

The photograph has a startling effect on me, causing my throat to swell up, my heart to beat faster and faster until my fingers come to rest on the edge of the photo, my legs pressing into the front of his desk as I sway.

"When did you take this?" I shake my head, and rephrase. The photo is of Boxer and I locked in a sensual kiss, his hands on my lower back, my fingers entwined through his hair. "I realize when, but . . . never mind. It doesn't matter. You blackmailed him?"

"I wouldn't say that. I merely showed him these images and explained what it might look like to the rest of the community should these get out and about."

"You threatened to ruin my reputation," I say quietly. "And he did whatever you asked of him to spare me the repercussions."

"Love makes a man do strange things. Though, I really think it will be a great partnership between the two of us. Maybe I'll see you around."

I pick up the contract, reading it over. It's firm, locked in solid, and my heart sinks with each paragraph.

"Looks pretty, doesn't it?" Andy says.

My throat is too tight to speak. I gaze over the rest of it, my eyes coming to land on his name down below. I stutter, cough, and then cover it up by clasping a hand to my forehead. "I don't want to see this anymore."

Andy clucks sympathetically. "It'll be okay, sweetheart."

I don't trust myself not to give everything away, so I forgo a retort on his term of endearment. Before leaving, I swipe the photo from his desk.

"Tell my newest client hello for me, will you?" Andy calls after me.

Once again, I don't have the willpower to respond.

However, I do find it in me to smile.

As I walk out the front door, I look down at the photo, and I know exactly what I must do. Because on that dotted line there was a signature, but it didn't read Landon Boxer.

He'd left me a sign, and thank goodness I hadn't been so blinded that I missed it.

Instead of his own name, he'd signed mine. With one tiny addition—my first name, and his last name.

Jocelyn Boxer, I murmur, trying the name on for size. Not half bad.

Even better, it was a little sign from him that he'd been thinking of me, and a simultaneous message to Rumpert. Nobody is coming between us.

I climb into the car, grinning like a madwoman which spikes Lindsay into overdrive mode. "Where to? Tell me what happened in there, boss."

"What's that reporter's name who keeps calling?"

"Diana, why?"

"Get her on the phone, please. Now."

CHAPTER 41

Boxer

"AND SHE LIVES happily ever after."

"Dad!" Charli shrieks. "You can't just say that and skip half of the story."

"I didn't skip half of the story," I grumble, smoothing my daughter's hair back from her forehead. We're in my parents' home, curled together in the room where I grew up as a child. Charli's eyes had been closed, her breathing somewhat heavy, and I'd thought she'd passed out pages ago. So, I'd skipped to the end of the book.

Apparently, that wasn't the case. The girl slept with one eye open and had Rapunzel memorized backward and forward.

"Tough crowd, huh?" I tell her.

"Flip back to the part where she lets her hair down," Charli says. "You're not pulling the wool over my eyeballs."

I prepare to resume the story, a reluctant smile taking over as I remind myself to slow down and enjoy this moment. Time has already flown by far too quickly—last time I looked, Charli was a pink cheeked infant. Today, she's six years old, and smarter than me.

But there's an anxiousness underneath all of the goodness, the sweetness of being united with my little girl. Jocelyn hasn't called me, hasn't texted me all evening. I landed a few hours ago, and with the time change, it's evening here, bedtime already.

I should've heard from her by now.

Charli's eyes sink closed again, but every time I slow my reading, my own eyes drowsy from the lack of sleep the previous evening, she pinches me gently until I keep going.

On the third pinch, I realize my mind has been wandering, and I've been reading the same words over and over again for the last few minutes. Charli's eyes have left the pages of the book, and have turned to watch my face.

"What's wrong, dad?"

"Wrong?" I shift, straightening in bed. "Nothing's wrong. Just lost my place."

"Ten times."

I sigh and reach out to draw her closer to my side. "Fine, I have something on my mind. And I'd like to talk to you about it."

"Okay." Charli scoots higher, too, pulling her favorite blanket with her. "But you still didn't finish the book."

"We'll finish it," I promise. "But first, I want to talk to you about Jocelyn."

"What about Jocelyn?"

"What do you think about her? Do you like her?"

"She's nice. She's pretty, sort of like Rapunzel."

I laugh at the image, but it's not completely wrong. Long blonde hair, the only difference being Jocelyn rarely wears it down. "What would you say if I wanted my happily ever after to be with Jocelyn?"

"You love her?"

"Yes, I think I do."

"More than me?"

"In a different way than I love you." I pull Charli to me, kiss the soft skin of her cheek. "Nobody can ever compare to you."

"Well, okay then."

"Okay?"

"Okay!" She yawns. "You want to marry Jocelyn?"

Again, Charli's ten steps ahead of me, and it's throwing me for a loop. "I think I'd like that, eventually. For now, though, I want to know if I have your permission to date her."

She frowns. "I thought she was just your business friend."

"She was . . ." I sigh. The benefits of having an intelligent daughter are balanced out by her using that perceptiveness against me. "But I want that to change. It already has a little bit, but before things change anymore, I want to make sure it's okay with you."

"Are you going to start leaving me at nights to go away with her?"

"No! No, not at all. It will just mean the three of us spend more time together."

"Will she live with us?"

"Maybe down the line, if we decide to get married."

"Okay."

"Okay . . . what?"

"That sounds good. Can you finish the book?"

"Oh, uh . . . sure. Do you have any questions?"

"Can you finish the book?"

"About Jocelyn. I want to make sure it's okay with you, honey."

"Dad." Charli wiggles around until she's facing me. Her hands circle around my wrists as she looks into my eyes. "Rapunzel gets to live happily ever after. You should, too."

"Charli—" I'm stunned into silence, but it only lasts a moment.

"Can we keep reading, please?"

I smile, nuzzle in against the comforter as the story, this time, sounds weightier. Almost a little too close to home, despite the magic and witches and fairytales between the pages. Who knows?

Maybe there's a bit of magic in this world, too.

I continue, flipping pages until we've reached the last one. Finally, the words *The End* appear with sweet relief, and I kiss Charli's bouncy curls goodnight as her eyelids flutter with dreams.

I make my way into the living room to say goodnight to my parents. They're both waiting up, and I can see in their eyes I'm not getting off easy. They're chatterboxes by nature, and my mother's got this look in her eye that means she's got some questions she wants answered.

"Where are you off to so quickly?" she asks. "Charli's down for the night?"

"She is," I say. "Rapunzel knocks her out every time."

My dad sits next to my mom, his eyes half closed. He's more interested in snoozing in his chair, but my mother likely dragged him to the kitchen table. His only incentive to stay here is the glass of whiskey she fixed him.

"So . . ." My mother says, her birdlike nose pointed in the air. "Did you have a nice trip?"

"I did." I lean against the edge of the table, knuckles curled over the back of the chair, but I can tell it's not going to be enough. Even so, I give it one last go. "I'm pretty tired, so I might hit the hay—"

"Take a seat, honey," my mother croons. "We barely see you these days. Give me five minutes of your time."

I heave myself into the seat.

"Want some whiskey?" my dad asks. "Get it yourself. It's in the kitchen."

I wave it off. "Playoffs Friday. I'll pass this time."

"Good job, honey," my mother says. "We're proud of you. Aren't we, Arnold?"

My dad grunts and takes a sip of his drink.

"Yes, we are," my mother repeats. "But more importantly, we hear you have a new best friend."

Neither of my parents are particularly wowed by my career, my money, or the hint of fame that comes with it. Keeps me humble.

If anything, I felt their disappointment when Lauren left harder than anything. They didn't blame it on me, they just . . . wanted to see me happy. With a neat little family unit just like their own and, though it came from a good place, it hurt me, too.

I wanted that family unit. I wanted a wife, and I thought I'd wanted it to be Lauren. I'm not sure if they ever understood that. For my mother, a woman who lived for her children, she couldn't understand why a woman would ever want to leave her family. She always suspected there was something else going on when, the sad truth was, I just wasn't enough for her.

I'd given up on arguing a long while back. My dad probably had a stern talk with my mother about it, and since then, we've ignored the issue. The missing mother, the absent wife. My lack of interest in finding either.

"And which little birdie told you this?" I ask, stalling.

"Well, Charli of course," my mother says. "She catches onto a lot, you know. Pays to be careful what you say, who you introduce to her."

"I am very careful, ma."

"She seems quite taken with your new friend."

"Her name is Jocelyn, and you can stop calling her my friend. We're dating."

My dad's eyebrows shoot up. "Hell hath frozen over."

I roll my eyes to the ceiling. "Look, I appreciate the support, or whatever this is, but I'm a grown man. I can handle my own affairs, and I can handle how I raise my daughter and who she meets. Thank you for the input."

"Oh, honey, we're not trying to get those undies of yours in a twist," my mother says. "Honestly, we're just here to help. I am just wondering why we haven't heard anything about her before?"

"Her name is Jocelyn Jones, and we met through work," I tell them. "She's a sports agent, and she's fantastic at her job. She's beautiful, and smart, and kind, and if you come down and visit, you'll get to meet her."

"Meet her?" My mother appears on the verge of shock. "You are going to let us meet a woman in your life, Landon Boxer?"

"God, ma. Not if you're going to act like this."

"Steven told us that—"

"Hold on, you've talked to Steven about this, too? I thought you said Charli."

"Well, we had to do our research once we heard you had a special friend," my mother says. "Steven says she's very beautiful. I can't believe your brother met her before us. Your own parents!"

"Bring her up here," my dad says. "I hate the city."

"You live in San Fran," I tell him. "That's a city. LA is an hour flight."

He snorts in derision.

"Arnold, we'll go visit. When can we visit, honey?" My mother looks between us. "Come on, boys, cooperate."

"After playoffs," I tell them, standing. "Now, I have to get going. I have a phone call to make and sleep to catch up on."

My mother spreads her arms wide, and I play the dutiful son as I make my way around the table and wrap her in my arms. She feels small, more fragile, and I'm reminded that she's not growing younger. I clasp her a little bit tighter, warmed by the scent of cinnamon rolls lingering on her clothes.

"Love you, ma."

"Thank you for coming, honey." My mother's nails dig into

my shoulders. "You can tell us things, you know. We're very happy for you."

My dad claps me on the shoulder, and that's as much affection as I'll get from him, which is fine by me. We have a *no emotions are good emotions* policy between us.

"I will, ma. Come and meet her. I think you'll really be pleased."

"As long as you're happy."

When I straighten, I'm surprised to find tears in her eyes. She's got blue eyes like me, and there's a happiness radiating there, the same sort of happiness that I feel when I think of Jocelyn Jones.

"You love her, don't you?" she whispers.

I smile and bow my head. "I do."

My mother reaches out and clasps my father's hand in hers. Then without a word, she nods and waves me off with her hands. As I leave the room, I hear the gentle sound of sobs—happy tears, I assume—and my father's sympathetic grunts.

I get my emotions from my father.

Except for the underlying current of nerves that've had my stomach in knots all evening. I know that I threw the contract with Andy Rumpert and signed a mixture of Jocelyn's name and my own, adding insult to injury, but did she? Had she stormed straight to his office the second he spilled the news like I expected, or had she assumed the worst?

I pull out my phone and debate waiting for her to call me, but that's a dick move. I'm not playing games; I want her to know my intentions loud and clear. If Jocelyn and I don't work out, it's not going to be for lack of trying.

I'm a grown man, a father, and I know what I want. Her name is Jocelyn Jones, and I'm going after her.

Luckily, she picks up on the first ring. "Thank God," I groan.

"I've been thinking of you all day."

"Is that right?"

"I'm so sorry, I assume you've heard the news," I tell her. "I didn't mean—"

"I saw it."

"Saw . . ."

"The signature."

There's a coolness to her voice that I can't quite place. "And?"

"Clever."

"Are you upset? Look, I should've talked to you first, but everything happened so fast."

"Did you know about the meeting the day before?"

I run a hand through my hair. Her voice isn't accusatory, but there's a thin line of curiosity there. "Yes."

"And you didn't tell me about it."

"Rumpert surprised both of us in the dressing room—I had no idea he'd be there. I only agreed to a meeting with him because he wouldn't get the hell out of there, and I wanted to be alone with you. I swear."

"And the rest of the night, it didn't come up?"

"No, because I had other areas of focus."

She gives a light laugh, and I take this as a positive.

So I continue. "Seriously, Joss. We did the shoot, and after that, I had about two thoughts on my mind."

"I can guess one of them, but what's the other?"

"Besides getting you into bed, I had to let you know how I felt. I hadn't planned to tell you I loved you, but . . . I do. I did then. I mean it and I meant it, and that's why the idiot didn't enter my mind. I forgot about it right up until the meeting."

"I'm not mad," she says softly. "I just wanted to hear you say that. I love you."

"I love you too. I need to see you this week—tomorrow when I get back." I pause, rub a hand over my forehead. "Shit, I have practice. And the next day, Charli's got something at school. With playoffs—"

"Hey, stop talking," she says gently. "I've got a better idea. Take this week to get back on schedule. Spend time with Charli. I stole you for the whole weekend, so I can be patient. Friday night, after your game, maybe we can make plans."

This woman is a godsend. I can't afford to focus elsewhere on the week of playoffs, but for her I would, if it meant I could keep her. "Do you mean that?"

"I do," she says. "Friday night."

"When Rumpert realizes what happened—"

"Don't worry about it," she says, her voice soothing. "I have a plan. Let's just wait until Friday, and we can talk in person."

"Friday it is," I tell her. "Joss, before I tell you goodnight . . . do you trust me?"

"Of course I do."

I nod, swallowing hard. "Good. I should've talked to you before the meeting, I know. I'm sorry. But when he pulled out those photos, I didn't think, I just reacted and—"

"I get it," she says. "Thanks for calling. I hope you finished Rapunzel first."

"Yes, but you might have to meet my parents."

"What?!"

"Goodnight, Joss," I tell her. "I'll call you tomorrow."

"Goodnight, Landon. Sweet dreams."

I climb into bed, the sound of her words fresh on my ears. When I dream, it's of holding her close, and when I wake, the bed is too cold and empty.

Sometime in the middle of the night, I move into the room where I slept as a child and join Charli. She curls into my arms, a warm little figure, and finally, I rest.

CHAPTER 42

Jocelyn

FRIDAY NIGHT BEGINS with a plan.

I hang up the phone with Boxer, smiling about the evening ahead. He's supposed to go on and win his game. I'm supposed to watch from the stands, and then head straight to his house afterward where Marie and Charli will surely be waiting up. He'll deal with his post-game business and meet us at home.

To say I'm anxious is an understatement. Between his schedule and my workload, we haven't been able to see one another all week. It works out fine, really, since I have a surprise for him that wasn't ready until tonight.

"Headed home," I call to Lindsay as I pack up my things from the office. "I'm sorry there wasn't an extra ticket. I could've used moral support."

"No problem," she says with a grin in my direction. "I don't think you'll miss me as much as you think. I'm going to watch it from home with Mark."

I raise my eyebrows. "The boyfriend's still going strong?"

"Knock on wood," she says. Then she raps her knuckles against the desk with a cheeky wink. "You and me both. Look at us being adults and romantic and all of that crap."

I do something I rarely do, but I'm in a giddy mood. I waltz around the desk and pull her into a hug. "Mark is a lucky guy."

"Oh, boss," she groans. "I don't know how to handle the new you."

"The new me?"

"Emotions and hugs, and all of this . . ." She gives a faux shudder. "You're so . . . human."

I shake my head, making my way to the door. "Oh! The thing with Diana? How's that coming along?"

"She has it ready. Swing by on your way to the rink."

"You're a rock star. Don't stay late today, okay?"

"Date with Mark, remember? I'm going to close up as soon as you leave."

I head down and retrieve my car, pulling it onto the streets of LA with just a hint of nerves fluttering in my stomach. Two hours until game time, and I have so much still to accomplish.

First order of business is to swing by my new reporter friend's office. I met Diana for one of my first ever interviews earlier this week, and she's prepared a little something in return. It could either be an ingenious solution to my problems, or it could completely backfire and ruin everything.

I'm crossing my fingers for the former.

"Thanks again for doing this," Diana says as I swing by her office. She's short, her skin a gorgeous shade of mocha, and she's wearing a bright shade of pink on her lips. "I'm really excited to share this with everyone. I hope I did the story justice."

I take a look at the bundle in my hands, nod and smile. "It's perfect. Thank you, Diana. Oh, and one more thing?"

"Anything."

"Where did you get that lipstick?"

★ ★ ★

TWO HOURS LATER, I'm running late to the game, hoping my tardiness is worth it. I'd decided that tonight, of all nights, called for a colorful occasion—and since I didn't own many colorful clothes, I took Diana up on her suggestion and hit the mall.

There, I'd found a summery yellow dress that hung to just above my knees, tapered through my waist, and fluttered in wispy sleeves high on my shoulder. It wasn't *exactly* appropriate attire for a hockey game, but I wasn't focused on the game; I was intent on making sure the evening which followed it went perfectly.

When I arrive at the arena, the emptiness of a line outside makes it clear that I'm running behind. I hand over my car to the valet, hustle inside, and find my seat. I'm halfway through scanning the seats for a familiar face, when my eyes lock on the one face more familiar than any other.

Boxer gives a wave from down on the ice. He's waiting for his name to be called, and he must've been scanning the stands relentlessly to find me so quickly. My breath hitches at the realization that it's me he was waiting to see.

I feel a little like a neon highlighter standing amid a sea of black sweaters and hug my dark shawl closer to my chest. Then, I wave back.

The game kicks off with the typical fanfare, and the first two periods fly by with such intensity I don't even have the chance to consider my sitting here alone. It's not until a familiar voice calls my name that I realize there's only a few minutes left in the game.

"Good one, huh?" Duke nods at the rink below. The score is tied one to one. "Boxer's having a fantastic game. Wonder if he's showing off for a special someone?"

I glance at my shoes—also new, very cute pumps—to hide the blush in my cheeks. "Showing off for future agents, I'm sure. You heard the news about him signing with Rumpert, I suppose?"

To my surprise, Duke shakes his head and worms his way into a seat next to me. We sit in silence for a long moment, whistles blowing in the background. "You've changed."

"Me?" It comes out sounding a little squeaky. "No, I don't think so."

"Your cheeks are doing that thing where they go all red. Never used to do that. I say Boxer's name, and you light up like a Christmas tree."

"Sorry."

He clears his throat. "Was that an apology? You're going soft, Jones."

I let my eyes slide closed for a second, alone despite the roar of the crowd. "He's ruined me."

Duke reaches over and squeezes my knee. "Any good man, or woman, will."

I feign a smile. "I haven't ruined him, at least."

Duke barks laughter. "Are you kidding me? The man's putty in your hands. I'll bet the only reason he's playing so hard today is to prove to himself he's not turning all googly eyed with love."

"So?" I offer a truce of a smile. "How'd you guess?"

"I know these things." He crosses his arms. "Sounds like you had a nice weekend in New York?"

"We did."

"Thanks for the endorsement lead. I'm going to take the missus on a quick trip to Palm Springs. We're renewing our vows the week after I retire."

"Congratulations."

"Nah, it's an excuse for a vacation." He blows it off, but I can see there's a hint of happiness underneath that hard exterior. "She deserves to be spoiled a bit."

I laugh. "I guess she's ruined you, too."

"Suppose you're right. So, give me the details. What happened with Andy?"

I bob my head to either side. "I'm still not sure."

"How did that happen?" Duke seems genuinely shocked, and more flatteringly, quite confused. "The man's a jackass."

"Yeah, well . . . don't count me out just yet." I sigh, cross my legs, and gaze at the ice for a second. "I think I have a way to fix it."

"I'm glad to see you haven't completely lost your touch."

We both turn to face the rink, the clock ticking down from a minute.

"Hey, Duke," I start. "What do you think—"

A collective gasp from the crowd mutes my next words. I turn back to the ice to see what's happening just in time to see Boxer's body sailing through the air and into the boards.

He lands with a crash, the sort of crunch of bones hitting surface that causes an entire room to cringe. Without realizing it, my hand reaches for Duke's and squeezes—so tight I'm not sure circulation can get through. My heart nearly stops. My breathing becomes painful.

I fly to my feet. "We've got to get down there. How? Duke! Get up! We need—"

"Sit down, you're not getting anywhere," Duke says. "You're pale as a ghost, and I'm not carrying you if you pass out."

"I'm not . . ." I see stars, and I quit speaking once more. I can't feel Duke's hand squeezing me back, or his voice telling me to come with him. I just sit. Still.

Still as Boxer, who hasn't moved once since he hit the boards and then the ice.

"What happened?" I manage to gasp as medics approach him. "Is he alive?"

"He'll be fine," Duke says. "It's hockey, men get banged up."

But there's an antsiness in the crowd that doesn't accompany all injuries, the sort of car wreck anxiety that at once has people unable to look away and brimming with sympathy all in one.

"But what if . . . is he unconscious?" I ask. I glance to Duke for the first time, really seeing him, and there's a note of worry there that undercuts everything else. "You're worried! What's happening with him?"

"Let's get out of here," he tells me. "Come on, he won't be finishing this game."

"But—"

"Come on."

We squeeze into the hallway with a few others struggling to leave before the rush of the final moments. As luck would have it, I recognize the man squeezing out right next to me.

"Jocelyn," Rumpert says. "Hello, Duke."

I'm too distracted to respond, but Duke mumbles something more sensible.

"I can handle this," Rumpert says. "Y'all can go on home. I'll head to the hospital with Boxer."

"Shut up, Rumpert, and go the hell home," Duke snaps. "You don't have to 'handle' anything."

"The hospital?" I murmur more quietly.

"I'll go to the hospital with you," Duke says as he sends Andy packing with a murderous glare. "Boxer clocked his head good, and I imagine they'll want to check him out. I won't leave you alone with Rumpert."

"No, it's okay, I have to go." I find myself speaking hollow words, as if it's a voice outside of my body that's speaking, and the rest of me is just listening. I turn to Duke. "Are you sure he's going to be okay?"

"Boxer? Yeah, the man's a wall of brick. He'll wake up, they'll poke at his bruises, and we'll all be on our merry little way."

"Then I . . . I can't make it to the hospital right now. I have to be somewhere else."

"Where the hell else do you have to be on a Friday night when your boyfriend's injured?" Duke asks, scanning my face for answers. With a jolt of understanding, he sees exactly where I'm headed, and he nods again in agreement. "Go on," he says more gently. "He'll appreciate it."

"Promise you'll call me with any updates."

"Only thing I'll be updating is Rumpert's nose. Flatten it a little, and . . ." He shakes his head as the dream fades. "I will, kid. Get going."

I climb in the car and cruise away from the rink.

There is only one person in the world who might need me more than Boxer. I point my car in her direction and press the pedal to the floor.

CHAPTER 43

Boxer

"MY DAMN HEAD hasn't hurt this bad since college," I moan. Someone's thrown me into a hospital bed, and I've got some beeps and buzzes and lights peering at me. "I'm alive, I'm fine. Let me out of here."

"Soon enough," Duke growls. "Stop being a princess and sit still."

I listen to his voice; I'm used to following orders from Duke. He has a no bullshit policy, and it has never led me astray.

The doctors and nurses finish up whatever they're doing, and I motion Duke over. While he approaches, I glance behind him. Through the door, I can see the shiny helmet that's Andy Rumpert's greasy hair, and the image makes me want to vomit. Or maybe that's the concussion.

"Why the hell did you let them bring me to the hospital?" I ask. "I'm fine. You know I'm fine."

"Red tape," Duke snarks. "Give them a few more hours, and I'll personally drive you home."

"My car?"

"At the rink."

"Great."

"It's fine, I'm sure there's someone who'll be happy to drive you back when you're not cross-eyed."

There's an ache inside that has nothing to do with my injuries at his insinuation. "Is she here?"

"No."

A hot flash of anger burns through me, along with a shred of hurt, but my reaction is interrupted as the doctor whisks me away for a few more exams. They poke and prod and whatever they do, while the only thing I can do is to sit and think.

Where is Jocelyn?

By the time I manage to free myself from the hospital, it's nearly morning. Save for a lingering dullness in my head and some instructions to take things easy for a few weeks—*yeah, right*—I'm free as a bird.

Duke pulls the car up to the hospital door, and as I slide into the passenger seat, he shoots me a questioning glance. "Did you figure it out in there?"

"Jocelyn? Yes."

"Good. Don't fuck this one up."

"Thanks for the advice."

"I'm serious, she's a keeper."

"You don't think I know that?"

Duke raises his eyebrow in response, and that's the rest of our conversation for the duration of the car ride. When we pull up in front of my house, I thank him and slide out.

"Hey," Duke says. "Congratulations. I want an invitation to your big day."

I shake my head, a smile toying on my lips, but it's too painful to continue, so I stop.

Duke pulls away from the curb, his old sports car too loud for my neighborhood at this time of night. Either that, or it's my head—hard to say. I'm just glad to be home.

The door creaks open to the darkened house. It's nearly five in the morning. Marie had planned to stay over in the guest bedroom, but I'd told her that if Jocelyn beat me home, she could take off early.

I duck back outside to check the hiding spot underneath the potted plant, but the key's still there. Either Marie let Jocelyn inside, or I was wrong, and she's not here at all.

I ease through the front door, not bothering to turn on the lights as I head straight to the staircase. Up I go, peeking into the open door of the guest bedroom as I pass it. Nothing, not even a ruffle on the bed.

I continue on, my heart thumping loud enough to wake the dead as I reach Charli's room. Her room is always my first stop when I come home late from a game.

I push open the door, as quietly as possible, and there is the answer to all of my questions. Jocelyn is curled on the bed with Charli, both of them fast asleep. Charli's little arms are wrapped tight around Joss's neck, her lips turned into a little pout.

Charli's curls bounce across Jocelyn's blonde strands, the two intermingling on the pillow, straight mixed with curly. I take a step into the room to watch them both for a long second, my heart constricting until it might very well explode.

Whatever love I'd confessed for her this weekend in New York seems already small, insignificant to what I'm feeling now. I want more than anything to tuck her in my arms and carry her to bed with me. To be mine, forever.

But I can't possibly break up the sleeping beauties, not when their faces look so peaceful. Surely they're dreaming of fairytales, of long-haired maidens dropping their hair out tower windows.

I take one step back, but I'm so intent on watching them sleep that I miss the squeaky floorboard, and under my weight, it sounds like the house is breaking in half.

Charli hardly stirs, but Jocelyn's eyes fly open, and she brings a hand to her forehead, brushing hair back from her face.

"What? I . . . where—oh." She glances first at Charli, then at me. "Boxer, oh, I'm so sorry. I hope you don't mind I came here—"

"Come with me." I extend my hand, clasp her soft fingers in mine. "Please."

I guide her through the house, feeling like a ghost of myself, until we reach the bedroom door. Pushing it open, I lead her into the room and pause, letting her scan the surroundings, her vision adjusting to the bright room washed with moonlight.

"How are you? Your head, your injury." She presses me into the room without a second thought, urging me onto the bed. Her hands stroke through my hair, her fingers cool and gentle, and it feels glorious. "I came here because I figured Charli would be worried, and you'd wanted me to relieve Marie, and I'm so sorry I couldn't be at the hospital for you."

"No, thank you. Thank you for everything."

She inhales a breath and glances at the open door. I'm trying to tug her in for a kiss, but she's hesitant. "Charli."

I solve that problem by sliding out from under Jocelyn and locking the door.

"But your injury," she says.

"I'm fine," I tell her. "I've had worse."

"You need rest."

"No," I rest a hand on her shoulder. "I need you. Stay here tonight?"

"Of course, but—"

"Stop," I tell her. "Whatever you were going to say can wait."

"But—"

"It can wait."

"You're injured," she says again, stroking her hand across my face.

"Not so injured that I don't want you."

"Believe me, I want you too." She pauses for a tender moment. "But for now, let's just be together."

I groan aloud, but I know she's right. So I settle for tugging on the yellow fabric fluttering high on her thigh. "By the way, you looked beautiful in the stands tonight. I love this dress on you."

"It doesn't look silly?"

I close my eyes for a long moment. "Silly? You never look silly. Stunning, perfect, feminine, maybe. Never silly."

"Do you have a t-shirt or something I could borrow? I didn't know if packing an overnight bag would be presumptuous."

I move to my closet and pull out an extra-large t-shirt that's old enough to be worn soft. "Will this work?"

"Thank you."

"If I had my say, you could just put that overnight bag in my closet and let it stay," I tell her. "You could even stay here with it."

"Are you asking me to move in with you?"

I give what I think is a seductive one shoulder shrug, but I probably look like an idiot. "If that's not too forward."

She strips out of her yellow dress, turning half sideways, as if that would do anything to keep my eyes off her. At my sharp inhalation of breath, she shoots a flirtatious smile in my direction that has me shedding clothes like I'm on fire.

"You're injured!" She tells me for the umpteenth time. Then she looks down, and her mouth parts in surprise. "Jesus, Boxer. You just walked out of the hospital."

"You have a way of making me crazy."

"Wait. Before anything else, I have something to show you."

I blink in surprise. "Show me?"

"Yes," she says. "I promised you I'd take care of things, and I need an opinion."

"Now?"

"Yes." Her fingers shake as she tugs my shirt onto her body. "Tonight."

I harden just seeing her in my clothes. I never want her to leave them. Or me. Or this house. To be here together, forever, is a dream.

"Okay," I agree. "But I can't possibly imagine what's more important than this."

When she blinks, confused, I finally pull her into my arms. The scent of her holds me hostage there, captive, and I plan on staying still until she pushes me away.

My fingers explore underneath the edge of her shirt, her soft bottom the perfect fit for my hands. Then I tease upward, playing with the edge of the lace panties. It's like a treasure chest just waiting to be opened.

"Boxer," she says, once my fingers begin to dance under the edges. "I have something to show you."

"Right." I clear my throat and pretend I'm not about to explode like a firecracker. "Business, then pleasure."

She smiles up at me. "If it weren't important, I wouldn't bother you with it now, but it's time sensitive."

"Fine," I tell her. "I'll behave. But for the record, in this house, we eat dessert first. Then business."

Her cheeks go pink, and she looks down at her hands. "Well, I think that sounds perfectly un-backwards."

"While you run downstairs, I'm going to jump in the shower quickly." I lean in, kiss her gently on the cheek. "And then you can show me whatever it is you have to show me."

CHAPTER 44

Jocelyn

AFTER A BRIEF trip downstairs to grab my purse, I return to Boxer's bedroom, pausing only to peek into Charli's room on the way back and ensure she's still sound asleep.

She is, drifting away in dreamland, eyelashes fluttering and small breaths puffing against her pillow. The word to use is sweet, but it's not strong enough. Her cheeks are strawberry pink, her lips matching, her hair like golden threads curled over the pillow. There's more beauty in one moment of watching her sleep than a lifetime of what I've known so far. The thought is sobering.

"There you are." Boxer appears at the door to his bedroom, his expression soft. "Come here, Joss."

I let my feet drag me toward him, my heart pulling me along for the ride. It's only once we're tucked safely inside, door shut and locked, that a breath rattles from my chest.

"I told you the other night that I'd fix this whole situation," I tell him. "And I had an idea."

"This is your idea?"

I nod, fingers shaking as I dig into my purse. "Please don't be mad."

"Mad?"

Boxer rinsed off in a five minute shower while I ran downstairs to collect my purse, and he is now dressed in shorts and an old Lightning sweatshirt. His hair is somewhat ruffled, and he smells like cedar and soap. I'd give just about everything to sink into his arms and forget about everything else.

"I'm . . ." I clear my throat. "I'll let it speak for itself."

I pull out a celebrity magazine commonly found in the check-out lines at grocery stores and, judging by his expression, he recognizes the name. *StarCrossed*.

"Page twenty-two," I say. "It's dog-eared."

He flips through the pages, every second taking a bit of my resolve away. My palms are sweaty, my breaths shallow. This might just be the stupidest thing I've ever done. If I've sabotaged everything with Boxer because of this move, I'll be devastated.

He reads through page twenty-two once, and it takes ages. Years. Centuries.

I clear my throat again, louder, reminding him that *hello*, I'm still here.

He doesn't bother to glance up, his expression completely unreadable.

"So?" I prompt. "Initial thoughts? It's a little late to do anything about it since these'll hit the stands shortly, but I wanted you to know, to see it first, and . . . now that I'm here, I'm realizing I should've probably talked to you about it first—"

"Lightning Love," Boxer reads aloud, one eyebrow twitching upward. "Catchy title."

"Do you hate it? You hate it."

"I haven't read it."

"What?!" I cross the distance between us in two steps. "What have you been doing this whole time?"

"Staring at you—your picture. You are beautiful."

Boxer turns the magazine around, his finger pointing to the image of me in my pink dress. It's the very same photo that Rumpert handed over to me on Sunday—the very one he'd been using to blackmail Boxer into signing with him.

"You handed this over to a reporter . . . voluntarily?" he asks.

"I didn't want you to feel trapped into a contract with Andy. I know you only signed it in the first place to protect me."

"But I didn't sign it accurately."

"No, but if we tried to keep this a secret, he'd make our life a living hell," I say, a note of frustration leaking out into my words. "If we're going to try to make this work, it's going to come out sooner or later. Me and you. Us. I figured—why not announce it early when we can control it?"

"You'd do this for me?"

"No."

He looks surprised.

I clear my throat. "For us."

His eyes return to the photograph. It's a beautiful moment captured; if I'd seen it on a magazine rack, I'd call it the picture of love.

"Jocelyn Jones sits down with me for what might be her first ever personal interview, Diana Morse writes," Boxer reads further, his eyes scanning the next sentence. "It seems love is brewing for this well-known . . ."

Boxer stalls, stumbling over the next words.

"Ice queen," I fill in. "It's okay. I approved the story."

He shakes his head, skips a few paragraphs, and resumes reading the questions from the text. *"Do you love him?"* His eyes look up, meet mine, and recite the words I'd stated quite clearly for Diana. *"Without a doubt."*

I blink, unable to hold his gaze.

"Do you mean it, Joss?"

I nod, raise a hand to wipe the edges of one of my eyes. "Yes, I do," I tell him. "I mean it a million times over."

Boxer sets the magazine down on the dresser and pulls me over to the bed in one motion. He's got his hands on my shoulders, our bare skin zinging against one another.

"You're hurt," I whisper, as his mouth trails tantalizing kisses down my neck. "Let's wait, we'll have plenty of opportunities."

"I'm fine."

"You were in the hospital."

"Then be gentle." He pauses for long enough to wink at me. "If you can stand it."

"Yes, of course. I'm just worried about—"

"Don't be," he murmurs, his hands reaching for the bottom of my shirt. "Thank you. For being here, for coming to Charli, for what you said to Diana."

I'm too sensitive, too tender to respond, so I close my eyes and let the sensations of his fingers wash over my body, caress my skin like a gentle waterfall.

He twirls me around, spinning me onto the bed like we're in some sort of slow dance, a tornado of sensuality. It begins like a gentle gust of wind, soft and tender, spiraling around us like stardust.

His mouth, his hands, our skin brushes against one another. Every touch is electric—building, burning until the breeze turns into a gust, and this thing, this relationship between us is clawing for more, demanding all the other has to give.

Landon lays me on the bed, my nakedness no longer a source of discomfort, but a measure of trust, a display for all that I am. The good, the cold, the fire burning deep within that is melting away the shields I've built up year over year.

Fingertips brush over my skin while my own dig into his hips. I pull him close. He pulls me closer. I let my hands roam free underneath his sweatshirt, guiding it gently over his head. His shorts go next. From the nightstand, he retrieves a condom and rolls it on before cradling me in his arms.

We're tangled together in the bed, my arms around his back, his hands pulling my hips toward him, lifting me off the comforter. The fabric, smooth to the touch, burns against my skin, every sensation intensified.

When his mouth meets mine, he presses against me and pauses, holding there for a long second.

"Please," I whisper finally.

He moans my name, nestles into my neck as my legs wrap around his back. When he eases inside, our breaths hiss together.

The gentle breeze that started everything now circles us in torrents, wild and free, desperate and crazed in our need to claim one another, to destroy all walls, boundaries, obstacles between us. To destroy the old, to weed away the dead to make room for the new.

We're spiraling together in a perfect parallel, each of his beats matched with one of my own, until we're driven to the edge, the fury, when suddenly it breaks, and we slip into the eye of the storm.

He stills, our breathing heavy, and he gives the slightest shake of his head. "I love you, Jocelyn Jones."

"I love you, too, Landon Boxer," I say, aching with the fullness of the words, of him.

His hand rises to stroke my cheek, his eyes the most piercing blue as they cut through every facade I've created, every layer of protection that exists around my heart.

I close my eyes. I feel too much, too hard when he looks at me. I'm not used to feeling worthy of such love, but when I'm with Boxer, he makes me feel every bit deserving of it, and that's what scares me the most.

He slides back, presses into me one last time, and together, we release. His name spills from my lips, stifled as I press my mouth to his neck and he rocks us both to a finish that leaves my body limp, my mind drained, my spirit wrung.

When the waves subside, he rolls me to him and curls me into his body.

"Promise me one thing, Miss Jones," he says.

I turn to face him, my hand rising to press through his hair of its own accord. "Anything."

"Will you be my agent?"

I still, my hand still ensnarled in his locks. "Are you serious?"

"Who says business and pleasure can't mix?"

I can only blink.

"I mean it," he says again. "I want you to be my partner. In love, in life, in business. In everything. If we're going into this, I'm not going to half-ass it."

"So we'll full ass it together?"

He gives a serious nod. "What do you say?"

I lean in, press my lips to his. "I say you've got yourself a deal, Mr. Boxer."

EPILOGUE

One Year Later

"GOOD MORNING, GORGEOUS."

His voice wakes me, eases me into reality from a peaceful slumber. Sunlight streams through the windows, washing Boxer's newly decorated bedroom with bright light.

He had the mancave decorations re-done when I moved in, and the outcome was a clean and cozy, refreshing style. Black furniture, gauzy curtains, colorful pops from pillows on the window seat. A plush white comforter rustles over me as I push it down, glancing up at the gorgeous face staring back at me.

"Hello, handsome." I push myself to a seated position, stretching, yawning as his eyes follow my every movement. I catch sight of the breakfast tray in his hands and frown. "What's the special occasion?"

Boxer sets the tray on the bedside table, then eases onto the bed next to me. "Happy Mother's Day to the most wonderful mother I know."

I rest a hand on my belly, not yet feeling the curve of the baby beneath my fingers. "We can't celebrate yet," I tell him, though the thought is so sweet it sends tears to tease my eyes. "We haven't told Charli."

After Boxer asked me to marry him last summer, we spent the fall adjusting to life as an engaged couple, moving in, testing out our new family unit. It'd been like a dream—smooth and simple and right.

We finally tied the official knot in a small ceremony just before Valentine's Day. *Small* ceremony being relative. I'd wanted it private and intimate, but Boxer had a zillion and one teammates and family members that needed an invitation, so the party had grown to nearly a hundred people.

Lindsay was there, too, of course, as was Duke. He was responsible for this whole thing starting in the first place, as he mentioned loudly and tipsily in his speech. Also present had been Diana, the reporter who'd run the magazine article for us—an article which, surprisingly, hadn't upset the world all that much with its release.

As it turned out, nobody cared about my dating Boxer. The people who did care were supportive. All except for one. Andy Rumpert. But he was forced to get over the article, and the failed contract, if he wanted to stay in the game.

Thankfully, a newer, shinier recruit had popped up for the next season looking for an agent. When I didn't challenge Andy for the new player, it'd led to an odd sort of truce between us. In exchange for Boxer, he got an easy card for a surefire moneymaker. I'd say I came out on top.

Maybe the best surprise guests of all had been Andi and Ryan Pierce. After Boxer had proposed, I'd finally taken Lindsay up on her offer to set up a meeting with the Minnesota Star, and my former recruiting interest, Ryan Pierce. I'd hosted the couple at a private lunch—without a word to Boxer—and apologized. For everything.

I apologized for the way I'd treated them, for the way I'd pushed apart a relationship that should've been left to flourish. A relationship that, in retrospect, was so clearly perfect.

I apologized for not believing Ryan, and for dismissing Andi, and most of all, for not listening when they'd tried to explain. Not only had they forgiven me, but they'd become some of our closest friends.

Shortly after the ceremony, we'd taken off for a long weekend in Hawaii. We were hesitant to leave Charli for too long, but we needn't have worried. She adored having her grandparents shuttle her to and from school and spoil her rotten.

Even so, it'd been a productive honeymoon as evidenced by my growing belly. What a surprise it had been to find out a baby had happened so quickly, and though we savored the news and excitement together, we'd decided not to tell anyone—not yet, at least.

There was something about keeping the news quiet, private for a few months, that felt special. However, the expiration date on our secret was fast approaching. I'd been pushing to tell Charli for the last couple of weeks, but Boxer had resisted, claiming we'd tell her when the time was right.

"I'm not talking about *this* Mother's Day." Boxer slides behind me so his back is resting against the headboard, his hands circling my waist to land over mine, gesturing toward the baby. "I'm talking about Charli."

"Charli?"

"Even before we were married, you loved Charli like your own. And these past few months . . ." Boxer trails off, his voice catching in his throat. "It's been incredible. Watching the two of you together. You complete our family in more ways than I ever could've imagined."

I swallow hard, blinking back tears that'd pricked the second he began talking. Spinning, I face him in bed, my hands coming to rest on either side of his face. My throat, still thick with emotion, can't seem to bear words, so I press a kiss to his lips, instead.

A tender, gentle kiss. He responds immediately. Then more urgently, then with wild desperation. This sort of love, this overbearing, soul crushing need for him is beyond anything I had thought possible. I hadn't seen the capacity for it before, not in myself, not in anyone, but as his tongue presses into my mouth, possessive, demanding, I can't help but believe.

He pulls up my nightie, slides down my panties as he adjusts his position. His boxers fly off, kicked to the floor before he returns to sit against the headboard. "You are so damn beautiful," he whispers, his hands snaking under my shirt to caress my breasts. "I came in here with the intention to feed you breakfast, and there it sits, forgotten."

"This is much more delicious," I tell him with a smile. "I'm not complaining."

"I need a taste." He leans in, kisses me on one breast, then the other. His hands gently run over my stomach for a long moment, and he studies it, me, us. "God, I love you so much."

"I love you, too." I wriggle closer against him. "Did you lock the door?"

"Of course."

"Then what are you waiting for?"

His mouth covers mine, plundering and hot, taking all that I can give. My arms circle his neck, my entire body pulsing with need for him. I raise to my knees as his hands grip my hips, hold me close, help me to rise.

I hover above him as he presses his length against my entrance, teasing, playing, his mouth distracting me with little kisses across my neck. Finally, the tension builds, twists until there's a spiral of heat running between us, and his fingers dig into my skin, sliding me onto him.

I gasp at the feel of him, even after all this time. The fullness of him, the hardness of him, of his chest as I lean against him, of the contrasting softness in his eyes as he begins to move. We meet each other in a dance, a building, terrifying crescendo until it's too much, and I cry out with release.

His mouth covers mine, swallowing my cries, holding me against him, against his lap, shattering together as the waves crest, carry us over, and gently fade into the distance.

His hands run through my hair, holding my head to his shoulder as the calm returns. His arms lock behind my back as he sighs with pleasure. "Damn."

It's all I can do not to drool on him, so I merely nod as a response.

"That was amazing," he says. "I'll have to make you breakfast more often."

We climb from the bed, ease into the shower together where we take turns washing each other, peppering the moment with kisses, caresses until we can't keep our hands from each other any longer. A second wave of need rocks through us, eases, and leaves us exhausted and satiated. The honeymoon might've ended, but our need for each other has only grown stronger.

An hour later, we're still lounging in bed, finally making use of the toast and orange juice from the tray. The cereal is beyond repair, and the eggs have cooled. But it's the most delicious meal I've ever eaten in my life.

A knock on the door sounds, and Boxer climbs from bed, taking a quick look to make sure we're both decent. He opens the door and, to nobody's surprise, reveals a head full of curly hair positively sizzling with energy.

"Hello," Charli says with a cryptic smile. "How are you?"

"We're good," Boxer says. "Care for some breakfast?"

Charli eyes the tray, wrinkles her nose at the cereal. "Gross."

I laugh, move to stand. "Let's go make you some real breakfast."

"Wait," she instructs, eyes landing on her dad with real severity. "I have something for Jocelyn."

"You do?" Boxer appears genuinely surprised. "What is it?"

"It's a secret."

She solemnly moves across the room, and I look over her head to Boxer, then ease my way back onto the bed. He shrugs, mouths *no idea,* and follows her to my side.

We all pile in, three people deep, when she finally pulls something out from behind her back.

"I made this for you," Charli said. "I hope you like it."

I look down, accept a handmade card on bright green construction paper. There's crooked writing on the front, and it's these letters that make my eyes well up with tears all over again.

Dear Joss,
Happy Mother's Day.
Thank you for being my mom.
Love,
Charli

"Oh, Charli . . ." I read the card from to back one more time. A tear slides down my cheek. "Did you make this in school?"

"No. I made it because I felt like it."

Boxer's hand comes down, runs along his daughter's hair. "Jocelyn's pretty great, isn't she?"

Charli nods. "You're a really great mom."

I open my arms and pull Charli into them. I kiss her forehead, her curls, and force myself to stop crying so she doesn't get the wrong idea. "Thank you." I clutch the card to my chest. "I'm going to keep this forever."

"Okay," Charli says. "What about breakfast?"

"We have a surprise for you, too," Boxer says, easing down onto the bed next to us. His eyes make contact with mine, and I nod. He puts an arm around Charli, rests her head against him. "You're going to be a big sister."

Her eyes go wide, the size of saucers. "What?"

"A big sister!" Boxer breaks into a broad smile, unable to hide his own excitement at the news. "Jocelyn's pregnant."

"Jocelyn's having a baby?" Charli turns to look at me. "Is it a boy or a girl? I want a boy. Girls are too sissy. Except for me. I don't want to play Barbies."

"We don't know yet. It's too soon to tell." Boxer pulls her tight, kisses her curls.

"What do you think, Charli?" I ask. "Are you excited to be a big sister?"

"Depends. Do I have to share my room?"

I grin. "No, not right away."

"Are there more coming after this one?" She shoots a skeptical look at both of us. "Because we only have one extra bedroom."

"Probably," Boxer says.

"We'll talk about it," I add.

Boxer laughs, leans over and kisses my forehead. "Whatever you say, boss."

The End

AUTHOR'S NOTE

Thank you so much for reading! I hope you enjoyed Joss and Boxer's story!

If you'd like to be kept posted on the release date for the next book in the series—another standalone coming soon!—please sign up for *Love Letters from Lily* at LilyKateAuthor.com or find me on Facebook.

Lastly, if you happened to enjoy the story and can spare five minutes out of your day, honest reviews at the retailer of your choice are always welcome and appreciated.

Thank you so much in advance!

Stay tuned for more from the Minnesota Ice team, and a brand-new spin-off series!

ABOUT THE AUTHOR

MY NAME IS Lily Kate, and I work a pretttttty boring day By night, I write books filled with heat, heart, and humor. My debut novel, Delivery Girl, released in early 2017. When I'm not writing books, you may find me watching Christmas movies before Thanksgiving, eating whipped cream from the can, or hanging out with my family..

www.lilykateauthor.com

Printed in the USA
CPSIA information can be obtained
at www.ICGtesting.com
JSHW031957150824
68134JS00063B/3577